The
Science Fiction
Stories of
Rudyard Kipling

The
Science Fiction
Stories of
Rudyard Kipling

Edited by John Brunner

A Citadel Twilight Book
Published by Carol Publishing Group

A Citadel Twilight Book
Published by Carol Publishing Group
Citadel Twilight is a registered trademark of Carol Communications Group
Editorial Offices: 600 Madison Avenue, New York, N.Y. 10022
Sales and Distribution Offices: 120 Enterprise Avenue, Secaucus, N.J. 07094
In Canada: Canadian Manda Group, P.O. Box 920, Station U, Toronto,
    Ontario M8Z 5P9
Queries regarding rights and permissions should be addressed to
Carol Publishing Group, 600 Madison Avenue, New York, N.Y. 10022

First published under the title *Kipling's Science Fiction* by Tom
Doherty Associates, New York, 1992.

Carol Publishing books are available at special
discounts for bulk purchases, for sales promotions, fund-raising, or
educational purposes. Special editions can be created to
specifications. For details, contact Special Sales Department, Carol
Publishing Group, 120 Enterprise Avenue, Secaucus, N.J. 07094

Manufactured in the United States of America
10 9 8 7 6 5 4 3 2 1

ISBN 0-8065-1508-2

Contents

For much of the information on Kipling's career I am indebted to Charles Carrington's excellent study *Rudyard Kipling: His Life and Work* (Pelican Books, London, 1970), and the twenty contributors to *Rudyard Kipling: The Man, His Work and His World* edited by John Gross (Weidenfeld & Nicolson, London, 1972). The opinions are of course my own.

—JKHB

Kipling's Major
Publications

About Rudyard Kipling

In a book by David Frost entitled *I Could Have Kicked Myself*, a compilation of decisions that their makers lived to regret, it is asserted that in 1869 the editor of the *San Francisco Examiner* sacked Rudyard Kipling from his job as a cub reporter, saying, "I'm sorry, Mr. Kipling, but you just don't know how to use the English language."

Which was, I suppose, scarcely surprising, since at the time RK was rather less than five years old.

But he was a prodigy, even if not quite on Mr. Frost's scale. His first collection of verse, *Schoolboy Lyrics*, was published when he was sixteen, albeit without his permission. On learning what his mother had done with his juvenile effusions, reportedly he "sulked for three days." And one might almost say that that epitomized the pattern of his life. During his lifetime approximately 15,000,000 copies of his works were sold in English alone. So popular were they in French translation that on one visit to France he was described as being treated "like a national hero." He was the first British author to receive the Nobel Prize for Literature. He would never admit to writing poetry, only "verses," yet T. S. Eliot was among his staunchest champions. He was twice offered, twice refused, a knighthood. He was made a Companion of Honour, but that was much to his annoyance. He declined the Order of Merit, arguably the most coveted distinction in Britain, and forbade his name to be put

forward for the post of Poet Laureate. Universities and
learned societies awarded him medals and honorary
degrees—those he did accept—and toward the end of his
life he became a close friend of King George V.

Yet he was never able truly to enjoy his astonishing
achievement, for the passage of his days was marred by
suffering, both physical and mental, and by such tragedies
as, perhaps, the ancient Greeks would have attributed to
Nemesis. Here, in outline, is his story.

Born in 1865 in Bombay, where his father was the
principal of a recently founded school of art, he was sent
to Britain for his education and spent most of his
childhood separated from his parents, although his sister
Alice (known as "Trix") went with him. The woman to
whose care they were confided maltreated the boy to such
a degree that when, during an unexpected visit, his mother
came to kiss him good night, he automatically flung up his
arm to ward off the blow he had been conditioned to
expect. In later life Trix became deranged and, their
parents being dead, RK had to accept responsibility for
her care; perhaps it was at this time that the seeds of that
burden were sown.

However, he spent a month each year with his mother's
sister, who was married to the prominent artist Sir
Edward Burne-Jones, and later described their home as "a
paradise which I verily believe saved me." This and other
links with the artistic and literary life of London were in
young adulthood to stand him in equally good stead.

He was far happier at the school where he passed his early
teens, which he later adapted as the setting for his
"Stalky" stories; in particular, the headmaster gave him
the run of his study and encouraged his omnivorous
reading. By now it was obvious he was both intelligent
and gifted. But university fees were beyond his parents'
means, so just before his seventeenth birthday in 1882 he
returned to India, where they had obtained him a job on a
newspaper.

The next few years marked him for life. Although, after
being lionized in London in 1889–90, he paid only one

more visit to India, his apprenticeship there as a journalist
and commentator on the social and political scene
provided the first significant outlet for his talents and
shaped his preference for the range of styles and choice of
subjects that were to earn him his almost incredible
popularity. To the end of his days he retained his
admiration, dating from his late teens, for the tough
hard-headed individualist; for "the man who's good at
what he has to do," be his calling villager or Viceroy; for
the skillful engineer, the cunning strategist, the
silver-tongued confidence man. . . . And, perhaps above
all else, for India's fantastic, colorful, endlessly varied
store of tales and myths and legends, with which his
childhood had so richly stocked his mind.

Such was the success of his early stories that he could
afford to travel to England via Japan, the U.S.A., and
Canada—quite a voyage for a twenty-four-year-old. He
was made much of in London, but despite his many
acquaintances felt desperately lonely until he fell in with a
young American named Wolcott Balestier. They became
close friends and even collaborated on a novel, *The
Naulahka.*
　　Tragedy, though, was waiting in the wings; while RK
was making another long voyage, to South Africa,
Australia, and New Zealand, Wolcott was struck down in
Germany by typhoid fever and died at thirty.
　　Conceivably *in memoriam* (no one will ever be sure), RK
proposed to and married Wolcott's sister, Carrie
Balestier, and they settled on her family's estate in
Vermont. The next few years ensured that America
became the second great influence on his work, after
India. In addition they saw the birth of children, the
publication of *Many Inventions* and the two *Jungle Books*
. . . and an almost farcical but most unpleasant feud with
his brother-in-law, which in the end drove him and Carrie
back to England.
　　It was on a return trip to the U.S.A., to visit the
Balestier family, that tragedy again invaded their lives. In a
bitter New York winter RK fell ill with inflammation of
the lungs. Often delirious, he fought for his life for nearly

seven weeks. Meantime, his baby son developed
bronchitis and both his daughters succumbed to
whooping cough . . . from which the elder died.

Despite his background in journalism (or maybe
because of it) he always hated publicity. Perhaps, though,
it was on some level a consolation that by now he was so
famous and indeed so beloved a writer that when, at the
same time, Pope Leo XIII also fell ill, the *Pall Mall
Gazette* issued posters with the headline KIPLING AND
POPE—in *that* order.

Then, for a while, the Kiplings' life grew calmer and more
bearable. Having rented houses in various parts of
Southern England, in 1902 they found the home
("Bateman's," near Burwash in Sussex) where they were
to settle for the rest of their lives—the place where
evolved the third and ultimately greatest of the influences
on his writing. After India, after America, it was the turn
of the mother country: England.

For whose future RK was becoming increasingly
concerned. Having served as a war correspondent during
the Boer Wars, he foresaw the likelihood of a major
European conflict at a time when most "experts" regarded
it as out of the question. In the event he was proved only
too right—and fate dealt him yet another blow in
consequence. Serving with the Irish Guards in 1915, his
only son John Kipling was reported missing, and though
the family clung to hope as long as possible they were
forced in the end to admit that he must be dead.

During and after the war, although he would never accept
the seat in Parliament that was his for the asking, RK
played a distinguished part in politics and public affairs,
notably on behalf of the War Graves Commission. (It was
he who proposed that in Westminster Abbey a tomb be
erected to The Unknown Soldier.) However . . .

Though he continued to write—*A Diversity of Creatures,
Land and Sea Tales,* and the story collection many people
regard as his finest, *Debits and Credits*—a permanent
shadow had fallen over his life. He lightened it with
travel; having been a keen motorist since the pioneering
days, he often enjoyed tours in France, a country he had

come to love almost as much as his own, and he even visited parts of the world that he had missed in his youth: Brazil, and the West Indies. But he, who had always appreciated good food and had even written a story whose hero was hopeless at everything except cooking ("His Gift," in *Land and Sea Tales*), was chronically ill with abdominal pains, so even the pleasures of the table were denied him. When a French doctor finally diagnosed that for fifteen years he had endured untreated gastric ulcers, he was too weak for the operation that might have given him relief. He died in January 1936.

He was a baffling, paradoxical man: fiercely patriotic, yet among the keenest and most unrelenting critics of his country; an advocate of Empire, who made no secret of his lifelong affection and respect for those whom others casually dismissed as "wogs" or worse; a man of letters whose greatest admiration was reserved for men of action; a confidant of at least one president and one king, whose reputation was founded on his tales and songs concerning peasants, barbarians, and that next-to-barbarian, the common soldier; a dreamer who, despite being endlessly fascinated by practical details—of government, of steam engines, of medicine and electricity and radio—did not hesitate to apply his talent to far-out tales of the fantastic, to horror stories, even to what in his day people had scarcely begun to refer to as science fiction . . . a truth, I trust, amply demonstrated in this and its companion volume.

He has been dead for more than half a century. But what other writer of his generation could, in the 1980s, have inspired an American editor to invite contributions for an anthology of SF stories modeled on or influenced by that person's work?*

In the manner of Robert Louis Stevenson, whom he corresponded with but never met, Kipling wrote his own

---

*The editor was David Drake. The collection, entitled *Heads to the Storm*, is published by Baen Books, and I'm delighted that it includes my story "Mowgli." RK influenced my work more than anybody, more even than did Wells—who, surprisingly, a decade later, echoed and approved RK's opinion of crowds as expressed in "As Easy as A.B.C." (See Book Three, Chapter Two of *Men Like Gods*.)

epitaph. Perhaps we should not attempt to resolve the contradictions of his nature, but be content to obey the injunction with which it concludes:

> *Seek not to question other than*
> *The books I leave behind.*

—JKHB
South Petherton
1988

A Matter of Fact
FROM MANY INVENTIONS (1893)

By the time this collection appeared, Kipling, then married and living in Vermont, was no longer a full-time journalist, though he was to serve as a war correspondent during the Boer War. Nonetheless, as he says at the beginning, "once a journalist, always and forever a journalist." Few of his stories illustrate more graphically the talent he had honed while working for newspapers in India, for assembling chance scraps of information into a concise and convincing whole.

Certainly he was never aboard a tramp steamer caught in an underwater volcanic eruption. But there are elements in his description of what happens to the sea in such a case that could not possibly have been invented. He must have spoken to someone who had survived the real event, and stored away what he was told until he needed it . . . as he continued to do throughout his working life.

When, a few years ago, Ellen Datlow of *Omni* decided to print an occasional "classic" SF story and asked me what of Kipling's I would recommend, I had no hesitation in naming "A Matter of Fact." It's the best sea-serpent story I have ever read. And, as you'll see, it has a perfectly marvelous ending.

A Lascar (from a Persian word meaning soldier, mercenary) was an Asiatic working on a European ship. A Board of Trade pump was one complying with British government standards. *"Hur illa!"* means literally "how queer." And The Needles are a group of rocks at the western tip of the Isle of Wight, off the south coast of England.

A Matter of Fact

And if ye doubt the tale I tell,
Steer through the South Pacific swell;
Go where the bracing coral hives
Unending strife of endless lives,
Where, leagued about the 'wildered boat,
The rainbow jellies fill and float;
And, lilting where the laver lingers,
The starfish trips on all her fingers;
Where, 'neath his myriad spines ashock,
The sea-egg ripples down the rock;
An orange wonder dimly guessed,
From darkness where the cuttles rest,
Moored o'er the darker deeps that hide
The blind white Sea-snake and his bride
Who, drowsing, nose the long-lost ships
Let down through darkness to their lips.

THE PALMS

Once a priest, always a priest; once a mason, always a mason; but once a journalist, always and forever a journalist.

There were three of us, all newspaper men, the only passengers on a little tramp steamer that ran where her owners told her to go. She had once been in the Bilbao iron ore business, had been lent to the Spanish Government for service at Manilla; and was ending her days in the Cape Town coolie-trade, with occasional trips to Madagascar and even as far as England. We found her going to Southampton in ballast, and shipped in her because the fares were nominal. There was Keller, of an American paper, on his way back to the States from palace executions in Madagascar; there was a burly half-Dutchman, called Zuyland, who owned and edited a paper up country near Johannesburg; and there was myself, who had solemnly put away all journalism, vowing to forget that I had ever known the difference between an imprint and a stereo advertisement.

Ten minutes after Keller spoke to me, as the *Rathmines* cleared Cape Town, I had forgotten the aloofness I desired to feign, and was in heated discussion on the immorality of expanding telegrams beyond a certain fixed point. Then Zuyland came out of his cabin, and we were all at home instantly, because we were men of the same profession needing no introduction. We annexed the boat formally, broke open the passengers' bathroom door—on the Manilla lines the Dons do not wash—cleaned out the orange-peel and cigar-ends at the bottom of the bath, hired a Lascar to shave us throughout the voyage, and then asked each other's names.

Three ordinary men would have quarreled through sheer boredom before they reached Southampton. We, by virtue of our craft, were anything but ordinary men. A large percentage of the tales of the world, the thirty-nine that cannot be told to ladies and the one that can, are common property coming of a common stock. We told them all, as a matter of form, with all their local and specific variants which are surprising. Then came, in the intervals of steady card-play, more personal histories of adventure and things seen and suffered: panics among white folk, when the blind terror ran from man to man on the Brooklyn Bridge, and the people crushed each other to death they knew not why; fires, and faces that opened and shut their mouths horribly at red-hot window frames; wrecks in frost and snow, reported from the sleet-sheathed rescue-tug at the risk of frostbite; long rides after diamond thieves; skirmishes on the veldt and in municipal committees with the Boers; glimpses of lazy tangled Cape politics and the mule-rule in the Transvaal; card-tales, horse-tales, woman-tales, by the score and the half hundred; till the first mate, who had seen more than us all put together, but lacked words to clothe his tales with, sat open-mouthed far into the dawn.

When the tales were done we picked up cards till a curious hand or a chance remark made one or other of us say, "That reminds me of a man who—or a business which—" and the anecdotes would continue while the *Rathmines* kicked her way northward through the warm water.

In the morning of one specially warm night we three were sitting immediately in front of the wheel-house, where an old Swedish boatswain whom we called "Frithiof the Dane" was at the wheel, pretending that he could not hear our stories. Once or twice Frithiof spun the spokes curiously, and Keller lifted his head from a long chair to ask, "What is it? Can't you get any steerage-way on her?"

"There is a feel in the water," said Frithiof, "that I cannot understand. I think that we run down-hills or somethings. She steers bad this morning."

Nobody seems to know the laws that govern the pulse of the big waters. Sometimes even a landsman can tell that the solid ocean is atilt, and that the ship is working herself up a long unseen slope; and sometimes the captain says, when neither full steam nor fair wind justifies the length of a day's run, that the ship is sagging downhill; but how these ups and downs come about has not yet been settled authoritatively.

"No, it is a following sea," said Frithiof; "and with a following sea you shall not get good steerage-way."

The sea was as smooth as a duck-pond, except for a regular oily swell. As I looked over the side to see where it might be following us from, the sun rose in a perfectly clear sky and struck the water with its light so sharply that it seemed as though the sea should clang like a burnished gong. The wake of the screw and the little white streak cut by the log-line hanging over the stern were the only marks on the water as far as eye could reach.

Keller rolled out of his chair and went aft to get a pineapple from the ripening stock that was hung inside the after awning.

"Frithiof, the log-line has got tired of swimming. It's coming home," he drawled.

"What?" said Frithiof, his voice jumping several octaves.

"Coming home," Keller repeated, leaning over the stern. I ran to his side and saw the log-line, which till then had been drawn tense over the stern railing, slacken, loop, and come up off the port quarter. Frithiof called up the speaking-tube to the bridge, and the bridge answered, "Yes, nine knots." Then Frithiof spoke again, and the answer was, "What do you want of the skipper?" and Frithiof bellowed, "Call him up."

By this time Zuyland, Keller, and myself had caught something of Frithiof's excitement, for any emotion on shipboard is most contagious. The captain ran out of his cabin, spoke to Frithiof, looked at the log-line, jumped on the bridge, and in a minute we felt the steamer swing round as Frithiof turned her.

"Going back to Cape Town?" said Keller.

Frithiof did not answer, but tore away at the wheel. Then he beckoned us three to help, and we held the wheel down till the *Rathmines* answered it, and we found ourselves looking into the white of our own wake, with the still oily sea tearing past our bows, though we were not going more than half steam ahead.

The captain stretched out his arm from the bridge and shouted. A minute later I would have given a great deal to have shouted too, for one-half of the sea seemed to shoulder itself above the other half, and came on in the shape of a hill. There was neither crest, comb, nor curl-over to it; nothing but black water with little waves chasing each other about the flanks. I saw it stream past and on a level with the *Rathmines'* bow-plates before the steamer hove up her bulk to rise, and I argued that this would be the last of all earthly voyages for me. Then we lifted forever and ever and ever, till I heard Keller saying in my ear, "The bowels of the deep, good Lord!" and the *Rathmines* stood poised, her screw racing and drumming on the slope of a hollow that stretched downwards for a good half-mile.

We went down that hollow, nose under for the most part, and the air smelt wet and muddy, like that of an emptied aquarium. There was a second hill to climb; I saw that much: but the water came aboard and carried me aft till it jammed me against the wheel-house door, and before I could catch breath or clear my eyes again we were rolling to and fro in torn water, with the scuppers pouring like eaves in a thunderstorm.

"There were three waves," said Keller; "and the stokehold's flooded."

The firemen were on deck waiting, apparently, to be drowned. The engineer came and dragged them below, and the crew, gasping, began to work the clumsy Board of Trade pump. That showed nothing serious, and when I understood that the *Rathmines* was really on the water, and not beneath it, I asked what had happened.

"The captain says it was a blow-up under the sea—a volcano," said Keller.

"It hasn't warmed anything," I said. I was feeling bitterly cold, and cold was almost unknown in those waters. I went below to change my clothes, and when I came up everything was wiped out in clinging white fog.

"Are there going to be any more surprises?" said Keller to the captain.

"I don't know. Be thankful you're alive, gentlemen. That's a tidal wave thrown up by a volcano. Probably the bottom of the sea has been lifted a few feet somewhere or other. I can't quite understand this cold spell. Our sea-thermometer says the surface water is 44°, and it should be 68° at least."

"It's abominable," said Keller, shivering. "But hadn't you better attend to the fog-horn? It seems to me that I heard something."

"Heard! Good heavens!" said the captain from the bridge, "I

should think you did." He pulled the string of our fog-horn, which was a weak one. It sputtered and choked, because the stoke-hold was full of water and the fires were half-drowned, and at last gave out a moan. It was answered from the fog by one of the most appalling steam-sirens I have ever heard. Keller turned as white as I did, for the fog, the cold fog, was upon us, and any man may be forgiven for fearing a death he cannot see.

"Give her steam there!" said the captain to the engine-room. "Steam for the whistle, if we have to go dead slow."

We bellowed again, and the damp dripped off the awnings on to the deck as we listened for the reply. It seemed to be astern this time, but much nearer than before.

"The *Pembroke Castle* on us!" said Keller; and then, viciously, "Well, thank God, we shall sink her too."

"It's a side-wheel steamer," I whispered. "Can't you hear the paddles?"

This time we whistled and roared till the steam gave out, and the answer nearly deafened us. There was a sound of frantic threshing in the water, apparently about fifty yards away, and something shot past in the whiteness that looked as though it were gray and red.

"The *Pembroke Castle* bottom up," said Keller, who, being a journalist, always sought for explanations. "That's the colors of a Castle liner. We're in for a big thing."

"The sea is bewitched," said Frithiof from the wheel-house. "There are *two* steamers!"

Another siren sounded on our bow, and the little steamer rolled in the wash of something that had passed unseen.

"We're evidently in the middle of a fleet," said Keller quietly. "If one doesn't run us down, the other will. Phew! What in creation is that?"

I sniffed, for there was a poisonous rank smell in the cold air—a smell that I had smelt before.

"If I was on land I should say that it was an alligator. It smells like musk," I answered.

"Not ten thousand alligators could make that smell," said Zuyland; "I have smelt them."

"Bewitched! Bewitched!" said Frithiof. "The sea she is turned upside down, and we are walking along the bottom."

Again the *Rathmines* rolled in the wash of some unseen ship, and a silver-gray wave broke over the bow, leaving on the deck a sheet of sediment—the gray broth that has its place in the fathomless deeps of the sea. A sprinkling of the wave fell on my face, and it was so cold that it stung as boiling water stings. The dead and most untouched deep water of the sea had been heaved to the top by the submarine volcano—the chill still water that kills all life and smells of desolation and emptiness. We did not need either the blinding fog or that indescribable smell of musk to make us unhappy—we were shivering with cold and wretchedness where we stood.

"The hot air on the cold water makes this fog," said the captain; "it ought to clear in a little time."

"Whistle, oh! whistle, and let's get out of it," said Keller.

The captain whistled again, and far and far astern the invisible twin steam-sirens answered us. Their blasting shriek grew louder, till at last it seemed to tear out of the fog just above our quarter, and I cowered while the *Rathmines* plunged bows under on a double swell that crossed.

"No more," said Frithiof, "it is not good anymore. Let us get away, in the name of God."

"Now if a torpedo-boat with a *City of Paris* siren went mad and broke her moorings and hired a friend to help her, it's just conceivable that we might be carried as we are now. Otherwise this thing is—"

The last words died on Keller's lips, his eyes began to start from his head, and his jaw fell. Some six or seven feet above the port bulwarks, framed in fog, and as utterly unsupported as the full moon, hung a Face. It was not human, and it certainly was not animal, for it did not belong to this earth as known to man. The mouth was open, revealing a ridiculously tiny tongue—as absurd as the tongue of an elephant; there were tense wrinkles of white skin at the angles of the drawn lips, white feelers like those of a barbel sprung from the lower jaw, and there was no sign of teeth within the mouth. But the horror of the face lay in the eyes, for those were sightless—white, in sockets as white as scraped bone, and blind. Yet for all this the face, wrinkled as the mask of a lion is drawn in Assyrian sculpture, was alive with rage and terror. One long white feeler touched our bulwarks. Then the face disappeared with the swiftness of a blindworm popping into its burrow, and the next thing that I remember is my own voice in my own ears, saying gravely to the mainmast, "But the air-bladder ought to have been forced out of its mouth, you know."

Keller came up to me, ashy white. He put his hand into his pocket, took a cigar, bit it, dropped it, thrust his shaking thumb into his mouth and mumbled, "The giant gooseberry and the raining frogs!

Gimme a light—gimme a light! Say, gimme a light." A little bead of blood dropped from his thumb-joint.

I respected the motive, though the manifestation was absurd. "Stop, you'll bite your thumb off," I said, and Keller laughed brokenly as he picked up his cigar. Only Zuyland, leaning over the port bulwarks, seemed self-possessed. He declared later that he was very sick.

"We've seen it," he said, turning round. "That is it."

"What?" said Keller, chewing the unlighted cigar.

As he spoke the fog was blown into shreds, and we saw the sea, gray with mud, rolling on every side of us and empty of all life. Then in one spot it bubbled and became like the pot of ointment that the Bible speaks of. From that wide-ringed trouble a Thing came up—a gray and red Thing with a neck—a Thing that bellowed and writhed in pain. Frithiof drew in his breath and held it till the red letters of the ship's name, woven across his jersey, straggled and opened out as though they had been type badly set. Then he said with a little cluck in his throat, "Ah me! It is blind. *Hur illa!* That thing is blind," and a murmur of pity went through us all, for we could see that the thing on the water was blind and in pain. Something had gashed and cut the great sides cruelly and the blood was spurting out. The gray ooze of the undermost sea lay in the monstrous wrinkles of the back, and poured away in sluices. The blind white head flung back and battered the wounds, and the body in its torment rose clear of the red and gray waves till we saw a pair of quivering shoulders streaked with weed and rough with shells, but as white in the clear spaces as the hairless, maneless, blind, toothless head. Afterwards, came a dot on the horizon and the sound of a shrill scream, and it was as though a shuttle shot all across the sea in one breath, and a second head and neck tore through the levels, driving a whispering wall of water to right and left. The two Things met—the one untouched and the other in its death-throe—male and female, we said, the female coming to the male. She circled round him bellowing, and laid her neck across the curve of his great turtle-back, and he disappeared under water for an instant, but flung up again, grunting in agony while the blood ran. Once the entire head and neck shot clear of the water and stiffened, and I heard Keller saying, as though he was watching a street accident, "Give him air. For God's sake, give him air." Then the death-struggle began, with crampings and twistings and jerkings of the white bulk to and fro, till our little steamer rolled again, and each gray wave coated her plates with the gray slime. The sun was clear, there was no wind, and we watched, the whole crew, stokers and all, in wonder and pity, but chiefly pity. The Thing was so helpless, and, save for his mate, so alone. No human eye should have beheld him; it was monstrous and indecent to exhibit him there in trade waters between atlas degrees of latitude. He had been spewed up, mangled and dying, from his rest on the sea-floor, where he might have lived till the Judgment Day, and we saw the tides of his life go from him as an angry tide goes out across rocks in the teeth of a landward gale. His mate lay rocking on the water a little distance off, bellowing continually, and the smell of musk came down upon the ship making us cough.

At last the battle for life ended in a batter of colored seas. We saw the writhing neck fall like a flail, the carcass turn sideways, showing the glint of a white belly and the inset of a gigantic hind leg or flipper. Then all sank, and sea boiled over it, while the mate swam round and round, darting her head in every direction. Though we might have feared that she would attack the steamer, no power on earth could have drawn any one of us from our places that hour. We watched, holding our breaths. The mate paused in her search; we could hear the wash beating along her sides; reared her neck as high as she could reach, blind and lonely in all that loneliness of the sea, and sent one desperate bellow booming across the swells as an oyster-shell skips across a pond. Then she made off to the westward, the sun shining on the white head and the wake behind it, till nothing was left to see but a little pinpoint of silver on the horizon. We stood on our course again; and the *Rathmines,* coated with the sea-sediment from bow to stern, looked like a ship made gray with terror.

"We must pool our notes," was the first coherent remark from Keller. "We're three trained journalists—we hold absolutely the biggest scoop on record. Start fair."

I objected to this. Nothing is gained by collaboration in journalism when all deal with the same facts, so we went to work each according to his own lights. Keller triple-headed his account, talked about our "gallant captain," and wound up with an allusion to American enterprise in that it was a citizen of Dayton, Ohio, that had seen the sea-serpent. This sort of thing would have discredited the Creation, much more a mere sea tale, but as a specimen of the picture-writing of a half-civilized people it was very interesting. Zuyland took a heavy column and a half, giving approximate lengths and breadths, and the whole list of the crew whom he had

sworn on oath to testify to his facts. There was nothing fantastic or
flamboyant in Zuyland. I wrote three-quarters of a leaded bourgeois
column, roughly speaking, and refrained from putting any jour-
nalese into it for reasons that had begun to appear to me.

Keller was insolent with joy. He was going to cable from Southampton to the New York *World,* mail his account to America on the
same day, paralyze London with his three columns of loosely knit-
ted headlines, and generally efface the earth. "You'll see how I work
a big scoop when I get it," he said.

"Is this your first visit to England?" I asked.

"Yes," said he. "You don't seem to appreciate the beauty of our
scoop. It's pyramidal—the death of the sea-serpent! Good heavens
alive, man, it's the biggest thing ever vouchsafed to a paper!"

"Curious to think that it will never appear in any paper, isn't it?"
I said.

Zuyland was near me, and he nodded quickly.

"What do you mean?" said Keller. "If you're enough of a Brit-
isher to throw this thing away, I shan't. I thought you were a
newspaperman."

"I am. That's why I know. Don't be an ass, Keller. Remember,
I'm seven hundred years your senior, and what your grandchildren
may learn five hundred years hence, I learned from my grandfathers
about five hundred years ago. You won't do it, because you can't."

This conversation was held in open sea, where everything seems
possible, some hundred miles from Southampton. We passed the
Needles Light at dawn, and the lifting day showed the stucco villas
on the green and the awful orderliness of England—line upon line,
wall upon wall, solid stone dock and monolithic pier. We waited an
hour in the Customs shed, and there was ample time for the effect
to soak in.

"Now, Keller, you face the music. The *Havel* goes out today.
Mail by her, and I'll take you to the telegraph-office," I said.

I heard Keller gasp as the influence of the land closed about him,
cowing him as they say Newmarket Heath cows a young horse
unused to open courses.

"I want to retouch my stuff. Suppose we wait till we get to
London?" he said.

Zuyland, by the way, had torn up his account and thrown it
overboard that morning early. His reasons were my reasons.

In the train Keller began to revise his copy, and every time that
he looked at the trim little fields, the red villas, and the embank-
ments of the line, the blue pencil plunged remorselessly through the

slips. He appeared to have dredged the dictionary for adjectives. I could think of none that he had not used. Yet he was a perfectly sound poker-player and never showed more cards than were sufficient to take the pool.

"Aren't you going to leave him a single bellow?" I asked sympathetically. "Remember, everything goes in the States, from a trouser-button to a double-eagle."

"That's just the curse of it," said Keller below his breath. "We've played 'em for suckers so often that when it comes to the golden truth—I'd like to try this on a London paper. You have first call there, though."

"Not in the least. I'm not touching the thing in our papers. I shall be happy to leave 'em all to you; but surely you'll cable it home?"

"No. Not if I can make the scoop here and see the Britishers sit up."

"You won't do it with three columns of slushy headline, believe me. They don't sit up as quickly as some people."

"I'm beginning to think that too. Does *nothing* make any difference in this country?" he said, looking out of the window. "How old is that farmhouse?"

"New. It can't be more than two hundred years at the most."

"Um. Fields, too?"

"That hedge there must have been clipped for about eighty years."

"Labor cheap—eh?"

"Pretty much. Well, I suppose you'd like to try the *Times*, wouldn't you?"

"No," said Keller, looking at Winchester Cathedral. "Might as well try to electrify a haystack. And to think that the *World* would take three columns and ask for more—with illustrations too! It's sickening."

"But the *Times* might," I began.

Keller flung his paper across the carriage, and it opened in its austere majesty of solid type—opened with the crackle of an encyclopedia.

"Might! You *might* work your way through the bow-plates of a cruiser. Look at that first page!"

"It strikes you that way, does it?" I said. "Then I'd recommend you to try a light and frivolous journal."

"With a thing like this of mine—of ours? It's sacred history!"

I showed him a paper which I conceived would be after his own heart, in that it was modeled on American lines.

"That's homey," he said, "but it's not the real thing. Now, I should like one of these fat old *Times* columns. Probably there'd be a bishop in the office, though."

When we reached London Keller disappeared in the direction of the Strand. What his experiences may have been I cannot tell, but it seems that he invaded the office of an evening paper at 11:45 A.M. (I told him English editors were most idle at that hour), and mentioned my name as that of a witness to the truth of his story.

"I was nearly fired out," he said furiously at lunch. "As soon as I mentioned you, the old man said that I was to tell you that they didn't want any more of your practical jokes, and that you knew the hours to call if you had anything to sell, and that they'd see you condemned before they helped to puff one of your infernal yarns in advance. Say, what record do you hold for truth in this country, anyway?"

"A beauty. You ran up against it, that's all. Why don't you leave the English papers alone and cable to New York? Everything goes over there."

"Can't you see that's just why?" he repeated.

"I saw it a long time ago. You don't intend to cable, then?"

"Yes, I do," he answered, in the over-emphatic voice of one who does not know his own mind.

That afternoon I walked him abroad and about, over the streets that run between the pavements like channels of grooved and tongued lava, over the bridges that are made of enduring stone, through subways floored and sided with yard-thick concrete, between houses that are never rebuilt, and by river-steps hewn, to the eye, from the living rock. A black fog chased us into Westminster Abbey, and, standing there in the darkness, I could hear the wings of the dead centuries circling round the head of Litchfield A. Keller, journalist, of Dayton, Ohio, U.S.A., whose mission it was to make the Britishers sit up.

He stumbled gasping into the thick gloom, and the roar of the traffic came to his bewildered ears.

"Let's go to the telegraph-office and cable," I said. "Can't you hear the New York *World* crying for news of the great sea-serpent, blind, white, and smelling of musk, stricken to death by a submarine volcano, and assisted by his loving wife to die in mid-ocean, as visualized by an American citizen, the breezy, newsy, brainy newspaper man of Dayton, Ohio? 'Rah for the Buckeye State. Step lively! Both gates! Szz! Boom! Aah!" Keller was a Princeton man, and he seemed to need encouragement.

"You've got me on your own ground," said he, tugging at his overcoat pocket. He pulled out his copy, with the cable forms—for he had written out his telegram—and put them all into my hand, groaning, "I pass. If I hadn't come to your cursed country—If I'd sent it off at Southampton—If I ever get you west of the Alleghennies, if—"

"Never mind, Keller. It isn't your fault. It's the fault of your country. If you had been seven hundred years older you'd have done what I am going to do."

"What are you going to do?"

"Tell it as a lie."

"Fiction?" This with the full-blooded disgust of a journalist for the illegitimate branch of the profession.

"You can call it that if you like. I shall call it a lie."

And a lie it has become; for Truth is a naked lady, and if by accident she is drawn up from the bottom of the sea, it behooves a gentleman either to give her a print petticoat or to turn his face to the wall and vow that he did not see.

The Ship That Found Herself

FROM *THE DAY'S WORK* (1898)

Science fiction? Yes, of course. What else would you call a story about intelligent machines? (The same goes, by the way, for the next item in this collection, "·007.")

It's perhaps hard for us to realize, in this day and age, how relatively little contact most people at the end of the last century had with machines of the sort that we take for granted. We own cars and computers, typewriters and tape recorders, chain saws and kitchen blenders . . . but our forebears depended on muscle-power. Certainly they traveled by train and sometimes steamer, but buses were still horse-drawn, as for the most part were plows and reapers, and they were still building sailing-ships. A moderately prosperous household might have a bicycle or two, a treadle-operated sewing-machine, a manual washing-machine and wringer, possibly a bellows camera, and one or two other items, but in *The Bazaar, Exchange and Mart* for June 28, 1889, these, plus guns and watches, were virtually the only machines on offer apart from industrial and scientific equipment.

It was one of RK's gifts that he sensed the counterpart of magic in machinery. He became, in a sense, a poet of the machine age (e.g., describing the departure of the liner *Mauretania:* "The captain moves a lever 'neath his hand,/ And the monstrous nine-decked city goes to sea.").

The idea of building a story around the shake-down voyage of a new ship may not seem so striking to us, who are familiar with such matters as the need to run-in a new car. But in its day this was a trail-blazing piece of work,

and I still find it remarkable how RK, with masterly econ-
omy of words, managed to endow all those inanimate objects with individual personalities.

Falls are the lines with which a ship's boat is let down
from the davits that swing it outboard of the deck for
launching. The Banks are presumably the Grand Banks,
off Newfoundland; the *Dimbula* would have passed them
on a Great Circle course. As to the song at the end, RK
learned it in Chicago from a group of newspapermen who
called themselves the Whitechapel Club. You can find it
in full, and the tune, on pages 202–3 of Carl Sandburg's
American Songbag.

The Ship That Found Herself

We now, held in captivity,
    Spring to our labour nor grieve!
See now, how it is blesseder,
    Brothers, to give than receive!
Keep trust, wherefore ye were made
    Paying the duty ye owe;
For a clean thrust and the sheer of the blade
    Shall carry us where we should go.

SONG OF THE ENGINES

I t was her first voyage, and though she was but a cargo-steamer of
twelve hundred tons, she was the very best of her kind, the
outcome of forty years of experiments and improvements in frame-
work and machinery; and her designers and owner thought as much
of her as though she had been the *Lucania.* Anyone can make a
floating hotel that will pay expenses, if he puts enough money into
the saloon, and charges for private baths, suites of rooms, and such
like; but in these days of competition and low freights every square
inch of a cargo-boat must be built for cheapness, great hold-capac-
ity, and a certain steady speed. This boat was, perhaps, two hundred
and forty feet long and thirty-two feet wide, with arrangements that
enabled her to carry cattle on her main and sheep on her upper deck
if she wanted to; but her great glory was the amount of cargo that

she could store away in her holds. Her owners—they were a very well-known Scotch firm—came round with her from the north, where she had been launched and christened and fitted, to Liverpool, where she was to take cargo for New York; and the owner's daughter, Miss Frazier, went to and fro on the clean decks, admiring the new paint and the brass work, and the patent winches, and particularly the strong, straight bow, over which she had cracked a bottle of champagne when she named the steamer the *Dimbula*. It was a beautiful September afternoon, and the boat in all her newness—she was painted lead-color with a red funnel—looked very fine indeed. Her house-flag was flying, and her whistle from time to time acknowledged the salutes of friendly boats, who saw that she was new to the High and Narrow Seas and wished to make her welcome.

"And now," said Miss Frazier delightedly, to the captain, "she's a real ship, isn't she? It seems only the other day father gave the order for her, and now—and now—isn't she a beauty!" The girl was proud of the firm, and talked as though she were the controlling partner.

"Oh, she's no so bad," the skipper replied cautiously. "But I'm sayin' that it takes more than christenin' to mak' a ship. In the nature o' things, Miss Frazier, if ye follow me, she's just irons and rivets and plates put into the form of a ship. She has to find herself yet."

"I thought father said she was exceptionally well found."

"So she is," said the skipper, with a laugh. "But it's this way wi' ships, Miss Frazier. She's all here, but the parts of her have not learned to work together yet. They've had no chance."

"The engines are working beautifully. I can hear them."

"Yes, indeed. But there's more than engines to a ship. Every inch of her, ye'll understand, has to be livened up and made to work wi' its neighbor—sweetenin' her, we call it, technically."

"And how will you do it?" the girl asked.

"We can no more than drive and steer her, and so forth; but if we have rough weather this trip—it's likely—she'll learn the rest by heart! For a ship, ye'll obsairve, Miss Frazier, is in no sense a reegid body closed at both ends. She's a highly complex structure o' various an' conflictin' strains, we' tissues that must give an' tak' accordin' to her personal modulus of elasteecity." Mr. Buchanan, the chief engineer, was coming towards them. "I'm sayin' to Miss Frazier, here, that our little *Dimbula* has to be sweetened yet, and nothin' but a gale will do it. How's all wi' your engines, Buck?"

"Well enough—true by plumb an' rule, o' course; but there's no spontaneeity yet." He turned to the girl. "Take my word, Miss Frazier, and maybe ye'll comprehend later; even after a pretty girl's christened a ship it does not follow that there's such a thing as a ship under the men that work her."

"I was sayin' the very same, Mr. Buchanan," the skipper interrupted.

"That's more metaphysical than I can follow," said Miss Frazier, laughing.

"Why so? Ye're good Scotch, an'—I knew your mother's father, he was fra' Dumfries—ye've a vested right in metapheesics, Miss Frazier, just as ye have in the *Dimbula*," the engineer said.

"Eh, well, we must go down to the deep waters, an' earn Miss Frazier her deevidends. Will you not come to my cabin for tea?" said the skipper. "We'll be in dock the night, and when you're goin' back to Glasgie ye can think of us loadin' her down an' drivin' her forth—all for your sake."

In the next few days they stowed some two thousand tons' dead weight into the *Dimbula,* and took her out from Liverpool. As soon as she met the lift of the open water, she naturally began to talk. If you lay your ear to the side of the cabin the next time you are in a steamer, you will hear hundreds of little voices in every direction, thrilling and buzzing, and whispering and popping, and gurgling and sobbing and squeaking exactly like a telephone in a thunderstorm. Wooden ships shriek and growl and grunt, but iron vessels throb and quiver through all their hundreds of ribs and thousands of rivets. The *Dimbula* was very strongly built, and every piece of her had a letter or number, or both, to describe it; and every piece had been hammered, or forged, or rolled, or punched by man, and had lived in the roar and rattle of the ship-yard for months. Therefore, every piece had its own separate voice in exact proportion to the amount of trouble spent upon it. Cast-iron, as a rule, says very little; but mild steel plates and wrought-iron, and ribs and beams that have been much bent and welded and riveted, talk continuously. Their conversation, of course, is not half as wise as our human talk, because they are all, though they do not know it, bound down one to the other in a black darkness, where they cannot tell what is happening near them, nor what will overtake them next.

As soon as she had cleared the Irish coast a sullen, gray-headed old wave of the Atlantic climbed leisurely over her straight bows, and sat down on her steam-capstan used for hauling up the anchor.

Now the capstan and the engine that drove it had been newly painted red and green; besides which, nobody likes being ducked.

"Don't you do that again," the capstan sputtered through the teeth of his cogs. "Hi! Where's the fellow gone?"

The wave had slouched overside with a plop and a chuckle; but "Plenty more where he came from," said a brother-wave, and went through and over the capstan, who was bolted firmly to an iron plate on the iron deck-beams below.

"Can't you keep still up there?" said the deck-beams. "What's the matter with you? One minute you weigh twice as much as you ought to, and the next you don't!"

"It isn't my fault," said the capstan. "There's a green brute outside that comes and hits me on the head."

"Tell that to the shipwrights. You've been in position for months and you've never wriggled like this before. If you aren't careful you'll strain *us*."

"Talking of strain," said a low, rasping, unpleasant voice, "are any of you fellows—you deck-beams, we mean—aware that those exceedingly ugly knees of yours happen to be riveted into our structure—*ours*?"

"Who might you be?" the deck-beams inquired.

"Oh, nobody in particular," was the answer. "We're only the port and starboard upper-deck stringers; and if you persist in heaving and hiking like this, we shall be reluctantly compelled to take steps."

Now the stringers of the ship are long iron girders, so to speak, that run lengthways from stern to bow. They keep the iron frames (what are called ribs in a wooden ship) in place, and also help to hold the ends of the deck-beams, which go from side to side of the ship. Stringers always consider themselves most important, because they are so long.

"You will take steps—will you?" This was a long echoing rumble. It came from the frames—scores and scores of them, each one about eighteen inches distant from the next, and each riveted to the stringers in four places. "We think you will have a certain amount of trouble in *that*"; and thousands and thousands of the little rivets that held everything together whispered: "You will. You will! Stop quivering and be quiet. Hold on, brethren! Hold on! Hot Punches! What's that?"

Rivets have no teeth, so they cannot chatter with fright; but they did their best as a fluttering jar swept along the ship from stern to bow, and she shook like a rat in a terrier's mouth.

An unusually severe pitch, for the sea was rising, had lifted the big throbbing screw nearly to the surface, and it was spinning round in a kind of soda-water—half sea and half air—going much faster than was proper, because there was no deep water for it to work in. As it sank again, the engines—and they were triple expansion, three cylinders in a row—snorted through all their three pistons. "Was that a joke, you fellow outside? It's an uncommonly poor one. How are we to do our work if you fly off the handle that way?"

"I didn't fly off the handle," said the screw, twirling huskily at the end of the screw-shaft. "If I had, you'd have been scrap-iron by this time. The sea dropped away from under me, and I had nothing to catch on to. That's all."

"That's all, d'you call it?" said the thrust-block, whose business it is to take the push of the screw; for if a screw had nothing to hold it back it would crawl right into the engine-room. (It is the holding back of the screwing action that gives the drive to a ship.) "I know I do my work deep down and out of sight, but I warn you I expect justice. All I ask for is bare justice. Why can't you push steadily and evenly, instead of whizzing like a whirligig, and making me hot under all my collars?" The thrust-block had six collars, each faced with brass, and he did not wish to get them heated.

All the bearings that supported the fifty feet of screw-shaft as it ran to the stern whispered: "Justice—give us justice."

"I can only give you what I can get," the screw answered. "Look out! It's coming again!"

He rose with a roar as the *Dimbula* plunged, and "whack—flack—whack—whack" went the engines, furiously, for they had little to check them.

"I'm the noblest outcome of human ingenuity—Mr. Buchanan says so," squealed the high-pressure cylinder. "This is simply ridiculous!" The piston went up savagely, and choked, for half the steam behind it was mixed with dirty water. "Help! Oiler! Fitter! Stoker! Help! I'm choking," it gasped. "Never in the history of maritime invention has such a calamity overtaken one so young and strong. And if I go, who's to drive the ship?"

"Hush! oh, hush!" whispered the Steam, who, of course, had been to sea many times before. He used to spend his leisure ashore in a cloud, or a gutter, or a flowerpot, or a thunderstorm, or anywhere else where water was needed. "That's only a little priming, a little carrying-over, as they call it. It'll happen all night, on and off. I don't say it's nice, but it's the best we can do under the circumstances."

"What difference can circumstances make? I'm here to do my

work—on clean, dry steam. Blow circumstances!" the cylinder roared.

"The circumstances will attend to the blowing. I've worked on the North Atlantic run a good many times—it's going to be rough before morning."

"It isn't distressingly calm now," said the extra-strong frames—they were called web-frames—in the engine-room. "There's an upward thrust that we don't understand, and there's a twist that is very bad for our brackets and diamond-plates, and there's a sort of west-north-westerly pull that follows the twist, which seriously annoys us. We mention this because we happened to cost a good deal of money, and we feel sure that the owner would not approve of our being treated in this frivolous way."

"I'm afraid the matter is out of the owner's hands for the present," said the Steam, slipping into the condenser. "You're left to your own devices till the weather betters."

"I wouldn't mind the weather," said a flat bass voice below; "it's this confounded cargo that's breaking my heart. I'm the garboard-strake, and I'm twice as thick as most of the others, and I ought to know something."

The garboard-strake is the lowest plate in the bottom of a ship, and the *Dimbula's* garboard-strake was nearly three-quarters of an inch mild steel.

"The sea pushes me up in a way I should never have expected," the strake grunted, "and the cargo pushes me down, and, between the two, I don't know what I'm supposed to do."

"When in doubt, hold on," rumbled the Steam, making head in the boilers.

"Yes; but there's only dark, and cold, and hurry, down here; and how do I know whether the other plates are doing their duty? Those bulwark-plates up above, I've heard, ain't more than five-sixteenths of an inch thick—scandalous, I call it."

"I agree with you," said a huge web-frame by the main cargo-hatch. He was deeper and thicker than all the others, and curved halfway across the ship in the shape of half an arch, to support the deck where deck-beams would have been in the way of cargo coming up and down. "I work entirely unsupported, and I observe that I am the sole strength of this vessel, so far as my vision extends. The responsibility, I assure you, is enormous. I believe the money-value of the cargo is over one hundred and fifty thousand pounds. Think of that!"

"And every pound of it is dependent on my personal exertions."

Here spoke a sea-valve that communicated directly with the water outside, and was seated not very far from the garboard-strake. "I rejoice to think that I am a Prince-Hyde Valve, with best Pará rubber facings. Five patents cover me—I mention this without pride—five separate and several patents, each one finer than the other. At present I am screwed fast. Should I open, you would immediately be swamped. This is incontrovertible!"

Patent things always use the longest words they can. It is a trick that they pick up from their inventors.

"That's news," said a big centrifugal bilge-pump. "I had an idea that you were employed to clean decks and things with. At least, I've used you for that more than once. I forget the precise number, in thousands, of gallons which I am guaranteed to throw per hour; but I assure you, my complaining friends, that there is not the least danger. I alone am capable of clearing any water that may find its way here. By my Biggest Deliveries, we pitched then!"

The sea was getting up in a workmanlike style. It was a dead westerly gale, blown from under a ragged opening of green sky, narrowed on all sides by fat, gray clouds; and the wind bit like pincers as it fretted the spray into lacework on the flanks of the waves.

"I tell you what it is," the foremast telephoned down its wire-stays. "I'm up here, and I can take a dispassionate view of things. There's an organized conspiracy against us. I'm sure of it, because every single one of these waves is heading directly for our bows. The whole sea is concerned in it—and so's the wind. It's awful!"

"What's awful?" said a wave, drowning the capstan for the hundredth time.

"This organized conspiracy on your part," the capstan gurgled, taking his cue from the mast.

"Organized bubbles and spindrift! There has been a depression in the Gulf of Mexico. Excuse me!" He leaped overside; but his friends took up the tale one after another.

"Which has advanced—" That wave hove green water over the funnel.

"As far as Cape Hatteras—" He drenched the bridge.

"And is now going out to sea—to sea—to sea!" The third went free in three surges, making a clean sweep of a boat, which turned bottom up and sank in the darkening troughs alongside, while the broken falls whipped the davits.

"That's all there is to it," seethed the white water roaring through the scuppers. "There's no animus in our proceedings. We're only meteorological corollaries."

"Is it going to get any worse?" said the bow-anchor chained down to the deck, where he could only breathe once in five minutes.

"Not knowing, can't say. Wind may blow a bit by midnight. Thanks awfully. Good-bye."

The wave that spoke so politely had traveled some distance aft, and found itself all mixed up on the deck amidships, which was a well-deck sunk between high bulwarks. One of the bulwark plates, which was hung on hinges to open outward, had swung out, and passed the bulk of the water back to the sea again with a clean smack.

"Evidently that's what I'm made for," said the plate, closing again with a sputter of pride. "Oh no, you don't, my friend!"

The top of a wave was trying to get in from the outside, but as the plate did not open in that direction, the defeated water spurted back.

"Not bad for five-sixteenths of an inch," said the bulwark-plate. "My work, I see, is laid down for the night"; and it began opening and shutting with the motion of the ship as it was designed to do.

"We are not what you might call idle," groaned all the frames together, as the *Dimbula* climbed a big wave, lay on her side at the top, and shot into the next hollow, twisting in the descent. A huge swell pushed up exactly under her middle, and her bow and stern hung free with nothing to support them. Then one joking wave caught her up at the bow, and another at the stern, while the rest of the water slunk away from under her just to see how she would like it; so she was held up at her two ends only, and the weight of the cargo and the machinery fell on the groaning iron keels and bilge-stringers.

"Ease off! Ease off, there!" roared the garboard-strake. "I want one-eighth of an inch fair play. D'you hear me, you rivets!"

"Ease off! Ease off!" cried the bilge-stringers. "Don't hold us so tight to the frames!"

"Ease off!" grunted the deck-beams, as the *Dimbula* rolled fearfully. "You've cramped our knees into the stringers, and we can't move. Ease off, you flat-headed little nuisances."

Then two converging seas hit the bows, one on each side, and fell away in torrents of streaming thunder.

"Ease off!" shouted the forward collision-bulkhead. "I want to crumple up, but I'm stiffened in every direction. Ease off, you dirty little forge-filings. Let me breathe!"

All the hundreds of plates that are riveted to the frames, and make the outside skin of every steamer, echoed the call, for each plate wanted to shift and creep a little, and each plate, according to its position, complained against the rivets.

"We can't help it! *We* can't help it!" they murmured in reply. "We're put here to hold you, and we're going to do it; you never pull us twice in the same direction. If you'd say what you were going to do next, we'd try to meet your views."

"As far as I could feel," said the upper-deck planking, and that was four inches thick, "every single iron near me was pushing or pulling in opposite directions. Now, what's the sense of that? My friends, let us all pull together."

"Pull any way you please," roared the funnel, "so long as you don't try your experiments on *me*. I need seven wire ropes, all pulling in different directions, to hold me steady. Isn't that so?"

"We believe you, my boy!" whistled the funnel-stays through their clenched teeth, as they twanged in the wind from the top of the funnel to the deck.

"Nonsense! We must all pull together," the decks repeated. "Pull lengthways."

"Very good," said the stringers; "then stop pushing sideways when you get wet. Be content to run gracefully fore and aft, and curve in at the ends as we do."

"No—no curves at the end! A very slight workmanlike curve from side to side, with a good grip at each knee, and little pieces welded on," said the deck-beams.

"Fiddle!" cried the iron pillars of the deep, dark hold. "Whoever heard of curves? Stand up straight; be a perfectly round column, and carry tons of good solid weight—like that! There!" A big sea smashed on the deck above, and the pillars stiffened themselves to the load.

"Straight up and down is not bad," said the frames, who ran that way in the sides of the ship, "but you must also expand yourselves sideways. Expansion is the law of life, children. Open out! open out!"

"Come back!" said the deck-beams savagely, as the upward heave of the sea made the frames try to open. "Come back to your bearings, you slack-jawed irons!"

"Rigidity! Rigidity! Rigidity!" thumped the engines. "Absolute, unvarying rigidity—rigidity!"

"You see!" whined the rivets in chorus. "No two of you will ever pull alike, and—and you blame it all on us. We only know how to go through a plate and bite down on both sides so that it can't, and mustn't, and shan't move."

"I've got one-fraction of an inch play, at any rate," said the garboard-strake, triumphantly. So he had, and all the bottom of the ship felt the easier for it.

"Then we're no good," sobbed the bottom rivets. "We were ordered—we were ordered—never to give; and we've given, and the sea will come in, and we'll all go to the bottom together! First we're blamed for everything unpleasant, and now we haven't the consolation of having done our work."

"Don't say I told you," whispered the Steam consolingly; "but, between you and me and the last cloud I came from, it was bound to happen sooner or later. You *had* to give a fraction, and you've given without knowing it. Now, hold on, as before."

"What's the use?" a few hundred rivets chattered. "We've given—we've given; and the sooner we confess that we can't keep the ship together, and go off our little heads, the easier it will be. No rivet forged can stand this strain."

"No one rivet was ever meant to. Share it among you," the Steam answered.

"The others can have my share. I'm going to pull out," said a rivet in one of the forward plates.

"If you go, others will follow," hissed the Steam. "There's nothing so contagious in a boat as rivets going. Why, I knew a little chap like you—he was an eighth of an inch fatter, though—on a steamer—to be sure, she was only nine hundred tons, now I come to think of it—in exactly the same place as you are. He pulled out in a bit of a bobble of a sea, not half as bad as this, and he started all his friends on the same butt-strap, and the plates opened like a furnace door, and I had to climb into the nearest fog-bank, while the boat went down."

"Now that's peculiarly disgraceful," said the rivet. "Fatter than me, was he, and in a steamer half our tonnage? Reedy little peg! I blush for the family, sir." He settled himself more firmly than ever in his place, and the Steam chuckled.

"You see," he went on, quite gravely, "a rivet, and especially a rivet in your position, is really the one indispensable part of the ship."

The Steam did not say that he had whispered the very same thing to every single piece of iron aboard. There is no sense in telling too much truth.

And all that while the little *Dimbula* pitched and chopped, and swung and slewed, and lay down as though she were going to die, and got up as though she had been stung, and threw her nose round and round in circles half a dozen times as she dipped; for the gale was at its worst. It was inky black, in spite of the tearing white froth on the waves, and, to top everything, the rain began to fall in sheets, so that you could not see your hand before your face. This did not make much difference to the ironwork below, but it troubled the foremast a good deal.

"Now it's all finished," he said dismally. "The conspiracy is too strong for us. There is nothing left but to—"

"*Hurraar! Brrrraaah! Brrrrrrp!*" roared the Steam through the foghorn, till the decks quivered. "Don't be frightened, below. It's only me, just throwing out a few words, in case anyone happens to be rolling round tonight."

"You don't mean to say there's anyone except *us* on the sea in such weather?" said the funnel in a husky snuffle.

"Scores of 'em," said the Steam, clearing its throat; "*Rrrrrraaa! Brraaaaa! Prrrrp!* It's a trifle windy up here; and, Great Boilers! how it rains!"

"We're drowning," said the scuppers. They had been doing nothing else all night, but this steady thrash of rain above them seemed to be the end of the world.

"That's all right. We'll be easier in an hour or two. First the wind and then the rain: Soon you may make sail again! *Grrraaaaaah! Drrrraaaa! Drrrp!* I have a notion that the sea is going down already. If it does you'll learn something about rolling. We've only pitched till now. By the way, aren't you chaps in the hold a little easier than you were?"

There was just as much groaning and straining as ever, but it was not so loud or squeaky in tone; and when the ship quivered she did not jar stiffly, like a poker hit on the floor, but gave with a supple little waggle, like a perfectly balanced golf-club.

"We have made a most amazing discovery," said the stringers, one after another. "A discovery that entirely changes the situation. We have found, for the first time in the history of ship-building, that the inward pull of the deck-beams and the outward thrust of the frames lock us, as it were, more closely in our places, and enables us to endure a strain which is entirely without parallel in the records of marine architecture."

The Steam turned a laugh quickly into a roar up the foghorn. "What massive intellects you great stringers have," he said softly, when he had finished.

"We also," began the deck-beams, "are discoverers and geniuses. We are of opinion that the support of the hold-pillars materially helps us. We find that we lock up on them when we are subjected to a heavy and singular weight of sea above."

Here the *Dimbula* shot down a hollow, lying almost on her side—righting at the bottom with a wrench and a spasm.

"In these cases—are you aware of this, Steam?—the plating at the bows, and particularly at the stern—we would also mention the floors beneath us—help *us* to resist any tendency to spring." The frames spoke, in the solemn, awed voice which people use when they have just come across something entirely new for the very first time.

"I'm only a poor puffy little flutterer," said the Steam, "but I have to stand a good deal of pressure in my business. It's all tremendously interesting. Tell us some more. You fellows are so strong."

"Watch us and you'll see," said the bow-plates, proudly. "Ready, behind there! Here's the Father and Mother of Waves coming! Sit tight, rivets all!" A great sluicing comber thundered by, but through the scuffle and confusion the Steam could hear the low, quick cries of the ironwork as the various strains took them—cries like these: "Easy, now—easy! *Now* push for all your strength! Hold out! Give a fraction! Hold up! Pull in! Shove crossways! Mind the strain at the ends! Grip, now! Bite tight! Let the water get away from under—and there she goes!"

The wave raced off into the darkness, shouting, "Not bad, that, if it's your first run!" and the drenched and ducked ship throbbed to the beat of the engines inside her. All three cylinders were white with the salt spray that had come down through the engine-room hatch; there was white fur on the canvas-bound steam-pipes, and even the bright-work deep below was speckled and soiled; but the cylinders had learned to make the most of steam that was half water, and were pounding along cheerfully.

"How's the noblest outcome of human ingenuity hitting it?" said the Steam, as he whirled through the engine-room.

"Nothing for nothing in this world of woe," the cylinders answered, as though they had been working for centuries, "and precious little for seventy-five pounds' head. We've made two knots this last hour and a quarter! Rather humiliating for eight hundred horse-power, isn't it?"

"Well, it's better than drifting astern, at any rate. You seem rather less—how shall I put it?—stiff in the back than you were."

"If you'd been hammered as we've been this night, you wouldn't be stiff—iff—iff, either. Theoreti—retti—retti—cally, of course, rigidity is the thing. Purr—purr—practically, there has to be a little give and take. *We* found that out by working on our sides for five minutes at a stretch—chch—chh. How's the weather?"

"Sea's going down fast," said the Steam.

"Good business," said the high-pressure cylinder. "Whack her up, boys. They've given us five pounds more steam"; and he began humming the first bars of "Said the Young Obadiah to the Old Obadiah," which, as you may have noticed, is a pet tune among engines not built for high speed. Racing-liners with twin-screws sing "The Turkish Patrol" and the overture to the "Bronze Horse," and "Madame Angot," till something goes wrong, and then they render Gounod's "Funeral March of a Marionette," with variations.

"You'll learn a song of your own some fine day," said the Steam, as he flew up the foghorn for one last bellow.

Next day the sky cleared and the sea dropped a little, and the *Dimbula* began to roll from side to side till every inch of iron in her was sick and giddy. But luckily they did not all feel ill at the same time: otherwise she would have opened out like a wet paper box.

The Steam whistled warnings as he went about his business: it is in this short, quick roll and tumble that follows a heavy sea that most of the accidents happen, for then everything thinks that the worst is over and goes off guard. So he orated and chattered till the beams and frames and floors and stringers and things had learned how to lock down and lock up on one another, and endure this new kind of strain.

They found ample time to practice, for they were sixteen days at sea, and it was foul weather till within a hundred miles of New York. The *Dimbula* picked up her pilot, and came in covered with salt and red rust. Her funnel was dirty gray from top to bottom; two boats had been carried away; three copper ventilators looked like hats after a fight with the police; the bridge had a dimple in the middle of it; the house that covered the steam steering-gear was split as with hatchets; there was a bill for small repairs in the engine-room almost as long as the screw-shaft; the forward cargo-hatch fell into bucket-staves when they raised the iron crossbars; and the steam-capstan had been badly wrenched on its bed. Altogether, as the skipper said, it was "a pretty general average."

"But she's soupled," he said to Mr. Buchanan. "For all her dead weight she rode like a yacht. Ye mind that last blow off the Banks? I am proud of her, Buck."

"It's verra good," said the chief engineer, looking along the disheveled decks. "Now, a man judgin' superfeecially would say we were a wreck, but we know otherwise—by experience."

Naturally everything in the *Dimbula* fairly stiffened with pride, and the foremast and the forward collision-bulkhead, who are pushing creatures, begged the Steam to warn the Port of New York of their arrival. "Tell those big boats all about us," they said. "They seem to take us quite as a matter of course."

It was a glorious, clear, dead calm morning, and in single file, with less than half a mile between each, their bands playing and their tug-boats shouting and waving handkerchiefs, were the *Majestic,* the *Paris,* the *Touraine,* the *Servia,* the *Kaiser Wilhelm II,* and the *Werkendam,* all statelily going out to sea. As the *Dimbula* shifted her helm to give the great boats clear way, the Steam (who knows far too much to mind making an exhibition of himself now and then) shouted:

"Oyez! Oyez! Oyez! Princes, Dukes, and Barons of the High Seas! Know ye by these presents, we are the *Dimbula,* fifteen days nine hours from Liverpool, having crossed the Atlantic with three thousand ton of cargo for the first time in our career! We have not foundered. We are here. *'Eer! 'Eer!* We are not disabled. But we have had a time wholly unparalleled in the annals of ship-building! Our decks were swept! We pitched; we rolled! We thought we were going to die! *Hi! Hi!* But we didn't. We wish to give notice that we have come to New York all the way across the Atlantic, through the worst weather in the world; and we are the *Dimbula!* We are—arr—ha—ha-r-r-r!"

The beautiful line of boats swept by as steadily as the procession of the Seasons. The *Dimbula* heard the *Majestic* say, "Hmph!" and the *Paris* grunted, "How!" and the *Touraine* said, "Oui!" with a little coquettish flicker of steam; and the *Servia* said, "Haw!" and the *Kaiser* and the *Werkendam* said, "Hoch!" Dutch-fashion—and that was absolutely all.

"I did my best," said the Steam, gravely, "but I don't think they were much impressed with us, somehow. Do you?"

"It's simply disgusting," said the bow-plates. "They might have seen what we've been through. There isn't a ship on the sea that has suffered as we have—is there, now?"

"Well, I wouldn't go so far as that," said the Steam, "because I've worked on some of those boats, and sent them through weather quite as bad as the fortnight that we've had, in six days; and some of them are a little over ten thousand tons, I believe. Now I've seen the *Majestic,* for instance, ducked from her bows to her funnel; and

I've helped the *Arizona,* I think she was, to back off an iceberg she met with one dark night; and I had to run out of the *Paris*'s engine-room, one day, because there was thirty foot of water in it. Of course, I don't deny—" The Steam shut off suddenly, as a tug-boat, loaded with a political club and a brass band, that had been to see a New York Senator off to Europe, crossed their bows, going to Hoboken. There was a long silence that reached, without a break, from the cut-water to the propeller-blades of the *Dimbula.*

Then a new, big voice said slowly and thickly, as though the owner had just waked up: "It's my conviction that I have made a fool of myself."

The Steam knew what had happened at once; for when a ship finds herself all the talking of the separate pieces ceases and melts into one voice, which is the soul of the ship.

"Who are you?" he said, with a laugh.

"I am the *Dimbula,* of course. I've never been anything else except that—and a fool!"

The tug-boat, which was doing its very best to be run down, got away just in time, its band playing clashily and brassily a popular but impolite air:

> In the days of old Rameses—are you on?
> In the days of old Rameses—are you on?
> In the days of old Rameses,
> That story had paresis,
> Are you on—are you on—are you on?

"Well, I'm glad you've found yourself," said the Steam. "To tell the truth I was a little tired of talking to all those ribs and stringers. Here's Quarantine. After that we'll go to our wharf and clean up a little, and—next month we'll do it all over again."

·007

FROM *THE DAY'S WORK* (1898)

What else do you call a story featuring intelligent machines . . . ?

Most of the remarks prefacing "The Ship That Found
Herself" apply equally to this story. Rereading it the
other day, picturing in imagination the marshaling-yard
where Poney does his switching, I found myself reminded
of the largest market-square in Europe, at Kraków in Po-
land, and the insight that overtook me there when I realized that for the first time in my life I was looking at a
land port. (It was where they used to break up caravans
that had come to Europe on the Silk Road, from as far
away as China.)

I suspect that a similar resemblance must have struck
RK while watching long-distance trains being made up for
their runs of hundreds or thousands of miles. And, since
he was who he was . . .

The number sounds familiar, doesn't it? (Not you,
Commander Bond—wait your turn!)

·007 is an American-class locomotive, a 4-4-0—that is,
with a four-wheeled truck (U.K. bogie) at the front, four
driving wheels, and no second truck under the cab. This
pattern had been common throughout the United States
since the 1840s, and constantly refined in detail. They had
an excellent reputation for versatility. A Mogul was a
2-6-0, i.e., with a two-wheel front truck and six driving
wheels. A Consolidation was a 2-8-0.

A cowcatcher, more formally known as a pilot, was a

frame mounted at the front of the locomotive that could be used to push obstructions such as fallen trees clear of the track. A switching-engine is what we call in Britain a shunting-engine, used for moving rolling-stock around the yards and making up and breaking down long-distance trains.

A parlor car has comfortable individual seats and often a bar. A vestibuled is what in Britain is called a corridor train, in which one can walk along and between the cars while the train is moving.

The Compound, described as N.G.—No Good!—would most likely have been a 4-6-2. Compounds have high-pressure cylinders to take the steam direct from the boiler and low-pressure ones to extract further work from it. According to J. T. van Riemsdijk (Encyclopedia of Railways) the compound uses less fuel and water, but is more expensive and requires a more highly trained driver.

The B. & A. was, I suspect, the Buffalo and Albany, but I don't possess a proper map of the Vanderbilt Lines.

Outrecuidance = presumptuousness. Faroucherie, according to Petit Robert, does not exist, but if it did it would mean unsociability. A loco was said to stick on a dead center when the main connecting-rod stopped exactly in line with the axle of the wheel, so it could move neither way.

One of RK's rare mistakes in the use of technical jargon occurs when Poney calls ·007 "eight-wheel coupled."

A grade is an incline. A Prince Albert was a double-breasted frock-coat. An injector is a device that opens the input valve to the boiler, allowing water to flow in against the resistance of the steam. A tender holds the reserve of water and fuel. A coupler links car to car, or car to loco. A switch (U.K. points) is a section of movable rail enabling a train to change from one track to another. M.T.K. is a misprint; it should be M.K.T. (Missouri, Kansas & Texas Railroad).

Lodge is used here in the Masonic sense; RK was inducted as a Freemason in India, and very proud of the fact that "I was entered by a member of the Brahmo Somaj (Hindu), passed by a Mohammedan, and raised by an Englishman. Our tyler was an Indian Jew" (1885). A "granger," by the way, was a member of the Patrons of

Husbandry, an organization of farmers divided into granges rather than lodges.

A caboose is a car attached to the rear of a freight or construction train, for the conductor or train crew. The Empire State and the Cannon-ball were legendary express trains. A naphtha-launch was a steam-launch using naphtha, an inflammable liquid distilled from petroleum or coal-tar, to heat her boiler.

·007

A locomotive is, next to a marine engine, the most sensitive thing man ever made; and No. ·007, besides being sensitive, was new. The red paint was hardly dry on his spotless bumper-bar, his headlight shone like a fireman's helmet, and his cab might have been a hardwood-finish parlor. They had run him into the round-house after his trial—he had said good-bye to his best friend in the shops, the overhead traveling-crane—the big world was just outside; and the other locos were taking stock of him. He looked at the semicircle of bold, unwinking headlights, heard the low purr and mutter of the steam mounting in the gauges—scornful hisses of contempt as a slack valve lifted a little—and would have given a month's oil for leave to crawl through his own driving-wheels into the brick ash-pit beneath him. ·007 was an eight-wheeled "American" loco, slightly different from others of his type, and as he stood he was worth ten thousand dollars on the Company's books. But if you had bought him at his own valuation, after half an hour's waiting in the darkish, echoing round-house, you would have saved exactly nine thousand nine hundred and ninety-nine dollars and ninety-eight cents.

A heavy Mogul freight, with a short cowcatcher and a fire-box that came down within three inches of the rail, began the impolite game, speaking to a Pittsburgh Consolidation, who was visiting.

"Where did this thing blow in from?" he asked, with a dreamy puff of light steam.

"It's all I can do to keep track of our makes," was the answer, "without lookin' after *your* back-numbers. Guess it's something Peter Cooper left over when he died."

·007 quivered; his steam was getting up, but he held his tongue. Even a hand-car knows what sort of locomotive it was that Peter

Cooper experimented upon in the far-away Thirties. It carried its coal and water in two apple-barrels, and was not much bigger than a bicycle.

Then up and spoke a small, newish switching-engine, with a little step in front of his bumper-timber, and his wheels so close together that he looked like a broncho getting ready to buck.

"Something's wrong with the road when a Pennsylvania gravel-pusher tells us anything about our stock, *I* think. That kid's all right. Eustis designed him, and Eustis designed me. Ain't that good enough?"

·007 could have carried the switching-loco round the yard in his tender, but he felt grateful for even this little word of consolation.

"We don't use hand-cars on the Pennsylvania," said the Consolidation. "That—er—peanut-stand's old enough and ugly enough to speak for himself."

"He hasn't bin spoken to yet. He's bin spoken *at*. Hain't ye any manners on the Pennsylvania?" said the switching-loco.

"You ought to be in the yard, Poney," said the Mogul, severely. "We're all long-haulers here."

"That's what you think," the little fellow replied. "You'll know more 'fore the night's out. I've bin down to Track 17, and the freight there—oh, Christmas!"

"I've trouble enough in my own division," said a lean, light suburban loco with very shiny brake-shoes. "My commuters wouldn't rest till they got a parlor-car. They've hitched her back of all, and she hauls worse'n a snow-plough. I'll snap her off some day sure, and then they'll blame every one except their foolselves. They'll be askin' me to haul a vestibuled next!"

"They made you in New Jersey, didn't they?" said Poney. "Thought so. Commuters and truck-wagons ain't any sweet haulin', but I tell *you* they're a heap better'n cuttin' out refrigerator-cars or oil-tanks. Why, I've hauled—"

"Haul! You?" said the Mogul contemptuously. "It's all you can do to bunt a cold-storage car up the yard. Now, I—" he paused a little to let the words sink in—"I handle the Flying Freight—e-leven cars worth just anything you please to mention. On the stroke of eleven I pull out; and I'm timed for thirty-five an hour. Costly—perishable—fragile—immediate—that's me! Suburban traffic's only but one degree better than switching. Express freight's what pays."

"Well, I ain't given to blowing, as a rule," began the Pittsburgh Consolidation.

"No? You was sent in here because you grunted on the grade," Poney interrupted.

"Where I grunt, you'd lie down, Poney; but, as I was saying, I don't blow much. Notwithstandin', *if* you want to see freight that is freight moved lively, you should see me warbling through the Alleghenies with thirty-seven ore-cars behind me, and my brake-men fightin' tramps so's they can't attend to my tooter. I have to do all the holdin' back then, and, though I say it, I've never had a load get away from me yet. *No*, sir. Haulin's one thing, but judgment and discretion's another. You want judgment in my business."

"Ah! But—but are you not paralyzed by a sense of your over-whelming responsibilities?" said a curious, husky voice from a corner.

"Who's that?" ·007 whispered to the Jersey commuter.

"Compound—experiment—N.G. She's bin switchin' in the B. & A. yards for six months, when she wasn't in the shops. She's economical (*I* call it mean) in her coal, but she takes it out in repairs. Ahem! I presume you found Boston somewhat isolated, madam, after your New York season?"

"I am never so well occupied as when I am alone." The Compound seemed to be talking from halfway up her smoke-stack.

"Sure," said the irreverent Poney, under his breath. "They don't hanker after her any in the yard."

"But, with my constitution and temperament—my work lies in Boston—I find your *outrecuidance*—"

"Outer which?" said the Mogul freight. "Simple cylinders are good enough for me."

"Perhaps I should have said *faroucherie*," hissed the Compound.

"I don't hold with any make of papier-mâché wheel," the Mogul insisted.

The Compound sighed pityingly, and said no more.

"Git 'em all shapes in this world, don't ye?" said Poney. "That's Mass'chusetts all over. They half start, an' then they stick on a dead-center, an' blame it all on other folk's ways o' treatin' them. Talkin' o' Boston, Comanche told me, last night, he had a hot-box just beyond the Newtons, Friday. That was why, *he* says, the Accommodation was held up. Made out no end of a tale, Comanche did."

"If I'd heard that in the shops, with my boiler out for repairs, I'd know 't was one o' Comanche's lies," the New Jersey commuter snapped. "Hot-box! Him! What happened was they'd put an extra car on, and he just lay down on the grade and squealed. They had to send 127 to help him through. Made it out a hot-box, did he? Time before that he said he was ditched! Looked me square in the headlight and told me that as cool as—as a water-tank in a cold wave. Hot-box! You ask 127 about Comanche's hot-box. Why, Comanche he was side-tracked, and 127 (*he* was just about as mad as they make 'em on account o' being called out at ten o'clock at night) took hold and whirled her into Boston in seventeen minutes. Hot-box! Hot fraud! That's what Comanche is."

Then ·007 put both drivers and his pilot into it, as the saying is, for he asked what sort of thing a hot-box might be?

"Paint my bell sky-blue!" said Poney, the switcher. "Make me a surface-railroad loco with a hardwood skirtin'-board round my wheels! Break me up and cast me into five-cent sidewalk-fakirs' mechanical toys! Here's an eight-wheel coupled 'American' don't know what a hot-box is! Never heard of an emergency-stop either, did ye? Don't know what ye carry jack-screws for? You're too innocent to be left alone with your own tender. Oh, you—you flat-car!"

There was a roar of escaping steam before any one could answer, and ·007 nearly blistered his paint off with pure mortification.

"A hot-box," began the Compound, picking and choosing the words as though they were coal, "a hot-box is the penalty exacted from inexperience by haste. Ahem!"

"Hot-box!" said the Jersey Suburban. "It's the price you pay for going on the tear. It's years since I've had one. It's a disease that don't attack short-haulers, as a rule."

"We never have hot-boxes on the Pennsylvania," said the Consolidation. "They get 'em in New York—same as nervous prostration."

"Ah, go home on a ferry-boat," said the Mogul. "You think because you use worse grades than our road 'ud allow, you're a kind of Allegheny angel. Now, I'll tell you what you . . . Here's my folk. Well, I can't stop. See you later, perhaps."

He rolled forward majestically to the turntable, and swung like a man-of-war in a tideway, till he picked up his track. "But as for you, you pea-green swivellin' coffee-pot [this to ·007], you go out and learn something before you associate with those who've made more mileage in a week than you'll roll up in a year. Costly—perishable— fragile—immediate—that's me! S'long."

"Split my tubes if that's actin' polite to a new member o' the Brotherhood," said Poney. "There wasn't any call to trample on ye like that. But manners was left out when Moguls was made. Keep up your fire, kid, an' burn your own smoke. 'Guess we'll all be wanted in a minute."

Men were talking rather excitedly in the round-house. One man, in a dingy jersey, said that he hadn't any locomotives to waste on the yard. Another man, with a piece of crumpled paper in his hand, said that the yard-master said that he was to say that if the other man said anything, he (the other man) was to shut his head. Then the other man waved his arms, and wanted to know if he was expected to keep locomotives in his hip-pocket. Then a man in a black Prince Albert, without a collar, came up dripping, for it was a hot August night, and said that what *he* said went; and between the three of them the locomotives began to go, too—first the Compound, then the Consolidation, then ·007.

Now, deep down in his fire-box, ·007 had cherished a hope that as soon as his trial was done, he would be led forth with songs and shoutings, and attached to a green-and-chocolate vestibuled flyer, under charge of a bold and noble engineer, who would pat him on his back, and weep over him, and call him his Arab steed. (The boys in the shops where he was built used to read wonderful stories of railroad life, and ·007 expected things to happen as he had heard.) But there did not seem to be many vestibuled flyers in the roaring, rumbling, electric-lighted yards, and his engineer only said:

"Now, what sort of a fool-sort of an injector has Eustis loaded on to this rig this time?" And he put the lever over with an angry snap, crying: "Am I supposed to switch with this thing, hey?"

The collarless man mopped his head, and replied that, in the present state of the yard and freight and a few other things, the engineer would switch and keep on switching till the cows came home. ·007 pushed out gingerly, his heart in his headlight, so nervous that the clang of his own bell almost made him jump the track. Lanterns waved, or danced up and down, before and behind him; and on every side, six tracks deep, sliding backward and forward, with clashings of couplers and squeals of hand-brakes, were cars—more cars than ·007 had dreamed of. There were oil-cars, and hay-cars, and stock-cars full of lowing beasts, and ore-cars, and potato-cars with stovepipe-ends sticking out in the middle; cold-storage and refrigerator cars dripping ice-water on the tracks; ventilated fruit- and milk-cars; flat-cars with truck-wagons full of market-stuff; flat-cars loaded with reapers and binders, all red and green and gilt under the sizzling electric lights; flat-cars piled high with strong-scented hides, pleasant hemlock-plank, or bundles of shingles; flat-cars creaking to the weight of thirty-ton castings, angle-irons, and rivet-boxes for some new bridge; and hundreds and hundreds and hundreds of box-cars loaded, locked and chalked. Men—hot and angry—crawled among and between and under the thousand wheels; men took flying jumps through his cab, when he halted for a moment; men sat on his pilot as he went forward, and on his tender as he returned; and regiments of men ran along the tops of the box-cars beside him, screwing down brakes, waving their arms, and crying curious things.

He was pushed forward a foot at a time, whirled backwards, his rear drivers clinking and clanking, a quarter of a mile; jerked into a switch (yard-switches are *very* stubby and unaccommodating), bunted into a Red D, or Merchant's Transport car, and, with no hint or knowledge of the weight behind him, started up anew. When his load was fairly on the move, three or four cars would be cut off, and ·007 would bound forward, only to be held hiccupping on the brake. Then he would wait a few minutes, watching the whirled lanterns, deafened with the clang of the bells, giddy with the vision of the sliding cars, his brake-pump panting forty to the minute, his front coupler lying sideways on his cow-catcher, like a tired dog's tongue in his mouth, and the whole of him covered with half-burnt coal-dust.

" 'Tisn't so easy switching with a straight-backed tender," said his little friend of the round-house, bustling by at a trot. "But you're comin' on pretty fair. Ever seen a flyin' switch? No? Then watch me."

Poney was in charge of a dozen heavy flat-cars. Suddenly he shot away from them with a sharp "*Whutt!*" A switch opened in the shadows ahead; he turned up it like a rabbit, it snapped behind him, and the long line of twelve-foot-high lumber jolted on into the arms of a full-sized road-loco, who acknowledged receipt with a dry howl.

"My man's reckoned the smartest in the yard at that trick," he said, returning. "Gives me cold shivers when another fool tries it, though. That's where my short wheel-base comes in. Likes as not you'd have your tender scraped off if *you* tried it."

·007 had no ambitions that way, and said so.

"No? Of course this ain't your regular business, but say, don't you think it's interestin'? Have you seen the yard-master? Well, he's the greatest man on earth, an' don't you forget it. When are we through? Why, kid, it's always like this, day *an'* night—Sundays and weekdays. See that thirty-car freight slidin' in four, no, five tracks off? She's all mixed freight, sent here to be sorted out into straight trains. That's why we're cuttin' out the cars one by one." He gave a vigorous push to a west-bound car as he spoke, and started back with a little snort of surprise, for the car was an old friend—an M. T. K. box-car.

"Jack my drivers, but it's Homeless Kate. Why, Kate, ain't there *no* gettin' you back to your friends? There's forty chasers out for you from your road, if there's one. Who's holdin' you now?"

"Wish I knew," whimpered Homeless Kate. "I belong in Topeka, but I've bin to Cedar Rapids; I've bin to Winnipeg; I've bin to Newport News; I've bin all down the old Atlanta and West Point;

an' I've bin to Buffalo. Maybe I'll fetch up at Haverstraw. I've only bin out ten months, but I'm homesick—I'm just achin' homesick."

"Try Chicago, Katie," said the switching-loco; and the battered old car lumbered down the track, jolting; "I want to be in Kansas when the sunflowers bloom."

"Yard's full o' Homeless Kates an' Wanderin' Willies," he explained to ·007. "I knew an old Fitchburg flat-car out seventeen months; an' one of ours was gone fifteen 'fore ever we got track of her. Dunno quite how our men fix it. Swap around, I guess. Anyway, I've done *my* duty. She's on her way to Kansas, via Chicago; but I'll lay my next boilerful she'll be held there to wait consignee's convenience, and sent back to us with wheat in the fall."

Just then the Pittsburgh Consolidation passed, at the head of a dozen cars.

"I'm goin' home," he said proudly.

"Can't get all them twelve on to the flat. Break 'em in half, Duchy!" cried Poney. But it was ·007 who was backed down to the last six cars, and he nearly blew up with surprise when he found himself pushing them on to a huge ferryboat. He had never seen deep water before, and shivered as the flat drew away and left his bogies within six inches of the black, shiny tide.

After this he was hurried to the freight-house, where he saw the yard-master, a smallish, white-faced man in shirt, trousers, and slippers, looking down upon a sea of trucks, a mob of bawling truckmen, and squadrons of backing, turning, sweating, spark-striking horses.

"That's shippers' carts loadin' on to the receivin' trucks," said the small engine reverently. "But *he* don't care. He let's 'em cuss. He's the Czar—King—Boss! He says 'Please,' and then they kneel down an' pray. There's three or four strings o' today's freight to be pulled before he can attend to *them*. When he waves his hand that way, things happen."

A string of loaded cars slid out down the track, and a string of empties took their place. Bales, crates, boxes, jars, carboys, frails, cases, and packages flew into them from the freight-house as though the cars had been magnets and they iron filings.

"Ki-yah!" shrieked little Poney. "Ain't it great?"

A purple-faced truckman shouldered his way to the yard-master, and shook his fist under his nose. The yard-master never looked up from his bundle of freight-receipts. He crooked his forefinger slightly, and a tall young man in a red shirt, lounging carelessly beside him, hit the truckman under the left ear, so that he dropped, quivering and clucking, on a hay-bale.

"Eleven, seven, ninety-seven, L. Y. S.; fourteen ought ought three; nineteen thirteen; one one four; seventeen ought twenty-one M. B.; *and* the ten west-bound. All straight except the two last. Cut 'em off at the junction. An' *that's* all right. Pull that string." The yard-master, with mild blue eyes, looked out over the howling truckmen at the waters in the moonlight beyond, and hummed:

> All things bright and beautiful,
> All creatures great and small,
> All things wise and wonderful,
> The Lawd Gawd He made all!

·007 moved the cars out and delivered them to the regular road-engine. He had never felt quite so limp in his life.

"Curious, ain't it?" said Poney, puffing, on the next track. "You an' me, if we got that man under our bumpers, we'd work him into red waste and not know what we'd done; but—up there—with the steam hummin' in his boiler that awful quiet way . . ."

"*I* know," said ·007. "Makes me feel as if I'd dropped my fire an' was getting cold. He *is* the greatest man on earth."

They were at the far north end of the yard now, under a switch-tower, looking down on the four-track way of the main traffic. The Boston Compound was to haul ·007's string to some faraway north-ern junction over an indifferent roadbed, and she mourned aloud for the ninety-six pound rails of the B. & A.

"You're young; you're young," she coughed. "You don't realize your responsibilities."

"Yes, he does," said Poney sharply; "but he don't lie down under 'em." Then, with a side-spurt of steam, exactly like a tough spitting: "There ain't more than fifteen thousand dollars' worth o' freight behind her anyway, and she carries on as if 'twere a hundred thou-sand—same as the Mogul's. Excuse me, madam, but you've the track. . . . She's stuck on a dead-center again—bein' specially de-signed not to."

The Compound crawled across the tracks on a long slant, groan-ing horribly at each switch, and moving like a cow in a snowdrift. There was a little pause along the yard after her taillights had disappeared; switches locked crisply, and every one seemed to be waiting.

"Now I'll show you something worth," said Poney. "When the

Purple Emperor ain't on time, it's about time to amend the Constitution. The first stroke of twelve is—"

"Boom!" went the clock in the big yard-tower, and far away ·007
heard a full vibrating "*Yah! Yah! Yah!*" A headlight twinkled on the
horizon like a star, grew an overpowering blaze, and whooped up
the humming track to the roaring music of a happy giant's song:

> With a michnai—ghignai—shtingal! Yah! Yah! Yah!
> Ein—zwei—drei—Mutter! Yah! Yah! Yah!
>   She climb upon der shteeple,
>   Und she frighten all der people,
> Singin' michnai—ghignai—shtingal! Yah! Yah!

The last defiant "yah! yah!" was delivered a mile and a half beyond
the passenger-depot; but ·007 had caught one glimpse of the superb
six-wheel-coupled racing-locomotive, who hauled the pride and
glory of the road—the gilt-edged Purple Emperor, the millionaires'
south-bound express, laying the miles over his shoulder as a man
peels a shaving from a soft board. The rest was a blur of maroon
enamel, a bar of white light from the electrics in the cars, and a
flicker of nickel-plated hand-rail on the rear platform.

"Ooh!" said ·007.

"Seventy-five miles an hour these five miles. Baths, I've heard;
barber's shop; ticker; and a library and the rest to match. Yes, sir;
seventy-five an hour! But he'll talk to you in the round-house just as
democratic as I would. And I—cuss my wheel-base!—I'd kick clean
off the track at half his gait. He's the master of our Lodge. Cleans
up at our house. I'll introdooce you some day. He's worth knowin'!
There ain't many can sing that song, either."

·007 was too full of emotions to answer. He did not hear a raging
of telephone-bells in the switch-tower, nor the man, as he leaned out
and called to ·007's engineer: "Got any steam?"

" 'Nough to run her a hundred mile out o' this, if I could," said
the engineer, who belonged to the open road and hated switching.

"Then get. The Flying Freight's ditched forty mile out, with fifty
rod o' track ploughed up. No; no one's hurt, but both tracks are
blocked. Lucky the wreckin'-car an' derrick are this end of the yard.
Crew'll be along in a minute. Hurry! You've the track."

"Well, I could jest kick my little sawed-off self," said Poney, as
·007 was backed, with a bang, on to a grim and grimy car like a
caboose, but full of tools—a flat-car and a derrick behind it. "Some
folks are one thing, and some are another; but *you're* in luck, kid.
They push a wrecking-car. Now, don't get rattled. Your wheel-base

will keep you on the track, and there ain't any curves worth mentionin'. Oh, say! Comanche told me there's one section o' saw-edged track that's liable to jounce ye a little. Fifteen an' a half out, *after* the grade at Jackson's crossin'. You'll know it by a farmhouse an' a windmill and five maples in the dooryard. Windmill's west o' the maples. An' there's an eighty-foot iron bridge in the middle o' that section with no guard-rails. See you later. Luck!"

Before he knew well what had happened, ·007 was flying up the track into the dumb dark world. Then fears of the night beset him. He remembered all he had ever heard of landslides, rain-piled boulders, blown trees, and strayed cattle, all that the Boston Compound had ever said of responsibility, and a great deal more that came out of his own head. With a very quavering voice he whistled for his first grade crossing (an event in the life of a locomotive), and his nerves were in no way restored by the sight of a frantic horse and a white-faced man in a buggy less than a yard from his right shoulder. Then he was sure he would jump the track; felt his flanges mounting the rail at every curve; knew that his first grade would make him lie down even as Comanche had done at the Newtons. He swept down the grade to Jackson's crossing, saw the windmill west of the maples, felt the badly laid rails spring under him, and sweated big drops all over his boiler. At each jarring bump he believed an axle had smashed; and he took the eighty-foot bridge without the guard-rail like a hunted cat on the top of a fence. Then a wet leaf stuck against the glass of his headlight and threw a flying shadow on the track, so that he thought it was some little dancing animal that would feel soft if he ran over it; and anything soft underfoot frightens a locomotive as it does an elephant. But the men behind seemed quite calm. The wrecking-crew were climbing carelessly from the caboose to the tender—even jesting with the engineer, for he heard a shuffling of feet among the coal, and the snatch of a song, something like this:

> Oh, the Empire State must learn to wait,
> And the Cannon-ball go hang,
> When the West-bound's ditched, and the tool-car's hitched,
> And it's 'way for the Breakdown Gang (Tara-ra!)
> 'Way for the Breakdown Gang!

"Say! Eustis knew what he was doin' when he designed this rig. She's a hummer. New, too."

"Snff! Phew! She *is* new. That ain't paint. That's—"

A burning pain shot through ·007's right rear driver—a crippling, stinging pain.

"This," said ·007, as he flew, "is a hot-box. Now I know what it means. I shall go to pieces, I guess. My first road-run, too!"

"Het a bit, ain't she?" the fireman ventured to suggest to the engineer.

"She'll hold for all we want of her. We're 'most there. 'Guess you chaps back had better climb into your car," said the engineer, his hand on the brake-lever. "I've seen men snapped off—"

But the crew fled laughing. They had no wish to be jerked on to the track. The engineer half turned his wrist, and ·007 found his drivers pinned firm.

"Now it's come!" said ·007, as he yelled aloud, and slid like a sleigh. For the moment he fancied that he would jerk bodily from off his under-pinning.

"That must be the emergency-stop Poney guyed me about," he gasped, as soon as he could think. "Hot-box—emergency-stop. They both hurt; but now I can talk back in the round-house."

He was halted, all hissing hot, a few feet in the rear of what doctors would call a compound-comminuted car. His engineer was kneeling down among his drivers, but he did not call ·007 his "Arab steed," nor cry over him, as the engineers did in the newspapers. He just bad-worded ·007, and pulled yards of charred cotton-waste from about the axles, and hoped he might some day catch the idiot who had packed it. Nobody else attended to him, for Evans, the Mogul's engineer, a little cut about the head, but very angry, was exhibiting, by lantern-light, the mangled corpse of a slim blue pig.

" 'T weren't even a decent-sized hog," he said. " 'T were a shoat."

"Dangerousest beasts they are," said one of the crew. "Get under the pilot an' sort o' twiddle ye off the track, don't they?"

"Don't they?" roared Evans, who was a red-headed Welshman. "You talk as if I was ditched by a hog every fool-day o' the week. *I* ain't friends with all the cussed half-fed shoats in the State o' New York. No, indeed! Yes, this is him—an' look what he's done!"

It was not a bad night's work for one stray piglet. The Flying Freight seemed to have flown in every direction, for the Mogul had mounted the rails and run diagonally a few hundred feet from right to left, taking with him such cars as cared to follow. Some did not. They broke their couplers and lay down, while rear cars frolicked over them. In that game, they had ploughed up and removed and twisted a good deal of the left-hand track. The Mogul himself had waddled into a corn-field, and there he knelt—fantastic wreaths of green twisted round his crank-pins; his pilot covered with solid clods of field, on which corn nodded drunkenly; his fire put out with dirt (Evans had done that as soon as he recovered his senses); and his broken headlight half full of half-burnt moths. His tender had thrown coal all over him, and he looked like a disreputable buffalo who had tried to wallow in a general store. For there lay, scattered over the landscape, from the burst cars, typewriters, sewing-machines, bicycles in crates, a consignment of silver-plated imported harness, French dresses and gloves, a dozen finely moulded hardwood mantels, a fifteen-foot naphtha-launch, with a solid brass bedstead crumpled around her bows, a case of telescopes and microscopes, two coffins, a case of very best candies, some gilt-edged dairy produce, butter and eggs in an omelette, a broken box of expensive toys, and a few hundred other luxuries. A camp of tramps hurried up from nowhere, and generously volunteered to help the crew. So the brakemen, armed with coupler-pins, walked up and down on one side, and the freight-conductor and the fireman patrolled the other with their hands in their hip-pockets. A long-bearded man came out of a house beyond the corn-field, and told Evans that if the accident had happened a little later in the year, all his corn would have been burned, and accused Evans of carelessness. Then he ran away, for Evans was at his heels shrieking, " 'Twas his hog done it—his hog done it! Let me kill him! Let me kill him!" Then the wrecking-crew laughed; and the farmer put his head out of a window and said that Evans was no gentleman.

But ·007 was very sober. He had never seen a wreck before, and it frightened him. The crew still laughed, but they worked at the same time; and ·007 forgot horror in amazement at the way they handled the Mogul freight. They dug round him with spades; they put ties in front of his wheels, and jack-screws under him; they embraced him with the derrick-chain and tickled him with crowbars; while ·007 was hitched on to wrecked cars and backed away till the knot broke or the cars rolled clear of the track. By dawn thirty or forty men were at work, replacing and ramming down the ties, gauging the rails and spiking them. By daylight all cars who could move had gone on in charge of another loco; the track was freed for traffic; and ·007 had hauled the old Mogul over a small pavement of ties, inch by inch, till his flanges bit the rail once more, and he settled down with a clank. But his spirit was broken, and his nerve was gone.

" 'T weren't even a hog," he repeated dolefully; " 't were a shoat; and you—*you* of all of 'em—had to help me on."

"But how in the whole long road did it happen?" asked ·007, sizzling with curiosity.

"Happen! It didn't happen! It just come! I sailed right on top of him around that last curve—thought he was a skunk. Yes; he was all as little as that. He hadn't more'n squealed once 'fore I felt my bogies lift (he'd rolled right under the pilot), and I couldn't catch the track again to save me. Swiveled clean off, I was. Then I felt him sling himself along, all greasy, under my left leadin' driver, and, oh, Boilers! that mounted the rail. I heard my flanges zippin' along the ties, an' the next I knew I was playin' 'Sally, Sally Waters' in the corn, my tender shuckin' coal through my cab, an' old man Evans lyin' still an' bleedin' in front o' me. Shook? There ain't a stay or a bolt or a rivet in me that ain't sprung to glory somewhere."

"Umm!" said ·007. "What d' you reckon you weigh?"

"Without these lumps o' dirt I'm all of a hundred thousand pound."

"And the shoat?"

"Eighty. Call him a hundred pounds at the outside. He's worth about four'n a half dollars. Ain't it awful? Ain't it enough to give you nervous prostration? Ain't it paralysin'? Why, I come just around that curve—" and the Mogul told the tale again, for he was very badly shaken.

"Well, it's all in the day's run, I guess," said ·007, soothingly; "an'—an' a corn-field's pretty soft fallin'."

"If it had bin a sixty-foot bridge, an' I could ha' slid off into deep water, an' blown up an' killed both men, same as others have done, I wouldn't ha' cared; but to be ditched by a shoat—an' you to help me out—in a corn-field—an' an old hayseed in his nightgown cussin' me like as if I was a sick truck-horse! . . . Oh, it's awful! Don't call me Mogul! I'm a sewin'-machine. They'll guy my sand-box off in the yard."

And ·007, his hot-box cooled and his experience vastly enlarged, hauled the Mogul freight slowly to the round-house.

"Hello, old man! Bin out all night, hain't ye?" said the irrepressible Poney, who had just come off duty. "Well, I must say you look it. Costly—perishable—fragile—immediate—that's you! Go to the shops, take them vine-leaves out o' your hair, an' git 'em to play the hose on you."

"Leave him alone, Poney," said ·007 severely, as he was swung on the turn-table, "or I'll—"

"Didn't know the old granger was any special friend o' yours, kid. He wasn't over civil to you last time I saw him."

"I know it; but I've seen a wreck since then, and it has about scared the paint off me. I'm not going to guy anyone as long as I steam—not when they're new to the business an' anxious to learn.

And I'm not goin' to guy the old Mogul either, though I did find him
wreathed around with roastin'-ears. 'Twas a little bit of a shoat—
not a hog—just a shoat, Poney—no bigger'n a lump of anthracite—I
saw it—that made all the mess. Anybody can be ditched, I guess."

"Found that out already, have you? Well, that's a good beginnin'."
It was the Purple Emperor, with his high, tight, plate-glass cab and
green velvet cushion, waiting to be cleaned for his next day's fly.

"Let me make you two gen'lemen acquainted," said Poney. "This
is our Purple Emperor, kid, whom you were admirin' and, I may
say, envyin' last night. This is a new brother, worshipful sir, with
most of his mileage ahead of him, but, so far as a serving-brother
can, I'll answer for him."

"Happy to meet you," said the Purple Emperor, with a glance
round the crowded round-house. "I guess there are enough of us
here to form a full meetin'. Ahem! By virtue of the authority vested
in me as Head of the Road, I hereby declare and pronounce No. ·007
a full and accepted Brother of the Amalgamated Brotherhood of
Locomotives, and as such entitled to all shop, switch, track, tank,
and round-house privileges throughout my jurisdiction, in the Degree of Superior Flier, it bein' well known and credibly reported to
me that our Brother has covered forty-one miles in thirty-nine minutes and a half on an errand of mercy to the afflicted. At a conve-
nient time, I myself will communicate to you the Song and Signal of
this Degree whereby you may be recognized in the darkest night.
Take your stall, newly entered Brother among Locomotives!"

Now, in the darkest night, even as the Purple Emperor said, if you
will stand on the bridge across the freight-yard, looking down upon
the four-track way, at 2:30 A.M., neither before nor after, when the
White Moth, that takes the overflow from the Purple Emperor, tears
south with her seven vestibuled cream-white cars, you will hear, as
the yard-clock makes the half-hour, a faraway sound like the bass
of a violincello, and then, a hundred feet to each word:

> With a michnai—ghignai—shtingal! Yah! Yah! Yah!
> Ein—zwei—drei—Mutter! Yah! Yah! Yah!
>> She climb upon der shteeple,
>> Und she frighten all der people,
> Singin' michnai—ghignai—shtingal! Yah! Yah!

That is ·007 covering his one hundred and fifty-six miles in two
hundred and twenty-one minutes.

"Wireless"
FROM *TRAFFICS AND DISCOVERIES*
(1904)

It is salutary to remember that devices which we take for
granted—radio among them—were within living memory
no more than experimental toys. Indeed, when this story
was written radio as such had not yet been invented; there
was only wireless telegraphy, a means of signaling with
Morse code. (Mike Royko, that great columnist of the
Chicago News, watched the first Moon-landing on television in company with an old man whose parents had
taken him west in a covered wagon. There have indeed
been changes, hmm?)

This story really is set in the pioneering days. *The Bazaar, Exchange and Mart* for February 10, 1905, includes
no reference at all to radio or W/T equipment, even
under "Scientific"; nor does the Sears Roebuck catalog
for 1908. One has to wait another five years before such
items are generally advertised. (There are several in Gam-
age's catalog for 1913.)

As is clear from this story, though, what excited RK's
imagination was less the technical detail of how it was
done, than the fact it was being done, no matter in what
way. Communication across space, with no tangible physical link between sender and receiver . . . Then why not
across time, too?

The scene is set in a drugstore—what the British call a
chemist's—in a seaside town. It is not identified, but the
reference to "eavesdropping across half South England"
suggests it may be somewhere on the East Coast, perhaps

Margate or Ramsgate, though this is hard to reconcile with a seafront on the English Channel. Geographical exactitude, however, is not of the essence. Poole is in Dorset, on the South Coast.

Guglielmo Marconi was the first person to send a wireless signal across the Atlantic. Apothecaries' Hall, in London, was and still is the headquarters of a professional association of pharmacists. An "Italian warehouse" sold a wide range of foods but specialized in pasta, olive oil, dried fruit and other Mediterranean produce.

Nicholas Culpepper or Culpeper (1616–54) was an astrologer and physician who wrote, among other works, *The English Physician and Complete Herbal*. RK devoted a story to him in *Rewards and Fairies* ("A Doctor of Medicine"). A job-master ran a livery stable, hiring out riding-horses and carriages. Paris diamonds were imitation jewels. The "superb glass jars;" which can still be seen occasionally, were a kind of symbol for a chemist's shop: carboys two or three feet high, partly filled with colored liquid. Orris is dried iris-root, used in perfumery and (then) pharmacy. Vulcanite was rubber hardened by heating it with sulphur, widely employed prior to the advent of plastics. The lethal-sounding chloric-ether in the "new and wildish drink" consisted, says my helpful local pharmacist, of one part chloroform to nineteen parts of 90 percent alcohol: lethal indeed! Hertzian waves are radio waves, so named after Heinrich Hertz (1857–94).

Benzoin or benjoin is gum benjamin, made from the juice of a tree that grows in Indonesia; it is an ingredient of incense. Chypre is a perfume made from sandalwood. Men-o'-war are naval ships.

"Wireless"

"It's a funny thing, this Marconi business, isn't it?" said Mr. Shaynor, coughing heavily. "Nothing seems to make any difference, by what they tell me—storms, hills, or anything; but if that's true we shall know before morning."

"Of course it's true," I answered, stepping behind the counter. "Where's old Mr. Cashell?"

"He's had to go to bed on account of his influenza. He said you'd very likely drop in."

"Where's his nephew?"

"Inside, getting the things ready. He told me that the last time they experimented they put the pole on the roof of one of the big hotels here, and the batteries electrified all the water-supply, and—" he giggled—"the ladies got shocks when they took their baths."

"I never heard of that."

"The hotel wouldn't exactly advertise it, would it? Just now, by what Mr. Cashell tells me, they're trying to signal from here to Poole, and they're using stronger batteries than ever. But, you see, he being the guvnor's nephew and all that (and it will be in the papers too), it doesn't matter how they electrify things in this house. Are you going to watch?"

"Very much. I've never seen this game. Aren't you going to bed?"

"We don't close till ten on Saturdays. There's a good deal of influenza in town, too, and there'll be a dozen prescriptions coming in before morning. I generally sleep in the chair here. It's warmer than jumping out of bed every time. Bitter cold, isn't it?"

"Freezing hard. I'm sorry your cough's worse."

"Thank you. I don't mind cold so much. It's this wind that fair cuts me to pieces." He coughed again hard and hackingly, as an old lady came in for ammoniated quinine. "We've just run out of it in bottles, madam," said Mr. Shaynor, returning to the professional tone, "but if you will wait two minutes, I'll make it up for you, madam."

I had used the shop for some time, and my acquaintance with the proprietor had ripened into friendship. It was Mr. Cashell who revealed to me the purpose and power of Apothecaries' Hall what time a fellow chemist had made an error in a prescription of mine, had lied to cover his sloth, and when error and lie were brought home to him had written vain letters.

"A disgrace to our profession," said the thin, mild-eyed man, hotly, after studying the evidence. "You couldn't do a better service to the profession than report him to Apothecaries' Hall."

I did so, not knowing what djinns I should evoke; and the result was such an apology as one might make who had spent a night on the rack. I conceived great respect for Apothecaries' Hall, and esteem for Mr. Cashell, a zealous craftsman who magnified his calling. Until Mr. Shaynor came down from the North his assistants had by no means agreed with Mr. Cashell. "They forget," said he, "that, first and foremost, the compounder is a medicine-man. On him depends the physician's reputation. He holds it literally in the hollow of his hand, sir."

Mr. Shaynor's manners had not, perhaps, the polish of the grocery and Italian warehouse next door, but he knew and loved his dispensary work in every detail. For relaxation he seemed to go no farther afield than the romance of drugs—their discovery, preparation, packing, and export—but it led him to the ends of the earth, and on this subject, and the Pharmaceutical Formulary, and Nicholas Culpepper, most confident of physicians, we met.

Little by little I grew to know something of his beginnings and his hopes—of his mother, who had been a schoolteacher in one of the northern counties, and of his red-headed father, a small job-master at Kirby Moors, who died when he was a child; of the examinations he had passed and of their exceeding and increasing difficulty; of his dreams of a shop in London; of his hate for the price-cutting Cooperative stores; and, most interesting, of his mental attitude towards customers.

"There's a way you get into," he told me, "of serving them carefully, and I hope, politely, without stopping your own thinking. I've been reading Christy's *New Commercial Plants* all this autumn, and that needs keeping your mind on it, I can tell you. So long as it isn't a prescription, of course, I can carry as much as half a page of Christy in my head, and at the same time I could sell out all that window twice over, and not a penny wrong at the end. As to prescriptions, I think I could make up the general run of 'em in my sleep, almost."

For reasons of my own, I was deeply interested in Marconi experiments at their outset in England; and it was of a piece with Mr. Cashell's unvarying thoughtfulness that, when his nephew the electrician appropriated the house for a long-range installation, he should, as I have said, invite me to see the result.

The old lady went away with her medicine, and Mr. Shaynor and I stamped on the tiled floor behind the counter to keep ourselves warm. The shop, by the light of the many electrics, looked like a Paris-diamond mine, for Mr. Cashell believed in all the ritual of his craft. Three superb glass jars—red, green, and blue—of the sort that led Rosamund to parting with her shoes—blazed in the broad plate-glass windows, and there was a confused smell of orris, Kodak films, vulcanite, tooth-powder, sachets, and almond-cream in the air. Mr. Shaynor fed the dispensary stove, and we sucked cayenne-pepper jujubes and menthol lozenges. The brutal east wind had cleared the streets, and the few passers-by were muffled to their puckered eyes. In the Italian warehouse next door some gay feathered birds and game, hung upon hooks, sagged to the wind across the left edge of our window-frame.

"They ought to take these poultry in—all knocked about like that," said Mr. Shaynor. "Doesn't it make you feel fair perishing? See that old hare! The wind's nearly blowing the fur off him."

I saw the belly-fur of the dead beast blown apart in ridges and streaks as the wind caught it, showing bluish skin underneath. "Bitter cold," said Mr. Shaynor, shuddering. "Fancy going out on a night like this! Oh, here's young Mr. Cashell."

The door of the inner office behind the dispensary opened, and an energetic, spade-bearded man stepped forth, rubbing his hands.

"I want a bit of tinfoil, Shaynor," he said. "Good-evening. My uncle told me you might be coming." This to me, as I began the first of a hundred questions.

"I've everything in order," he replied. "We're only waiting until Poole calls us up. Excuse me a minute. You can come in whenever you like—but I'd better be with the instruments. Give me that tinfoil. Thanks."

While we were talking, a girl—evidently no customer—had come into the shop, and the face and bearing of Mr. Shaynor changed. She leaned confidently across the counter.

"But I can't," I heard him whisper uneasily—the flush on his cheek was dull red, and his eyes shone like a drugged moth's. "I can't. I tell you I'm alone in the place."

"No, you aren't. Who's *that?* Let him look after it for half an hour. A brisk walk will do you good. Ah, come now, John."

"But he isn't—"

"I don't care. I want you to; we'll only go round by St. Agnes. If you don't—"

He crossed to where I stood in the shadow of the dispensary counter, and began some sort of broken apology about a lady-friend.

"Yes," she interrupted. "You take the shop for half an hour—to oblige *me,* won't you?"

She had a singularly rich and promising voice that well matched her outline.

"All right," I said. "I'll do it—but you'd better wrap yourself up, Mr. Shaynor."

"Oh, a brisk walk ought to help me. We're only going round by the church." I heard him cough grievously as they went out to-gether.

I refilled the stove, and, after reckless expenditure of Mr. Cashell's coal, drove some warmth into the shop. I explored many of the glass-knobbed drawers that lined the walls, tasted some disconcerting drugs, and, by the aid of a few cardamoms, ground ginger, chloric-ether, and dilute alcohol, manufactured a new and wildish drink, of which I bore a glassful to young Mr. Cashell, busy in the back office. He laughed shortly when I told him that Mr. Shaynor had stepped out—but a frail coil of wire held all his attention, and he had no word for me bewildered among the batteries and rods. The noise of the sea on the beach began to make itself heard as the traffic in the street ceased. Then briefly, but very lucidly, he gave me the names and uses of the mechanism that crowded the tables and the floor.

"When do you expect to get the message from Poole?" I demanded, sipping my liquor out of a graduated glass.

"About midnight, if everything is in order. We've got our installation-pole fixed to the roof of the house. I shouldn't advise you to turn on a tap or anything tonight. We've connected up with the plumbing, and all the water will be electrified." He repeated to me the history of the agitated ladies at the hotel at the time of the first installation.

"But what *is* it?" I asked. "Electricity is out of my beat altogether."

"Ah, if you knew *that* you'd know something nobody knows. It's just It—what we call Electricity, but the magic—the manifestations—the Hertzian waves—are all revealed by *this*. The coherer, we call it."

He picked up a glass tube not much thicker than a thermometer, in which, almost touching, were two tiny silver plugs, and between them an infinitesimal pinch of metallic dust. "That's all," he said, proudly, as though himself responsible for the wonder. "That is the thing that will reveal to us the Powers—whatever the Powers may be—at work—through space—a long distance away."

Just then Mr. Shaynor returned alone and stood coughing his heart out on the mat.

"Serves you right for being such a fool," said young Mr. Cashell, as annoyed as myself at the interruption. "Never mind—we've all the night before us to see wonders."

Shaynor clutched the counter, his handkerchief to his lips. When he brought it away I saw two bright red stains.

"I—I've got a bit of a rasped throat from smoking cigarettes," he panted. "I think I'll try a cubeb."

"Better take some of this. I've been compounding while you've been away." I handed him the brew.

" 'Twon't make me drunk, will it? I'm almost a teetotaller. My word! That's grateful and comforting."

He set down the empty glass to cough afresh.

"Brr! But it was cold out there! I shouldn't care to be lying in my grave a night like this. Don't *you* ever have a sore throat from smoking?" He pocketed the handkerchief after a furtive peep.

"Oh, yes, sometimes," I replied, wondering, while I spoke, into what agonies of terror I should fall if ever I saw those bright-red danger-signals under my nose. Young Mr. Cashell among the batteries coughed slightly to show that he was quite ready to continue his scientific explanations, but I was thinking still of the girl with the rich voice and the significantly cut mouth, at whose command I had taken charge of the shop. It flashed across me that she distantly resembled the seductive shape on a gold-framed toilet-water advertisement whose charms were unholily heightened by the glare from the red bottle in the window. Turning to make sure, I saw Mr. Shaynor's eyes bent in the same direction, and by instinct recognized that the flamboyant thing was to him a shrine. "What do you take for your—cough?" I asked.

"Well, I'm the wrong side of the counter to believe much in patent medicines. But there are asthma cigarettes, and there are pastilles. To tell you the truth, if you don't object to the smell, which is very like incense, I believe, though I'm not a Roman Catholic, Blaudett's Cathedral Pastilles relieve me as much as anything."

"Let's try." I had never raided a chemist's shop before, so I was thorough. We unearthed the pastilles—brown, gummy cones of benzoin—and set them alight under the toilet-water advertisement, where they fumed in thin blue spirals.

"Of course," said Mr. Shaynor, to my question, "what one uses in the shop for one's self comes out of one's pocket. Why, stock-taking in our business is nearly the same as with jewellers—and I can't say more than that. But one gets them"—he pointed to the pastille-box—"at trade prices." Evidently the censing of the gay, seven-tinted wench with the teeth was an established ritual which cost something.

"And when do we shut up shop?"

"We stay like this all night. The guv—old Mr. Cashell—doesn't believe in locks and shutters as compared with electric light. Besides, it brings trade. I'll just sit here in the chair by the stove and write a letter, if you don't mind. Electricity isn't my prescription."

The energetic young Mr. Cashell snorted within, and Shaynor settled himself up in his chair over which he had thrown a staring red, black, and yellow Austrian jute blanket, rather like a table-cover. I cast about, amid patent-medicine pamphlets, for something to read, but finding little, returned to the manufacture of the new drink. The Italian warehouse took down its game and went to bed. Across the street blank shutters flung back the gaslight in cold smears; the dried pavement seemed to rough up in goose-flesh under the scouring of the savage wind, and we could hear, long ere he passed, the policeman flapping his arms to keep himself warm. Within, the flavors of cardamoms and chloric-ether disputed those of the pastilles and a score of drugs and perfume and soap scents. Our electric lights, set low down in the windows before the tun-bellied Rosamund jars, flung inward three monstrous daubs of red, blue, and green, that broke into kaleidoscopic lights on the faceted knobs of the drug-drawers, the cut-glass scent flagons, and the bulbs of the sparklet bottles. They flushed the white-tiled floor in gorgeous patches; splashed along the nickel-silver counter-rails, and turned the polished mahogany counter-panels to the likeness of intricate grained marbles—slabs of porphyry and malachite. Mr. Shaynor unlocked a drawer, and ere he began to write, took out a meager bundle of letters. From my place by the stove, I could see the scalloped edges of the paper with a flaring monogram in the corner and could even smell the reek of chypre. At each page he turned toward the toilet-water lady of the advertisement and devoured her with over-luminous eyes. He had drawn the Austrian blanket over his shoulders, and among those warring lights he looked more than ever the incarnation of a drugged moth—a tiger-moth as I thought.

He put his letter into an envelope, stamped it with stiff mechanical movements, and dropped it in the drawer. Then I became aware of the silence of a great city asleep—the silence that underlaid the even voice of the breakers along the sea-front—a thick, tingling quiet of warm life stilled down for its appointed time, and unconsciously I moved about the glittering shop as one moves in a sick-room. Young Mr. Cashell was adjusting some wire that crackled from time to time with the tense, knuckle-stretching sound of the electric spark. Upstairs, where a door shut and opened swiftly, I could hear his uncle coughing abed.

"Here," I said, when the drink was properly warmed, "take some of this, Mr. Shaynor."

He jerked in his chair with a start and a wrench, and held out his hand for the glass. The mixture, of a rich port-wine color, frothed at the top.

"It looks," he said, suddenly, "it looks—those bubbles—like a string of pearls winking at you—rather like the pearls round that young lady's neck." He turned again to the advertisement where the female in the dove-colored corset had seen fit to put on all her pearls before she cleaned her teeth.

"Not bad, is it?" I said.

"Eh?"

He rolled his eyes heavily full on me, and, as I stared, I beheld all meaning and consciousness die out of the swiftly dilating pupils. His figure lost its stark rigidity, softened into the chair, and, chin on chest, hands dropped before him, he rested open-eyed, absolutely still.

"I'm afraid I've rather cooked Shaynor's goose," I said, bearing the fresh drink to young Mr. Cashell. "Perhaps it was the chloric-ether."

"Oh, he's all right." The spade-bearded man glanced at him pityingly. "Consumptives go off in those sort of doses very often. It's exhaustion . . . I don't wonder. I daresay the liquor will do him good. It's grand stuff," he finished his share appreciatively. "Well, as I was saying—before he interrupted—about this little coherer. The pinch of dust, you see, is nickel-filings. The Hertzian waves, you see, come out of space from the station that dispatches 'em, and all these little particles are attracted together—cohere, we call it— for just so long as the current passes through them. Now, it's important to remember that the current is an induced current. There are a good many kinds of induction—"

"Yes, but what *is* induction?"

"That's rather hard to explain untechnically. But the long and the short of it is that when a current of electricity passes through a wire there's a lot of magnetism present round that wire; and if you put another wire parallel to, and within what we call its magnetic field—why then, the second wire will also become charged with electricity."

"On its own account?"

"On its own account."

"Then let's see if I've got it correctly. Miles off, at Poole, or wherever it is—"

"It will be anywhere in ten years."

"You've got a charged wire—"

"Charged with Hertzian waves which vibrate, say, two hundred and thirty million times a second." Mr. Cashell snaked his forefinger rapidly through the air.

"All right—a charged wire at Poole, giving out these waves into space. Then this wire of yours sticking out into space—on the roof of the house—in some mysterious way gets charged with those waves from Poole—"

"Or anywhere—it only happens to be Poole tonight."

"And those waves set the coherer at work, just like an ordinary telegraph-office ticker?"

"No! That's where so many people make the mistake. The Hertzian waves wouldn't be strong enough to work a great heavy Morse instrument like ours. They can only just make that dust cohere, and while it coheres (a little while for a dot and a longer while for a dash) the current from this battery—the home battery"—he laid his hand on the thing—"can get through to the Morse printing-machine to record the dot or dash. Let me make it clearer. Do you know anything about steam?"

"Very little. But go on."

"Well, the coherer is like a steam-valve. Any child can open a valve and start a steamer's engines, because a turn of the hand lets in the main steam, doesn't it? Now, this home battery here ready to print is the main steam. The coherer is the valve, always ready to be turned on. The Hertzian wave is the child's hand that turns it."

"I see. That's marvelous."

"Marvelous, isn't it? And, remember, we're only at the beginning. There's nothing we shan't be able to do in ten years. I want to live—my God, how I want to live, and see it develop!" He looked through the door at Shaynor breathing lightly in his chair. "Poor beast! And he wants to keep company with Fanny Brand."

"Fanny *who*?" I said, for the name struck an obscurely familiar chord in my brain—something connected with a stained handkerchief, and the word "arterial."

"Fanny Brand—the girl you kept shop for." He laughed. "That's all I know about her, and for the life of me I can't see what Shaynor sees in her, or she in him."

"*Can't* you see what he sees in her?" I insisted.

"Oh, yes, if *that's* what you mean. She's a great, big, fat lump of a girl, and so on. I suppose that's why he's so crazy after her. She isn't his sort. Well, it doesn't matter. My uncle says he's bound to die before the year's out. Your drink's given him a good sleep, at any rate." Young Mr. Cashell could not catch Mr. Shaynor's face, which was half turned to the advertisement.

I stoked the stove anew, for the room was growing cold, and lighted another pastille. Mr. Shaynor in his chair, never moving, looked through and over me with eyes as wide and lusterless as those of a dead hare.

"Poole's late," said young Mr. Cashell, when I stepped back. "I'll just send them a call."

He pressed a key in the semidarkness, and with a rending crackle there leaped between two brass knobs a spark, streams of sparks, and sparks again.

"Grand, isn't it? *That's* the Power—our unknown Power—kicking and fighting to be let loose," said young Mr. Cashell. "There she goes—kick—kick—kick into space. I never get over the strangeness of it when I work a sending-machine—waves going into space, you know. T. R. is our call. Poole ought to answer with L. L. L."

We waited two, three, five minutes. In that silence, of which the boom of the tide was an orderly part, I caught the clear *"kiss—kiss—kiss"* of the halliards on the roof, as they were blown against the installation-pole.

"Poole is not ready. I'll stay here and call you when he is."

I returned to the shop, and set down my glass on a marble slab with a careless clink. As I did so, Shaynor rose to his feet, his eyes fixed once more on the advertisement, where the young woman bathed in the light from the red jar simpered pinkly over her pearls. His lips moved without cessation. I stepped nearer to listen. "And threw—and threw—and threw," he repeated, his face all sharp with some inexplicable agony.

I moved forward astonished. But it was then he found words—delivered roundly and clearly. These:—

And threw warm gules on Madeleine's young breast.

The trouble passed off his countenance, and he returned lightly to his place, rubbing his hands.

It had never occurred to me, though we had many times discussed reading and prize-competitions as a diversion, that Mr. Shaynor ever read Keats, or could quote him at all appositely. There was, after all, a certain stained-glass effect of light on the high bosom of the highly polished picture which might, by stretch of fancy, suggest, as a vile chromo recalls some incomparable canvas, the line he had spoken. Night, my drink, and solitude were evidently turning Mr.

Shaynor into a poet. He sat down again and wrote swiftly on his villainous note-paper, his lips quivering.

I shut the door into the inner office and moved up behind him. He made no sign that he saw or heard. I looked over his shoulder, and read, amid half-formed words, sentences, and wild scratches:—

> —Very cold it was. Very cold
> The hare—the hare—the hare—
> The birds—

He raised his head sharply, and frowned toward the blank shutters of the poulterer's shop where they jutted out against our window. Then one clear line came:—

> The hare, in spite of fur, was very cold.

The head, moving machine-like, turned right to the advertisement where the Blaudett's Cathedral pastille reeked abominably. He grunted, and went on:—

> Incense in a censer—
> Before her darling picture framed in gold—
> Maiden's picture—angel's portrait—

"Hsh!" said Mr. Cashell guardedly from the inner office, as though in the presence of spirits. "There's something coming through from somewhere; but it isn't Poole." I heard the crackle of sparks as he depressed the keys of the transmitter. In my own brain, too, something crackled, or it might have been the hair on my head. Then I heard my own voice, in a harsh whisper: "Mr. Cashell, there is something coming through here, too. Leave me alone till I tell you."

"But I thought you'd come to see this wonderful thing—Sir," indignantly at the end.

"Leave me alone till I tell you. Be quiet."

I watched—I waited. Under the blue-veined hand—the dry hand of the consumptive—came away clear, without erasure:—

> And my weak spirit fails
> To think how the dead must freeze—

he shivered as he wrote—

Beneath the churchyard mold.

Then he stopped, laid the pen down, and leaned back.

For an instant, that was half an eternity, the shop spun before me in a rainbow-tinted whirl, in and through which my own soul most dispassionately considered my own soul as that fought with an over-mastering fear. Then I smelt the strong smell of cigarettes from Mr. Shaynor's clothing, and heard, as though it had been the rending of trumpets, the rattle of his breathing. I was still in my place of observation, much as one would watch a rifle-shot at the butts, half-bent, hands on my knees, and head within a few inches of the black, red, and yellow blanket of his shoulder. I was whispering encouragement, evidently to my other self, sounding sentences, such as men pronounce in dreams.

"If he has read Keats, it proves nothing. If he hasn't—like causes *must* beget like effects. There is no escape from this law. *You* ought to be grateful that you know 'St. Agnes' Eve' without the book; because, given the circumstances, such as Fanny Brand, who is the key of the enigma, and approximately represents the latitude and longitude of Fanny Brawne; allowing also for the bright red color of the arterial blood upon the handkerchief, which was just what you were puzzling over in the shop just now; and counting the effect of the professional environment, here almost perfectly duplicated—the result is logical and inevitable. As inevitable as induction."

Still, the other half of my soul refused to be comforted. It was cowering in some minute and inadequate corner—at an immense distance.

Hereafter, I found myself one person again, my hands still gripping my knees, and my eyes glued on the page before Mr. Shaynor. As dreamers accept and explain the upheaval of landscapes and the resurrection of the dead, with excerpts from the evening hymn or the multiplication-table, so I had accepted the facts, whatever they might be, that I should witness, and had devised a theory, sane and plausible to my mind, that explained them all. Nay, I was even in advance of my facts, walking hurriedly before them, assured that they would fit my theory. And all that I now recall of that epoch-making theory are the lofty words: "If he has read Keats it's the chloric-ether. If he hasn't, it's the identical bacillus, or Hertzian wave of tuberculosis, *plus* Fanny Brand and the professional status which, in conjunction with the mainstream of subconscious thought common to all mankind, has thrown up temporarily an induced Keats."

Mr. Shaynor returned to his work, erasing and rewriting as before with swiftness. Two or three blank pages he tossed aside. Then he wrote, muttering:—

The little smoke of a candle that goes out.

"No," he muttered. "Little smoke—little smoke—little smoke. What else?" He thrust his chin forward toward the advertisement, whereunder the last of the Blaudett's Cathedral pastilles fumed in its holder. "Ah!" Then with relief:—

The little smoke that dies in moonlight cold.

Evidently he was snared by the rhymes of his first verse, for he wrote and rewrote "gold—cold—mold" many times. Again he sought inspiration from the advertisement, and set down, without erasure, the line I had overheard:—

And threw warm gules on Madeleine's young breast.

As I remembered the original it is "fair"—a trite word—instead of "young," and I found myself nodding approval, though I admitted that the attempt to reproduce "its little smoke in pallid moonlight died" was a failure.

Followed without a break ten or fifteen lines of bald prose—the naked soul's confession of its physical yearning for its beloved— unclean as we count uncleanliness; unwholesome, but human exceedingly; the raw material, so it seemed to me in that hour and in that place, whence Keats wove the twenty-sixth, seventh, and eighth stanzas of his poem. Shame I had none in overseeing this revelation; and my fear had gone with the smoke of the pastille.

"That's it," I murmured. "That's how it's blocked out. Go on! Ink it in, man. Ink it in!"

Mr. Shaynor returned to broken verse wherein "loveliness" was made to rhyme with a desire to look upon "her empty dress." He picked up a fold of the gay, soft blanket, spread it over one hand, caressed it with infinite tenderness, thought, muttered, traced some snatches which I could not decipher, shut his eyes drowsily, shook his head, and dropped the stuff. Here I found myself at fault, for I could not then see (as I do now) in what manner a red, black, and yellow Austrian blanket colored his dreams.

In a few minutes he laid aside his pen, and, chin on hand, considered the shop with thoughtful and intelligent eyes. He threw down the blanket, rose, passed along a line of drug-drawers, and read the names on the labels aloud. Returning, he took from his desk Christy's *New Commercial Plants* and the old Culpepper that I had given him, opened and laid them side by side with a clerkly air, all trace of passion gone from his face, read first in one and then in the other, and paused with pen behind his ear.

"What wonder of Heaven's coming now?" I thought.

"Manna—manna—manna," he said at last, under wrinkled brows. "That's what I wanted. Good! Now then! Now then! Good! Good! Oh, by God, that's good!" His voice rose and he spoke rightly and fully without a falter:—

> Candied apple, quince and plum and gourd,
> And jellies smoother than the creamy curd,
> And lucent syrups tinct with cinnamon,
> Manna and dates in Argosy transferred
> From Fez; and spiced dainties, every one
> From silken Samarcand to cedared Lebanon.

He repeated it once more, using "blander" for "smoother" in the second line; then wrote it down without erasure, but this time (my set eyes missed no stroke of any word) he substituted "soother" for his atrocious second thought, so that it came away under his hand as it is written in the book—as it is written in the book.

A wind went shouting down the street, and on the heels of the wind followed a spurt and rattle of rain.

After a smiling pause—and good right had he to smile—he began anew, always tossing the last sheet over his shoulder:—

> The sharp rain falling on the window-pane,
> Rattling sleet—the wind-blown sleet.

Then prose: "It is very cold of mornings when the wind brings rain and sleet with it. I heard the sleet on the window-pane outside, and thought of you, my darling. I am always thinking of you. I wish we could both run away like two lovers into the storm and get that little cottage by the sea which we are always thinking about, my own dear darling. We could sit and watch the sea beneath our windows. It would be a fairyland all of our own—a fairy sea—a fairy sea. . . ."

He stopped, raised his head, and listened. The steady drone of the Channel along the seafront that had borne us company so long leaped up a note to the sudden fuller surge that signals the change from ebb to flood. It beat in like the change of step throughout an army—this renewed pulse of the sea—and filled our ears till they, accepting it, marked it no longer.

> A fairyland for you and me
> Across the foam—beyond . . .
> A magic foam, a perilous sea.

He grunted again with effort and bit his underlip. My throat dried, but I dared not gulp to moisten it lest I should break the spell that was drawing him nearer and nearer to the high-water mark but two of the sons of Adam have reached. Remember that in all the millions permitted there are no more than five—five little lines—of which one can say: "These are the pure Magic. These are the clear Vision. The rest is only poetry." And Mr. Shaynor was playing hot and cold with two of them!

I vowed no unconscious thought of mine should influence the blindfold soul, and pinned myself desperately to the other three, repeating and re-repeating:—

> A savage spot as holy and enchanted
> As e'er beneath a waning moon was haunted
> By woman wailing for her demon lover.

But though I believed my brain thus occupied, my every sense hung upon the writing under the dry, bony hand, all brown-fingered with chemicals and cigarette smoke.

> Our windows fronting on the dangerous foam,

(he wrote, after long, irresolute snatches), and then—

> Our open casements facing desolate seas
> Forlorn—forlorn—

Here again his face grew peaked and anxious with that sense of loss I had first seen when the Power snatched him. But this time the agony was tenfold keener. As I watched it mounted like mercury in the tube. It lighted his face from within till I thought the visibly scourged soul must leap forth naked between his jaws, unable to endure. A drop of sweat trickled from my forehead down my nose and splashed on the back of my hand.

> Our windows facing on the desolate seas
> And pearly foam of magic fairyland—

"Not yet—not yet," he muttered, "wait a minute. *Please* wait a minute. I shall get it then—

> Our magic windows fronting on the sea,
> The dangerous foam of desolate seas . . .
> For aye.

Ouh, my God!"

From head to heel he shook—shook from the marrow of his bones outwards—then leaped to his feet with raised arms, and slid the chair screeching across the tiled floor where it struck the drawers behind and fell with a jar. Mechanically, I stooped to recover it.

As I rose, Mr. Shaynor was stretching and yawning at leisure.

"I've had a bit of a doze," he said. "How did I come to knock the chair over? You look rather—"

"The chair startled me," I answered. "It was so sudden in this quiet."

Young Mr. Cashell behind his shut door was offendedly silent.

"I suppose I must have been dreaming," said Mr. Shaynor.

"I suppose you must," I said. "Talking of dreams—I—I noticed you writing—before—"

He flushed consciously.

"I meant to ask you if you've ever read anything written by a man called Keats."

"Oh! I haven't much time to read poetry, and I can't say that I remember the name exactly. Is he a popular writer?"

"Middling. I thought you might know him because he's the only poet who was ever a druggist. And he's rather what's called the lover's poet."

"Indeed. I must dip into him. What did he write about?"

"A lot of things. Here's a sample that may interest you."

Then and there, carefully, I repeated the verse he had twice spoken and once written not ten minutes ago.

"Ah! Anybody could see he was a druggist from that line about the tinctures and syrups. It's a fine tribute to our profession."

"I don't know," said young Mr. Cashell, with icy politeness, opening the door one half-inch, "if you still happen to be interested in our trifling experiments. But, should such be the case—"

I drew him aside, whispering, "Shaynor seemed going off into some sort of fit when I spoke to you just now. I thought, even at the risk of being rude, it wouldn't do to take you off your instruments just as the call was coming through. Don't you see?"

"Granted—granted as soon as asked," he said, unbending. "I *did* think it a shade odd at the time. So that was why he knocked the chair down?"

"I hope I haven't missed anything," I said.

"I'm afraid I can't say that, but you're just in time for the end of a rather curious performance. You can come in too, Mr. Shaynor. Listen, while I read it off."

The Morse instrument was ticking furiously. Mr. Cashell interpreted: " 'K.K.V. *Can make nothing of your signals.*' " A pause. " '*M.M.V. M.M.V. Signals unintelligible. Purpose anchor Sandown Bay. Examine instruments tomorrow.*' " Do you know what that means? It's a couple of men-o'-war working Marconi signals off the Isle of Wight. They are trying to talk to each other. Neither can read the other's messages, but all their messages are being taken in by our receiver here. They've been going on for ever so long. I wish you could have heard it."

"How wonderful!" I said. "Do you mean we're overhearing Portsmouth ships trying to talk to each other—that we're eavesdropping across half South England?"

"Just that. Their transmitters are all right, but their receivers are out of order, so they only get a dot here and a dash there. Nothing clear."

"Why is that?"

"God knows—and Science will know tomorrow. Perhaps the induction is faulty; perhaps the receivers aren't tuned to receive just the number of vibrations per second that the transmitter sends. Only a word here and there. Just enough to tantalize."

Again the Morse sprang to life.

"That's one of 'em complaining now. Listen: '*Disheartening—most disheartening.*' It's quite pathetic. Have you ever seen a spiritualistic seance? It reminds me of that sometimes—odds and ends of messages coming out of nowhere—a word here and there—no good at all."

"But mediums are all impostors," said Mr. Shaynor, in the doorway, lighting an asthma-cigarette. "They only do it for the money they can make. I've seen 'em."

"Here's Poole, at last—clear as a bell. L.L.L. *Now* we shan't be long." Mr. Cashell rattled the keys merrily. "Anything you'd like to tell 'em?"

"No, I don't think so," I said. "I'll go home and get to bed. I'm feeling a little tired."

With the Night Mail
FROM ACTIONS AND REACTIONS
(1909)

Once upon a time I was sitting in the British Airways terminal at Kennedy on my way back to London. I was rather tired, after three extremely busy weeks in the States, and a bit depressed because I had a long while to wait and nothing much to occupy my time. I was, in sum, inclined to feel that the romance had gone out of travel with the passing of the *Mauretania* and the Cheltenham Flyer and the Twentieth Century Limited.

All of a sudden, though, my attention was caught by an announcement on the P.A. As I recall, what I heard was this:

"Pan American World Airways announce the departure of their Flight 501, for Frankfurt, Beirut, *and around the world.*"

A shiver crawled down my spine. No, the romance has not gone out of travel. It's just that nowadays it's a little harder to find.

Kipling was aware of this. (In another of his stories he makes a character suggest that the romance went out of travel with the advent of steam . . .) But he knew, and in this story demonstrated, that it will always be there if you look for it. And isn't that a science-fiction tenet?

"With the Night Mail" first appeared in 1905. How full it is of commonsensical predictions! Never mind how wrong RK was about the future of heavier-than-air craft. At a time when broadcasting was unknown, flying was in the experimental stage, and it was rare even for the finest ocean liners to carry wireless telegraphy equipment, he

recognized the need for a General Communication system
and Air Traffic Control. Our "cloud-breakers" may not
be as colorful and spectacular as his, but in principle the
radio beacons by which modern pilots navigate correspond to what he knew would be essential. I wish I had
space to include the imaginary advertisements, news re-
ports, and Letters to the Editor that he devised to accom-
pany the story on its original outing. He must have had a
lot of fun inventing his consistent, though imaginary, future world!

For those interested in the technicalities of writing: this
story is told in the historic present, then a rare mode in
English, though not uncommon in French.

The G.P.O. (now abolished) was Britain's General Post
Office. "Packet" meant a boat plying regularly between
one port and another; the term seems to have fallen into
disuse.

I can't help noting, from the reference to "little Ada
Warrleigh," that RK expected the flying aces of the future
to include women . . . I also thoroughly approve of his as-
sumption that war has gone "out of fashion"!

Highgate is in North London. Lift = U.S. elevator.
Colloid is what we would now call transparent plastic; RK
foresaw the need for a transparent material stronger than
glass and less liable to fracture, but Plexiglass was a generation off. A fathom = six feet. Aeolus in Greek mythol-
ogy was the keeper of the winds.

Clear speech, in the imaginary language International, is
relayed by RK's General Communicator. He was well up
with the most recent developments; it would be another
year before the Canadian Reginald Fessenden achieved
transmission of a spoken message across the Atlantic in
November 1906—by accident!

"Fleury's gas" does not of course exist, and can't, but
neither can faster-than-light drives. In this section RK
shows himself to have a firm grasp of the principles of
later science fiction. . . .

Boort I take to be an Afrikaans spelling of the Dutch
bort, coarse diamonds or diamond dust. (*Chambers Twentieth Century Dictionary* says the word is French; *Petit Rob-*

ert says it's English. *Collins Dictionary* also tries to claim it as English. I say it's spinach and the hell with it.)

"Area," in this context, means a space in front of a terraced (U.S. row) house, sunk to the same level as the basement, provided with steps and surrounded by a railing. It was used for deliveries of coal, kitchen supplies, and the like. A *wulli-wa* (and you'll have to own a better dictionary than any of mine before you find it!) is a violent squall; the term comes to English from Australian.

One of the things I most admire about RK is his gift for slang, even when he has to invent it. "Shunt the lift out of him with a spanner" is masterly! (Spanner = U.S. wrench.)

"A.B.C. regulations" are issued by the Aerial Board of Control; see the later explanation, and also "As Easy as A.B.C.," which follows. A corposant is "St. Elmo's fire"—a glow due to static electricity. Fastnet Rock is off the south coast of Ireland. Hydras in this sense are not aquatic micro-organisms, but the mythical monster with many heads.

The Banks, as in "The Ship That Found Herself," are the Grand Banks, off Newfoundland. (Trinity Bay, mentioned a few lines lower down, is on the Newfoundland coast.) The concept of compiling averaged records from the dip-dial tapes of every voyage for the edification of later captains is truly astonishing in the pre-computer age; RK saw through the manual labor of his own day to the time when machines would make such painstaking duties relatively easy.

He did not, admittedly, conceive how quickly we would vanquish the scourge of tuberculosis . . . but then, no more did H. G. Wells. And he made another of his rare mistakes when he sent his Tad-boats "ringing the world round the Fiftieth Meridian." He should have said Parallel. (Even the masters of the craft occasionally need help from a clear-eyed editor!)

But, in line with his praise of the G.P.O. as a "repository of ancientest tradition," RK outdoes himself by sending hostlers—called after those who tended horses at a stage-coach inn—to take care of the turbines when the engineers depart.

Enough, though! Enough! I mustn't keep you any longer from this fascinating and inventive story!

With the Night Mail
A STORY OF 2000 A.D.

At nine o'clock of a gusty winter night I stood on the lower stages of one of the G.P.O. outward mail towers. My purpose was a run to Quebec in "Postal Packet 162 or such other as may be appointed": and the Postmaster-General himself countersigned the order. This talisman opened all doors, even those in the dispatching-caisson at the foot of the tower, where they were delivering the sorted Continental mail. The bags lay packed close as herrings in the long grey underbodies which our G.P.O. still calls "coaches." Five such coaches were filled as I watched, and were shot up the guides to be locked on to their waiting packets three hundred feet nearer the stars.

From the dispatching-caisson I was conducted by a courteous and wonderfully learned official—Mr. L. L. Geary, Second Dispatcher of the Western Route—to the Captains' Room (this wakes an echo of old romance), where the mail captains come on for their turn of duty. He introduces me to the Captain of "162"—Captain Purnall, and his relief, Captain Hodgson. The one is small and dark; the other large and red; but each has the brooding sheathed glance characteristic of eagles and aeronauts. You can see it in the pictures of our racing professionals, from L. V. Rautsch to little Ada Warrleigh—that fathomless abstraction of eyes habitually turned through naked space.

On the notice-board in the Captains' Room, the pulsing arrows of some twenty indicators register, degree by geographical degree, the progress of as many homeward-bound packets. The word "Cape" rises across the face of a dial; a gong strikes: the South African mid-weekly mail is in at the Highgate Receiving Towers. That is all. It reminds one comically of the traitorous little bell which in pigeon-fanciers' lofts notifies the return of a homer.

"Time for us to be on the move," says Captain Purnall, and we are shot up by the passenger-lift to the top of the dispatch-towers. "Our coach will lock on when it is filled and the clerks are aboard. . . ."

"No. 162" waits for us in Slip E of the topmost stage. The great curve of her back shines frostily under the lights, and some minute alteration of trim makes her rock a little in her holding-down slips.

Captain Purnall frowns and dives inside. Hissing softly, "162" comes to rest as level as a rule. From her North Atlantic Winter nose-cap (worn bright as diamond with boring through uncounted leagues of hail, snow, and ice) to the inset of her three built-out propeller-shafts is some two hundred and forty feet. Her extreme diameter, carried well forward, is thirty-seven. Contrast this with the nine hundred by ninety-five of any crack liner, and you will realize the power that must drive a hull through all weathers at more than the emergency speed of the *Cyclonic*!

The eye detects no joint in her skin plating save the sweeping hair-crack of the bow-rudder—Magniac's rudder that assured us the dominion of the unstable air and left its inventor penniless and half-blind. It is calculated to Castelli's "gull-wing" curve. Raise a few feet of that all but invisible plate three-eighths of an inch and she will yaw five miles to port or starboard ere she is under control again. Give her full helm and she returns on her track like a whip-lash. Cant the whole forward—a touch on the wheel will suffice—and she sweeps at your good direction up or down. Open the complete circle and she presents to the air a mushroom-head that will bring her up all standing within a half mile.

"Yes," says Captain Hodgson, answering my thought, "Castelli thought he'd discovered the secret of controlling aeroplanes when he'd only found out how to steer dirigible balloons. Magniac invented his rudder to help war-boats ram each other; and war went out of fashion and Magniac he went out of his mind because he said he couldn't serve his country anymore. I wonder if any of us ever know what we're really doing."

"If you want to see the coach locked you'd better go aboard. It's due now," says Mr. Geary. I enter through the door amidships. There is nothing here for display. The inner skin of the gas-tanks comes down to within a foot or two of my head and turns over just short of the turn of the bilges. Liners and yachts disguise their tanks with decoration, but the G.P.O. serves them raw under a lick of grey official paint. The inner skin shuts off fifty feet of the bow and as much of the stern, but the bow-bulkhead is recessed for the lift-shunting apparatus as the stern is pierced for the shaft-tunnels. The engine-room lies almost amidships. Forward of it, extending to the turn of the bow tanks, is an aperture—a bottomless hatch at present—into which our coach will be locked. One looks down over the coamings three hundred feet to the dispatching-caisson whence voices boom upward. The light below is obscured to a sound of thunder, as our coach rises on its guides. It enlarges rapidly from a postage stamp to a playing card; to a punt and last a pontoon. The two clerks, its crew, do not even look up as it comes into place. The Quebec letters fly under their fingers and leap into the docketed racks, while both captains and Mr. Geary satisfy themselves that the coach is locked home. A clerk passes the way-bill over the hatch-coaming. Captain Purnall thumb-marks and passes it to Mr. Geary. Receipt has been given and taken. "Pleasant run," says Mr. Geary, and disappears through the door which a foot-high pneumatic compressor locks after him.

"A-ah!" sighs the compressor released. Our holding-down clips part with a tang. We are clear.

Captain Hodgson opens the great colloid underbody-porthole through which I watch over-lighted London slide eastward as the gale gets hold of us. The first of the low winter clouds cuts off the well-known view and darkens Middlesex. On the south edge of it I can see a postal packet's light ploughing through the white fleece. For an instant she gleams like a star ere she drops toward the Highgate Receiving Towers. "The Bombay Mail," says Captain Hodgson, and looks at his watch. "She's forty minutes late."

"What's our level?" I ask.

"Four thousand. Aren't you coming up on the bridge?"

The bridge (let us ever praise the G.P.O. as a repository of ancientest tradition!) is represented by a view of Captain Hodgson's legs where he stands on the Control Platform that runs thwart-ships overhead. The bow colloid is unshuttered and Captain Purnall, one hand on the wheel, is feeling for a fair slant. The dial shows 4,300 feet.

"It's steep tonight," he mutters, as tier on tier of cloud drops under. "We generally pick up an easterly draft below three thousand at this time o' the year. I hate slathering through fluff."

"So does Van Cutsem. Look at him huntin' for a slant!" says Captain Hodgson. A fog-light breaks cloud a hundred fathoms below. The Antwerp Night Mail makes her signal and rises between two racing clouds far to port, her flanks blood-red in the glare of Sheerness Double Light. The gale will have us over the North Sea in half an hour, but Captain Purnall let her go composedly—nosing to every point of the compass as she rises.

"Five thousand—six, six thousand eight hundred"—the dip-dial reads ere we find the easterly drift, heralded by a flurry of snow at the thousand fathom level. Captain Purnall rings up the engines and keys down the governor on the switch before him. There is no sense in urging machinery when Æolus himself gives you good knots for nothing. We are always in earnest now—our nose notched home on our chosen star. At this level the lower clouds are laid out, all neatly combed by the dry fingers of the East. Below that again is the strong westerly blow through which we rose. Overhead, a film of southerly drifting mist draws a theatrical gauze across the firmament. The moonlight turns the lower strata to silver without a stain except where our shadow underruns us. Bristol and Cardiff Double Lights (those statelily inclined beams over Severnmouth) are dead ahead of us; for we keep the Southern Winter Route. Coventry Central, the pivot of the English system, stabs upward once in ten seconds its spear of diamond light to the north; and a point or two off our starboard bow The Leek, the great cloud-breaker of Saint David's Head, swings its unmistakable green beam twenty-five degrees each way. There must be half a mile of fluff over it in this weather, but it does not affect The Leek.

"Our planet's overlighted if anything," says Captain Purnall at the wheel, as Cardiff-Bristol slides under. "I remember the old days of common white verticals that 'ud show two or three hundred feet up in a mist, if you knew where to look for 'em. In really fluffy weather they might as well have been under your hat. One could get lost coming home then, an' have some fun. Now, it's like driving down Piccadilly."

He points to the pillars of light where the cloud-breakers bore through the cloud-floor. We see nothing of England's outlines: only a white pavement pierced in all directions by these manholes of variously colored fire—Holy Island's white and red—St. Bee's interrupted white, and so on as far as the eye can reach. Blessed be Sargent, Ahrens, and the Dubois brothers, who invented the cloud-breakers of the world whereby we travel in security!

"Are you going to lift for The Shamrock?" asks Captain Hodgson. Cork Light (green, fixed) enlarges as we rush to it. Captain Purnall nods. There is heavy traffic hereabouts—the cloud-bank beneath us is streaked with running fissures of flame where the Atlantic boats are hurrying Londonward just clear of the fluff. Mail-packets are supposed, under the Conference rules, to have the five-thousand-foot lanes to themselves, but the foreigner in a hurry is apt to take liberties with English air. "No. 162" lifts to a long-

drawn wail of the breeze in the fore-flange of the rudder and we
make Valencia (white, green, white) at a safe 7,000 feet, dipping our
beam to an incoming Washington packet.

There is no cloud on the Atlantic, and faint streaks of cream
round Dingle Bay show where the driven seas hammer the coast. A
big S.A.T.A. liner *(Société Anonyme des Transports Aëriens)* is
diving and lifting half a mile below us in search of some break in the
solid west wind. Lower still lies a disabled Dane: she is telling the
liner all about it in International. Our General Communication dial
has caught her talk and begins to eavesdrop. Captain Hodgson
makes a motion to shut it off but checks himself. "Perhaps you'd
like to listen," he says.

"*Argol* of St. Thomas," the Dane whimpers. "Report owners
three starboard shaft collar-bearings fused. Can make Flores as we
are, but impossible farther. Shall we buy spares at Fayal?"

The liner acknowledges and recommends inverting the bearings.
The *Argol* answers that she has already done so without effect, and
begins to relieve her mind about cheap German enamels for collar-
bearings. The Frenchman assents cordially, cries "*Courage, mon
ami*," and switches off.

Their lights sink under the curve of the ocean.

"That's one of Lundt & Bleamers's boats," says Captain Hodgson. "Serves 'em right for putting German compos in their thrust-
blocks. *She* won't be in Fayal tonight! By the way, wouldn't you like
to look round the engine-room?"

I have been waiting eagerly for this invitation and I follow Captain Hodgson from the control-platform, stooping low to avoid the
bulge of the tanks. We know that Fleury's gas can lift anything, as
the world-famous trials of '89 showed, but its almost indefinite
powers of expansion necessitate vast tank room. Even in this thin air
the lift-shunts are busy taking out one-third of its normal lift, and
still "162" must be checked by an occasional downdraw of the
rudder or our flight would become a climb to the stars. Captain
Purnall prefers an overlifted to an underlifted ship; but no two
captains trim ship alike. "When *I* take the bridge," says Captain
Hodgson, "you'll see me shunt forty percent of the lift out of the gas
and run her on the upper rudder. With a swoop upwards instead of
a swoop downwards, *as* you say. Either way will do. It's only habit.
Watch our dip-dial! Tim fetches her down once every thirty knots
as regularly as breathing."

So is it shown on the dip-dial. For five or six minutes the arrow
creeps from 6,700 to 7,300. There is the faint "szgee" of the rudder,

and back slides the arrow to 6,000 on a falling slant of ten or fifteen knots.

"In heavy weather you jockey her with the screws as well," says Captain Hodgson, and, unclipping the jointed bar which divides the engine-room from the bare deck, he leads me on to the floor.

Here we find Fleury's Paradox of the Bulkheaded Vacuum—which we accept now without thought—literally in full blast. The three engines are H. T. & T. assisted-vacuo Fleury turbines running from 3,000 to the Limit—that is to say, up to the point when the blades make the air "bell"—cut out a vacuum for themselves precisely as over-driven marine propellers used to do. "162's" Limit is low on account of the small size of her nine screws, which, though handier than the old colloid Thelussons, "bell" sooner. The midships engine, generally used as a reinforce, is not running; so the port and starboard turbine vacuum-chambers draw direct into the return-mains.

The turbines whistle reflectively. From the low-arched expansion-tanks on either side the valves descend pillarwise to the turbine-chests, and thence the obedient gas whirls through the spirals of blades with a force that would whip the teeth out of a power-saw. Behind, is its own pressure held in leash or spurred on by the lift-shunts; before it, the vacuum where Fleury's Ray dances in violet-green bands and whirled turbillons of flame. The jointed U-tubes of the vacuum-chamber are pressure-tempered colloid (no glass would endure the strain for an instant) and a junior engineer with tinted spectacles watches the Ray intently. It is the very heart of the machine—a mystery to this day. Even Fleury who begat it and, unlike Magniac, died a multimillionaire, could not explain how the restless little imp shuddering in the U-tube can, in the fractional fraction of a second, strike the furious blast of gas into a chill greyish-green liquid that drains (you can hear it trickle) from the far end of the vacuum through the eduction-pipes and the mains back to the bilges. Here it returns to its gaseous, one had almost written sagacious, state and climbs to work afresh. Bilge-tank, upper tank, dorsal-tank, expansion-chamber, vacuum, main-return (as a liquid), and bilge-tank once more is the ordained cycle. Fleury's Ray sees to that; and the engineer with the tinted spectacles sees to Fleury's Ray. If a speck of oil, if even the natural grease of the human finger touch the hooded terminals Fleury's Ray will wink and disappear and must be laboriously built up again. This means half a day's work for all hands and an expense of one hundred and seventy-odd pounds to the G.P.O. for radium-salts and such trifles.

"Now look at our thrust-collars. You won't find much German compo there. Full-jeweled, you see," says Captain Hodgson as the engineer shunts open the top of a cap. Our shaft-bearings are C.M.C. (Commercial Minerals Company) stones, ground with as much care as the lens of a telescope. They cost £37 apiece. So far we have not arrived at their term of life. These bearings came from "No. 97," which took them over from the old *Dominion of Light* which had them out of the wreck of the *Perseus* aeroplane in the years when men still flew wooden kites over oil engines!

They are a shining reproof to all low-grade German "ruby" enamels, so-called *"boort"* facings, and the dangerous and unsatisfactory alumina compounds which please dividend-hunting owners and turn skippers crazy.

The rudder-gear and the gas lift-shunt, seated side by side under the engine-room dials, are the only machines in visible motion. The former sighs from time to time as the oil plunger rises and falls half an inch. The latter, cased and guarded like the U-tube aft, exhibits another Fleury Ray, but inverted and more green than violet. Its function is to shunt the lift out of the gas, and this it will do without watching. That is all! A tiny pump-rod wheezing and whining to itself beside a sputtering green lamp. A hundred and fifty feet aft down the flat-topped tunnel of the tanks a violet light, restless and irresolute. Between the two, three white-painted turbine-trunks, like eel-baskets laid on their side, accentuate the empty perspectives. You can hear the trickle of the liquefied gas flowing from the vacuum into the bilge-tanks and the soft *gluck-glock* of gas-locks closing as Captain Purnall brings "162" down by the head. The hum of the turbines and the boom of the air on our skin is no more than a cotton-wool wrapping to the universal stillness. And we are running an eighteen-second mile.

I peer from the fore end of the engine-room over the hatch-coamings into the coach. The mail-clerks are sorting the Winnipeg, Calgary, and Medicine Hat bags; but there is a pack of cards ready on the table.

Suddenly a bell thrills; the engineers run to the turbine-valves and stand by; but the spectacled slave of the Ray in the U-tube never lifts his head. He must watch where he is. We are hard-braked and going astern; there is language from the Control Platform.

"Tim's sparking badly about something," says the unruffled Captain Hodgson. "Let's look."

Captain Purnall is not the suave man we left half-an-hour since, but the embodied authority of the G.P.O. Ahead of us floats an ancient, aluminum-patched, twin-screw tramp of the dingiest, with no more right to the 5,000-foot lane than has a horse-cart to a modern road. She carries an obsolete "barbette" conning-tower—a six-foot affair with railed platform forward—and our warning beam plays on the top of it as a policeman's lantern flashes on the area sneak. Like a sneak-thief, too, emerges a shock-headed navigator in his shirt-sleeves. Captain Purnall wrenches open the colloid to talk with him man to man. There are times when Science does not satisfy.

"What under the stars are you doing here, you sky-scraping chimney-sweep?" he shouts as we two drift side by side. "Do you know this is a Mail-lane? You call yourself a sailor, sir? You ain't fit to peddle toy balloons to an Eskimo. Your name and number! Report and get down, and be—!"

"I've been blown up once," the shock-headed man cries, hoarsely, as a dog barking. "I don't care two flips of a contact for anything *you* can do, Postey."

"Don't you sir? But I'll make you care. I'll have you towed stern first to Disko and broke up. You can't recover insurance if you're broke for obstruction. Do you understand *that?*"

Then the stranger bellows: "Look at my propellers! There's been a wulli-wa down below that has knocked us into umbrella-frames! We've been blown up about forty thousand feet! We're all one conjuror's watch inside! My mate's arm's broke; my engineer's head's cut open; my Ray went out when the engines smashed; and ... and ... for pity's sake give me my height, Captain! We doubt we're dropping."

"Six thousand eight hundred. Can you hold it?" Captain Purnall overlooks all insults, and leans half out of the colloid, staring and snuffing. The stranger leaks pungently.

"We ought to blow into St. John's with luck. We're trying to plug the fore-tank now, but she's simply whistling it away," her captain wails.

"She's sinking like a log," says Captain Purnall in an undertone. "Call up the Banks Mark Boat, George." Our dip-dial shows that we, keeping abreast the tramp, have dropped five hundred feet the last few minutes.

Captain Purnall presses a switch and our signal beam begins to swing through the night, twizzling spokes of light across infinity.

"That'll fetch something," he says, while Captain Hodgson watches the General Communicator. He has called up the North

Banks Mark Boat, a few hundred miles west, and is reporting the case.

"I'll stand by you," Captain Purnall roars to the lone figure on the conning-tower.

"Is it as bad as that?" comes the answer. "She isn't insured. She's mine."

"Might have guessed as much," mutters Hodgson. "Owner's risk is the worst risk of all!"

"Can't I fetch St. John's—not even with this breeze?" the voice quavers.

"Stand by to abandon ship. Haven't you *any* lift in you, fore or aft?"

"Nothing but the midship tanks, and they're none too tight. You see, my Ray gave out and—" he coughs in the reek of the escaping gas.

"You poor devil!" This does not reach our friend. "What does the Mark Boat say, George?"

"Wants to know if there's any danger to traffic. Says she's in a bit of weather herself and can't quit station. I've turned in a General Call, so even if they don't see our beam someone's bound to help— or else we must. Shall I clear our slings? Hold on! Here we are! A Planet liner, too! She'll be up in a tick!"

"Tell her to have her slings ready," cries his brother captain. "There won't be much time to spare. . . . Tie up your mate," he roars to the tramp.

"My mate's all right. It's my engineer. He's gone crazy."

"Shunt the lift out of him with a spanner. Hurry!"

"But I can make St. John's if you'll stand by."

"You'll make the deep, wet Atlantic in twenty minutes. You're less than fifty-eight hundred now. Get your papers."

A Planet liner, east bound, heaves up in a superb spiral and takes the air of us humming. Her underbody colloid is open and her transporter-slings hang down like tentacles. We shut off our beam as she adjusts herself—steering to a hair—over the tramp's conning-tower. The mate comes up, his arm strapped to his side, and stumbles into the cradle. A man with a ghastly scarlet head follows, shouting that he must go back and build up his Ray. The mate assures him that he will find a nice new Ray all ready in the liner's engine-room. The bandaged head goes up wagging excitedly. A youth and a woman follow. The liner cheers hollowly above us, and we see the passengers' faces at the saloon colloid.

"That's a pretty girl. What's the fool waiting for now?" says Captain Purnall.

The skipper comes up, still appealing to us to stand by and see him fetch St. John's. He dives below and returns—at which we little human beings in the void cheer louder than ever—with the ship's kitten. Up fly the liner's hissing slings; her underbody crashes home and she hurtles away again. The dial shows less than 3,000 feet.

The Mark Boat signals we must attend to the derelict, now whistling her death-song, as she falls beneath us in long sick zigzags.

"Keep our beam on her and send out a General Warning," says Captain Purnall, following her down.

There is no need. Not a liner in air but knows the meaning of that vertical beam and gives us and our quarry a wide berth.

"But she'll drown in the water, won't she?" I ask.

"Not always," is his answer. "I've known a derelict up-end and sift her engines out of herself and flicker round the Lower Lanes for three weeks on her forward tanks only. We'll run no risks. Pith her, George, and look sharp. There's weather ahead."

Captain Hodgson opens the underbody colloid, swings the heavy pithing-iron out of its rack which in liners is generally cased as a smoking-room settee, and at two hundred feet releases the catch. We hear the whir of the crescent-shaped arms opening as they descend. The derelict's forehead is punched in, starred across, and rent diagonally. She falls stern first, our beam upon her; slides like a lost soul down that pitiless ladder of light, and the Atlantic takes her.

"A filthy business," says Hodgson. "I wonder what it must have been like in the old days?"

The thought had crossed my mind too. What if that wavering carcass had been filled with the men of the old days, each one of them taught (*that* is the horror of it!) that after death he would very possibly go forever to unspeakable torment?

And scarcely a generation ago, we (one knows now that we are only our fathers re-enlarged upon the earth), *we,* I say, ripped and rammed and pithed to admiration.

Here Tim, from the Control Platform, shouts that we are to get into our inflators and to bring him his at once.

We hurry into the heavy rubber suits—the engineers are already dressed—and inflate at the air-pump taps. G.P.O. inflators are thrice as thick as a racing man's "flickers," and chafe abominably under the armpits. George takes the wheel until Tim has blown himself up

to the extreme of rotundity. If you kicked him off the c.p. to deck
he would bounce back. But it is "162" that will do the kicking.

"The Mark Boat's mad—stark ravin' crazy," he snorts, returning
to command. "She says there's a bad blow-out ahead and wants me
to pull over to Greenland. I'll see her pithed first! We wasted half an
hour fussing over that dead duck down under, and now I'm expected to go rubbin' my back all round the Pole. What does she
think a postal packet's made of? Gummed silk? Tell her we're
coming on straight, George."

George buckles him into the Frame and switches on the Direct
Control. Now under Tim's left toe lies the port-engine Accelerator;
under his left heel the Reverse, and so with the other foot. The
lift-shunt stops stand out on the rim of the steering wheel where the
fingers of his left hand can play on them. At his right hand is the
midships engine lever ready to be thrown into gear at a moment's
notice. He leans forward in his belt, eyes glued to the colloid, and
one ear cocked toward the General Communicator. Henceforth he
is the strength and direction of "162," through whatever may befall.

The Banks Mark Boat is reeling out pages of A.B.C. Directions to
the traffic at large. We are to secure all "loose objects"; hood up our
Fleury Rays; and "on no account to attempt to clear snow from our
conning-towers till the weather abates." Underpowered craft, we
are told, can ascend to the limit of their lift, mail-packets to look out
for them accordingly; the lower lanes westward are pitting very
badly, "with frequent blow-outs, vortices, laterals, etc."

Still the clear dark holds up unblemished. The only warning is the
electric skin-tension (I feel as though I were a lacemaker's pillow)
and an irritability which the gibbering of the General Communicator increases almost to hysteria.

We have made eight thousand feet since we pithed the tramp and
our turbines are giving us an honest two hundred and ten knots.

Very far to the west an elongated blur of red, low down, shows
us the North Banks Mark Boat. There are specks of fire round her
rising and falling—bewildered planets about an unstable sun—helpless shipping hanging on to her light for company's sake. No wonder she could not quit station.

She warns us to look out for the backwash of the bad vortex in
which (her beam shows it) she is even now reeling.

The pits of gloom about us begin to fill with very faintly luminous
films—wreathing and uneasy shapes. One forms itself into a globe
of pale flame that waits shivering with eagerness till we sweep by.
It leaps monstrously across the blackness, alights on the precise tip

of our nose, pirouettes there an instant, and swings off. Our roaring bow sinks as though that light were lead—sinks and recovers to lurch and stumble again beneath the next blow-out. Tim's fingers on the lift-shunt strike chords of numbers—1:4:7:—2:4:6:—7:5:3, and so on; for he is running by his tanks only, lifting or lowering her against the uneasy air. All three engines are at work, for the sooner we have skated over this thin ice the better. Higher we dare not go. The whole upper vault is charged with pale krypton vapors, which our skin friction may excite to unholy manifestations. Between the upper and lower levels—5,000 and 7,000, hints the Mark Boat—we may perhaps bolt through if . . . Our bow clothes itself in blue flame and falls like a sword. No human skill can keep pace with the changing tensions. A vortex has us by the beak and we dive down a two-thousand-foot slant at an angle (the dip-dial and my bouncing body record it) of thirty-five. Our turbines scream shrilly; the propellers cannot bite on the thin air; Tim shunts the lift out of five tanks at once and by sheer weight drives her bulletwise through the maelstrom till she cushions with a jar on an up-gust, three thousand feet below.

"*Now* we've done it," says George in my ear. "Our skin-friction, that last slide, has played Old Harry with the tensions! Look out for laterals, Tim; she'll want some holding."

"I've got her," is the answer. "Come *up*, old woman."

She comes up nobly, but the laterals buffet her left and right like the pinions of angry angels. She is jolted off her course four ways at once, and cuffed into place again, only to be swung aside and dropped into a new chaos. We are never without a corposant grinning on our bows or rolling head over heels from nose to midships, and to the crackle of electricity around and within us is added once or twice the rattle of hail—hail that will never fall on any sea. Slow we must or we may break our back, pitch-poling.

"Air's a perfectly elastic fluid," roars George above the tumult. "About as elastic as a head sea off the Fastnet, ain't it?"

He is less than just to the good element. If one intrudes on the Heavens when they are balancing their volt-accounts; if one disturbs the High Gods' market-rates by hurling steel hulls at ninety knots across tremblingly adjusted electric tensions, one must not complain of any rudeness in the reception. Tim met it with an unmoved countenance, one corner of his under lip caught up on a tooth, his eyes fleeting into the blackness twenty miles ahead, and the fierce sparks flying from his knuckles at every turn of the hand. Now and again he shook his head to clear the sweat trickling from his eyebrows, and it was then that George, watching his chance, would slide down the life-rail and swab his face quickly with a big red handkerchief. I never imagined that a human being could so continuously labor and so collectedly think as did Tim through that Hell's half-hour when the flurry was at its worst. We were dragged hither and yon by warm or frozen suctions, belched up on the tops of wulli-was, spun down by vortices and clubbed aside by laterals under a dizzying rush of stars in the company of a drunken moon. I heard the rushing click of the midship-engine-lever sliding in and out, the low growl of the lift-shunts, and, louder than the yelling winds without, the scream of the bow-rudder gouging into any lull that promised hold for an instant. At last we began to claw up on a cant, bow-rudder and port-propeller together; only the nicest balancing of tanks saved us from spinning like the rifle-bullet of the old days.

"We've got to hitch to windward of that Mark Boat somehow," George cried.

"There's no windward," I protested feebly, where I swung shackled to a stanchion. "How can there be?"

He laughed—as we pitched into a thousand foot blow-out—that red man laughed beneath his inflated hood!

"Look!" he said. "We must clear those refugees with a high lift."

The Mark Boat was below and a little to the sou'west of us, fluctuating in the center of her distraught galaxy. The air was thick with moving lights at every level. I take it most of them were trying to lie head to wind but, not being hydras, they failed. An undertanked Moghrabi boat had risen to the limit of her lift, and, finding no improvement, had dropped a couple of thousand. There she met a superb wulli-wa, and was blown up spinning like a dead leaf. Instead of shutting off she went astern and, naturally, rebounded as from a wall almost into the Mark Boat, whose language (our G.C. took it in) was humanly simple.

"If they'd only ride it out quietly it 'ud be better," said George in a calm, while we climbed like a bat above them all. "But some skippers *will* navigate without enough lift. What does that Tad-boat think she is doing, Tim?"

"Playin' kiss in the ring," was Tim's unmoved reply. A Trans-Asiatic Direct liner had found a smooth and butted into it full power. But there was a vortex at the tail of that smooth, so the T.A.D. was flipped out like a pea from off a fingernail, braking madly as she fled down and all but over-ending.

"Now I hope she's satisfied," said Tim. "I'm glad I'm not a Mark

Boat . . . Do I want help?" The General Communicator dial had caught his ear. "George, you may tell that gentleman with my love—love, remember, George—that I do not want help. Who *is* the officious sardine-tin?"

"A Rimouski drogher on the lookout for a tow."

"Very kind of the Rimouski drogher. This postal packet isn't being towed at present."

"Those droghers will go anywhere on a chance of salvage," George explained. "We call 'em kittiwakes."

A long-beaked, bright steel ninety-footer floated at ease for one instant within hail of us, her slings coiled ready for rescues, and a single hand in her open tower. He was smoking. Surrendered to the insurrection of the airs through which we tore our way, he lay in absolute peace. I saw the smoke of his pipe ascend untroubled ere his boat dropped, it seemed, like a stone in a well.

We had just cleared the Mark Boat and her disorderly neighbors when the storm ended as suddenly as it had begun. A shooting star to northward filled the sky with the green blink of a meteorite dissipating itself in our atmosphere.

Said George: "That may iron out all the tensions." Even as he spoke, the conflicting winds came to rest; the levels filled; the laterals died out in long easy swells; the airways were smoothed before us. In less than three minutes the covey round the Mark Boat had shipped their power-lights and whirred away upon their businesses.

"What's happened?" I gasped. The nerve-storm within and the volt-tingle without had passed: my inflators weighed like lead.

"God He knows!" said Captain George soberly. "That old shooting star's skin-friction has discharged the different levels. I've seen it happen before. Phew! What a relief!"

We dropped from ten to six thousand and got rid of our clammy suits. Tim shut off and stepped out of the Frame. The Mark Boat was coming up behind us. He opened the colloid in that heavenly stillness and mopped his face.

"Hello, Williams!" he cried. "A degree or two out o' station, ain't you?"

"May be," was the answer from the Mark Boat. "I've had some company this evening."

"So I noticed. Wasn't that quite a little draft?"

"I warned you. Why didn't you pull out north? The east-bound packets have."

"Me? Not till I'm running a Polar consumptives' Sanatorium

boat. I was squinting through a colloid before you were out of your cradle, my son."

"I'd be the last man to deny it," the captain of the Mark Boat replies softly. "The way you handled her just now—I'm a pretty fair judge of traffic in a volt-flurry—it was a thousand revolutions beyond anything even *I*'ve ever seen."

Tim's back supples visibly to this oiling. Captain George on the c.p. winks and points to the portrait of a singularly attractive maiden pinned up on Tim's telescope-bracket above the steering wheel.

I see. Wholly and entirely do I see!

There is some talk overhead of "coming round to tea on Friday," a brief report of the derelict's fate, and Tim volunteers as he descends: "For an A.B.C. man young Williams is less of a high-tension fool than some . . . Were you thinking of taking her on, George? Then I'll just have a look round that port-thrust—seems to me it's a trifle warm—and we'll jog along."

The Mark Boat hums off joyously and hangs herself up in her appointed eyrie. Here she will stay, a shutterless observatory; a life-boat station; a salvage tug; a court of ultimate appeal-cum-meteorological bureau for three hundred miles in all directions, till Wednesday next when her relief slides across the stars to take her buffeted place. Her black hull, double conning-tower, and ever-ready slings represent all that remains to the planet of that odd old word authority. She is responsible only to the Aerial Board of Control—the A.B.C. of which Tim speaks so flippantly. But that semi-elected, semi-nominated body of a few score persons of both sexes, controls this planet. "Transportation is Civilization," our motto runs. Theoretically, we do what we please so long as we do not interfere with the traffic *and all it implies*. Practically, the A.B.C. confirms or annuls all international arrangements and, to judge from its last report, finds our tolerant, humorous, lazy little planet only too ready to shift the whole burden of public administration on its shoulders.

I discuss this with Tim, sipping maté on the c.p. while George fans her along over the white blur of the Banks in beautiful upward curves of fifty miles each. The dip-dial translates them on the tape in flowing freehand.

Tim gathers up a skein of it and surveys the last few feet, which record "162's" path through the volt-flurry.

"I haven't had a fever-chart like this to show up in five years," he says ruefully.

A postal packet's dip-dial records every yard of every run. The tapes then go to the A.B.C., which collates and makes composite photographs of them for the instruction of captains. Tim studies his irrevocable past, shaking his head.

"Hello! Here's a fifteen-hundred-foot drop at fifty-five degrees! We must have been standing on our heads then, George."

"You don't say so," George answers. "I fancied I noticed it at the time."

George may not have Captain Purnall's catlike swiftness, but he is all an artist to the tips of the broad fingers that play on the shunt-stops. The delicious flight-curves come away on the tape with never a waver. The Mark Boat's vertical spindle of light lies down to eastward, setting in the face of the following stars. Westward, where no planet should rise, the triple verticals of Trinity Bay (we keep still to the Southern route) make a low-lifting haze. We seem the only thing at rest under all the heavens; floating at ease till the earth's revolution shall turn up our landing-towers.

And minute by minute our silent clock gives us a sixteen-second mile.

"Some fine night," says Tim. "We'll be even with that clock's Master."

"He's coming now," says George, over his shoulder. "I'm chasing the night west."

The stars ahead dim no more than if a film of mist had been drawn under unobserved, but the deep air-boom on our skin changes to a joyful shout.

"The dawn-gust," says Tim. "It'll go on to meet the Sun. Look! Look! There's the dark being crammed back over our bows! Come to the after-colloid. I'll show you something."

The engine-room is hot and stuffy; the clerks in the coach are asleep, and the Slave of the Ray is ready to follow them. Tim slides open the aft colloid and reveals the curve of the world—the ocean's deepest purple—edged with fuming and intolerable gold. Then the Sun rises and through the colloid strikes out our lamps. Tim scowls in his face.

"Squirrels in a cage," he mutters. "That's all we are. Squirrels in a cage! He's going twice as fast as us. Just you wait a few years, my shining friend and we'll take steps that will amaze you. *We'll* Joshua you!"

Yes, that is our dream: to turn all earth into the Vale of Ajalon at our pleasure. So far, we can drag out the dawn to twice its normal length in these latitudes. But some day—even on the Equator—we shall hold the Sun level in his full stride.

Now we look down on a sea thronged with heavy traffic. A big submersible breaks water suddenly. Another and another follows with a swash and a suck and a savage bubbling of relieved pressures. The deep-sea freighters are rising to lung up after the long night, and the leisurely ocean is all patterned with peacock's eyes of foam.

"We'll lung up, too," says Tim, and when we return to the c.p. George shuts off, the colloids are opened, and the fresh air sweeps her out. There is no hurry. The old contracts (they will be revised at the end of the year) allow twelve hours for a run which any packet can put behind her in ten. So we breakfast in the arms of an easterly slant which pushes us along at a languid twenty.

To enjoy life, and tobacco, begin both on a sunny morning half a mile or so above the dappled Atlantic cloud-belts and after a volt-flurry which has cleared and tempered your nerves. While we discussed the thickening traffic with the superiority that comes of having a high level reserved to ourselves, we heard (and I for the first time) the morning hymn on a Hospital boat

She was cloaked by a skein of ravelled fluff beneath us and we caught the chant before she rose into the sunlight. *"Oh, ye Winds of God,"* sang the unseen voices: *"bless ye the Lord! Praise Him and magnify Him for ever!"*

We slid off our caps and joined in. When our shadow fell across her great open platforms they looked up and stretched out their hands neighborly while they sang. We could see the doctors and the nurses and the white-button-like faces of the cot-patients. She passed slowly beneath us, heading northward, her hull, wet with the dews of the night, all ablaze in the sunshine. So took she the shadow of a cloud and vanished, her song continuing. *"Oh, ye holy and humble men of heart, bless ye the Lord! Praise Him and magnify Him for ever."*

"She's a public lunger or she wouldn't have been singing the *Benedicite;* and she's a Greenlander or she wouldn't have snow-blinds over her colloids," said George at last. "She'll be bound for Frederikshavn or one of the Glacier sanatoriums for a month. If she was an accident ward she'd be hung up at the eight-thousand-foot level. Yes—consumptives."

"Funny how the new things are the old things. I've read in books," Tim answered, "that savages used to haul their sick and wounded up to the tops of hills because microbes were fewer there.

We hoist 'em into sterilized air for a while. Same idea. How much do the doctors say we've added to the average life of a man?"

"Thirty years," says George with a twinkle in his eye. "Are we going to spend 'em all up here, Tim?"

"Flap ahead, then. Flap ahead. Who's hindering?" the senior captain laughed, as we went in.

We held a good lift to clear the coastwise and Continental shipping; and we had need of it. Though our route is in no sense a populated one, there is a steady trickle of traffic this way along. We met Hudson Bay furriers out of the Great Preserve, hurrying to make their departure from Bonavista with sable and black fox for the insatiable markets. We over-crossed Keewatin liners, small and cramped; but their captains, who see no land between Trepassy and Blanco, know what gold they bring back from West Africa. Trans-Asiatic Directs, we met, soberly ringing the world round the Fiftieth Meridian at an honest seventy knots; and white-painted Ackroyd & Hunt fruiters out of the south fled beneath us, their ventilated hulls whistling like Chinese kites. Their market is in the North among the northern sanatoria where you can smell their grapefruit and bananas across the cold snows. Argentine beef boats we sighted too, of enormous capacity and unlovely outline. They, too, feed the northern health stations in ice-bound ports where submersibles dare not rise.

Yellow-bellied ore-flats and Ungava petrol-tanks punted down leisurely out of the north, like strings of unfrightened wild duck. It does not pay to "fly" minerals and oil a mile farther than is necessary; but the risks of transhipping to submersibles in the ice-pack off Nain or Hebron are so great that these heavy freighters fly down to Halifax direct, and scent the air as they go. They are the biggest tramps aloft except the Athabasca grain-tubs. But these last, now that the wheat is moved, are busy, over the world's shoulder, timber-lifting in Siberia.

We held to the St. Lawrence, (it is astonishing how the old waterways still pull us children of the air), and followed his broad line of black between its drifting ice-blocks, all down the Park that the wisdom of our fathers—but everyone knows the Quebec run.

We dropped to the Heights Receiving Towers twenty minutes ahead of time, and there hung at ease till the Yokohama Intermediate Packet could pull out and give us our proper slip. It was curious to watch the action of the holding-down clips all along the frosty river front as the boats cleared or came to rest. A big Hamburger was leaving Pont Levis and her crew, unshipping the platform railıňgs, began to sing "Elsinore"—the oldest of our chanteys. You know it of course:

> Mother Rugen's tea-house on the Baltic—
> Forty couple waltzing on the floor!
> And you can watch my Ray,
> For I must go away
> And dance with Ella Sweyn at Elsinore!

Then, while they sweated home the covering-plates:

> Nor-Nor-Nor-Nor-
> West from Sourabaya to the Baltic—
> Ninety knot an hour to the Skaw!
> Mother Rugen's tea-house on the Baltic
> And a dance with Ella Sweyn at Elsinore!

The clips parted with a gesture of indignant dismissal, as though Quebec, glittering under her snows, were casting out these light and unworthy lovers. Our signal came from the Heights. Tim turned and floated up, but surely then it was with passionate appeal that the great tower arms flung open—or did I think so because on the upper staging a little hooded figure also opened her arms wide towards her father?

In ten seconds the coach with its clerks clashed down to the receiving-caisson; the hostlers displaced the engineers at the idle turbines, and Tim, prouder of this than all, introduced me to the maiden of the photograph on the shelf. "And by the way," said he to her, stepping forth in sunshine under the hat of civil life, "I saw young Williams in the Mark Boat. I've asked him to tea on Friday."

As Easy as A.B.C.
FROM A DIVERSITY OF CREATURES
(1917)

Set in the same future as "With the Night Mail," this
—which was actually written in 1912—is one of Kipling's
most misunderstood stories.

Which is not altogether surprising. One needs to know
something of RK's life, his background, and the kind of
experiences which shaped his views, in order fully to
grasp the points that he was driving at. Confronted by a
bald statement like "Too much dam' Democracy!", one
can be forgiven for jumping to the conclusion that the author was in favor of authoritarian rule, even perhaps dic-
tatorship.

This isn't quite the way of it . . .

What RK did very deeply distrust was what we would
now call populism: shameless manipulation of the public
to provide a veneer of respectability for the seizure and
misuse of power. He knew about mobs, and the many-
headed monsters they become. In India he had seen religious riots between Muslim and Hindu; he had lived in
America at a time when lynch law was still common, and
regarded it as a betrayal of the ideals his wife's country
was supposed to stand for. The most effective symbol he
ever created, in my view, is the statue of "The Nigger in
Flames," with its inscription "To the Eternal Memory of
the Justice of the People" . . . (Yes, he did use the word
nigger. In his day it was conventional, deriving as it does
from the Spanish word for black, but he was strict about
confining its application to black Africans and their de-
scendants in the New World. He was in no sense a blind

racial bigot—witness his boast about the membership of
his Freemasons' Lodge, referred to in the preface to
"·007." In "On the City Wall" [*Soldiers Three*], wanting to
portray the repulsive character of an English officer, he
said: "The Captain was not a nice man. He called all natives 'niggers,' which, besides being extreme bad form,
shows gross ignorance.")

Presumably it was his detestation of mobs—shared, by
the way, with H. G. Wells, with whom he had almost nothing otherwise in common—that led him to foresee the dan-
gers of the population explosion at a time when most people
were arguing in favor of increasing the birthrate . . .

He was, in effect, what nowadays would be called a
libertarian. He expressed his attitude most clearly in a
speech he made in 1923, on being elected as Lord Rector
of the University of St. Andrews, in Scotland. This is
how he wound up his address:

At any price that I can pay, let me own myself. And the price is
worth paying if you keep what you have bought . . . A man may
apply his independence to what is called worldly advantage, and
discover too late that he laboriously has made himself dependent
on a mass of external conditions for the maintenance of which he
sacrificed himself. So he may be festooned with the whole haber-
dashery of success, and go to his grave a castaway. Some men hold
that the risk is worth taking. Others do not. It is to these that I have
spoken.

RK's choice of the name De Forest has caused much spec-
ulation; was it after the radio and television pioneer Lee
De Forest? Perhaps; but in America he was personally acquainted with a man of that name, not the inventor.

His reference to forced timber, so long before the discovery of auxins, is a fine example of his sense of what
might one day become possible. So is the notion of re-
mote control for farm machinery; so, too, is the way in
which despite the darkness the ship's position is displayed
on an illuminated map: a terrain-following system. And—
well, I'm not absolutely sure, but his "ground-circuits"
may be the first reference in science fiction to a force field

(as his "flying loop" is probably the first to a pressor beam). At any rate the Nicholls *Encyclopedia of Science Fiction* records no other before the 1930s.

We haven't yet got around to RK's road-surfacing machines, but they have always struck me as feasible, and economically a lot more sensible than transporting enormous quantities of concrete or asphalt over vast distances.

As Easy as A.B.C.

I sn't it almost time that our Planet took some interest in the proceedings of the Aerial Board of Control? One knows that easy communications nowadays, and lack of privacy in the past, have killed all curiosity among mankind, but as the Board's Official Reporter I am bound to tell my tale.

At 9:30 A.M., August 26, A.D. 2065, the Board, sitting in London, was informed by De Forest that the District of Northern Illinois had riotously cut itself out of all systems and would remain disconnected till the Board should take over and administer it direct.

Every Northern Illinois freight and passenger tower was, he reported, out of action; all District main, local, and guiding lights had been extinguished; all General Communications were dumb, and through traffic had been diverted. No reason had been given, but he gathered unofficially from the Mayor of Chicago that the District complained of "crowd-making and invasion of privacy."

As a matter of fact, it is of no importance whether Northern Illinois stay in or out of planetary circuit; as a matter of policy, any complaint of invasion of privacy needs immediate investigation, lest worse follow.

By 9:45 A.M. De Forest, Dragomiroff (Russia), Takahira (Japan), and Pirolo (Italy) were empowered to visit Illinois and "to take such steps as might be necessary for the resumption of traffic and *all that that implies.*" By 10 A.M. the Hall was empty, and the four Members and I were aboard what Pirolo insisted on calling "my leetle godchild"—that is to say, the new *Victor Pirolo.* Our Planet prefers to know Victor Pirolo as a gentle, grey-haired enthusiast who spends his time near Foggia, inventing or creating new breeds of Spanish-Italian olive-trees; but there is another side to his nature—the manufacture of quaint inventions, of which the *Victor Pirolo* is, perhaps, not the least surprising. She and a few score sister-craft of the same type embody his latest ideas. But she is not comfortable. An A.B.C. boat does not take the air with the level-keeled lift of a liner, but shoots up rocket-fashion like the "aeroplane" of our ancestors, and makes her height at top-speed from the first. That is why I found myself sitting suddenly on the large lap of Eustace Arnott, who commands the A.B.C. Fleet. One knows vaguely that there is such a thing as a Fleet somewhere on the Planet, and that, theoretically, it exists for the purposes of what used to be known as "war." Only a week before, while visiting a glacier sanatorium behind Gothaven, I had seen some squadrons making false auroras far to the north while they maneuvered round the Pole; but, naturally, it had never occurred to me that the things could be used in earnest.

Said Arnott to De Forest as I staggered to a seat on the chart-room divan: "We're tremendously grateful to 'em in Illinois. We've never had a chance of exercising all the Fleet together. I've turned in a General Call, and I expect we'll have at least two hundred keels aloft this evening."

"Well aloft?" De Forest asked.

"Of course, sir. Out of sight till they're called for."

Arnott laughed as he lolled over the transparent chart-table where the map of the summer-blue Atlantic slid along, degree by degree, in exact answer to our progress. Our dial already showed 320 m.p.h. and we were two thousand feet above the uppermost traffic lines.

"Now, where is this Illinois District of yours?" said Dragomiroff. "One travels so much, one sees so little. Oh, I remember! It is in North America."

De Forest, whose business it is to know the out districts, told us that it lay at the foot of Lake Michigan, on a road to nowhere in particular, was about half an hour's run from end to end, and, except in one corner, as flat as the sea. Like most flat countries nowadays, it was heavily guarded against invasion of privacy by forced timber—fifty-foot spruce and tamarack, grown in five years. The population was close on two millions, largely migratory be-tween Florida and California, with a backbone of small farms (they call a thousand acres a farm in Illinois) whose owners come into Chicago for amusements and society during the winter. They were, he said, noticeably kind, quiet folk, but a little exacting, as all flat countries must be, in their notions of privacy. There had, for in-stance, been no printed news-sheet in Illinois for twenty-seven years. Chicago argued that engines for printed news sooner or later developed into engines for invasion of privacy, which in turn might bring the old terror of Crowds and blackmail back to the Planet. So news-sheets were not.

"And that's Illinois," De Forest concluded. "You see, in the Old Days, she was in the forefront of what they used to call 'progress,' and Chicago—"

"Chicago?" said Takahira. "That's the little place where there is Salati's Statue of the Nigger in Flames? A fine bit of old work."

"When did you see it?" asked De Forest quickly. "They only unveil it once a year."

"I know. At Thanksgiving. It was then," said Takahira, with a shudder. "And they sang MacDonough's Song, too."

"Whew!" De Forest whistled. "I did not know that! I wish you'd told me before. MacDonough's Song may have had its uses when it was composed, but it was an infernal legacy for any man to leave behind."

"It's protective instinct, my dear fellows," said Pirolo, rolling a cigarette. "The Planet, she has had her dose of popular government. She suffers from inherited agoraphobia. She has no—ah—use for crowds."

Dragomiroff leaned forward to give him a light. "Certainly," said the white-bearded Russian, "the Planet has taken all precautions against crowds for the past hundred years. What is our total population today? Six hundred million, we hope; five hundred, we think; but—but if next year's census shows more than four hundred and fifty, I myself will eat all the extra little babies. We have cut the birthrate out—right out! For a long time we have said to Almighty God, 'Thank You, Sir, but we do not much like Your game of life, so we will not play.'"

"Anyhow," said Arnott defiantly, "men live a century apiece on the average now."

"Oh, that is quite well! I am rich—you are rich—we are all rich and happy because we are so few and we live so long. Only *I* think Almighty God He will remember what the Planet was like in the time of Crowds and the Plague. Perhaps He will send us nerves. Eh, Pirolo?"

The Italian blinked into space. "Perhaps," he said, "He has sent them already. Anyhow, you cannot argue with the Planet. She does not forget the Old Days, and—what can you do?"

"For sure we can't remake the world." De Forest glanced at the map flowing smoothly across the table from west to east. "We ought to be over our ground by nine tonight. There won't be much sleep afterwards."

On which hint we dispersed, and I slept till Takahira waked me for dinner. Our ancestors thought nine hours' sleep ample for their little lives. We, living thirty years longer, feel ourselves defrauded with less than eleven out of the twenty-four.

By ten o'clock we were over Lake Michigan. The west shore was lightless, except for a dull ground-glare at Chicago, and a single traffic-directing light—its leading beam pointing north—at Waukegan on our starboard bow. None of the Lake villages gave any sign of life; and inland, westward, so far as we could see, blackness lay unbroken on the level earth. We swooped down and skimmed low across the dark, throwing calls county by county. Now and again we picked up the faint glimmer of a house-light, or heard the rasp and rend of a cultivator being played across the fields, but Northern Illinois as a whole was one inky, apparently uninhabited, waste of high, forced woods. Only our illuminated map, with its little pointer switching from county to county, as we wheeled and twisted, gave us any idea of our position. Our calls, urgent, pleading, coaxing or commanding, through the General Communicator brought no answer. Illinois strictly maintained her own privacy in the timber which she grew for that purpose.

"Oh, this is absurd!" said De Forest. "We're like an owl trying to work a wheat-field. Is this Bureau Creek? Let's land, Arnott, and get hold of someone."

We brushed over a belt of forced woodland—fifteen-year-old maple sixty feet high—grounded on a private meadow-dock, none too big, where we moored to our own grapnels, and hurried out through the warm dark night towards a light in a verandah. As we neared the garden gate I could have sworn we had stepped knee-deep in quicksand, for we could scarcely drag our feet against the prickling currents that clogged them. After five paces we stopped, wiping our foreheads, as hopelessly stuck on dry smooth turf as so many cows in a bog.

"Pest!" cried Pirolo angrily. "We are ground-circuited. And it is my own system of ground-circuits too! I know the pull."

"Good evening," said a girl's voice from the verandah. "Oh, I'm sorry! We've locked up. Wait a minute."

We heard the click of a switch, and almost fell forward as the currents round our knees were withdrawn.

The girl laughed, and laid aside her knitting. An old-fashioned Controller stood at her elbow, which she reversed from time to time, and we could hear the snort and clank of the obedient cultivator half a mile away, behind the guardian woods.

"Come in and sit down," she said. "I'm only playing a plow. Dad's gone to Chicago to—Ah! Then it was *your* call I heard just now!"

She had caught sight of Arnott's Board uniform, leaped to the switch, and turned it full on.

We were checked, gasping, waist-deep in current this time, three yards from the verandah.

"We only want to know what's the matter with Illinois," said De Forest placidly.

"Then hadn't you better go to Chicago and find out?" she answered. "There's nothing wrong here. We own ourselves."

"How can we go anywhere if you won't loose us?" De Forest went on, while Arnott scowled. Admirals of Fleets are still quite human when their dignity is touched.

"Stop a minute—you don't know how funny you look!" She put her hands on her hips and laughed mercilessly.

"Don't worry about that," said Arnott, and whistled. A voice answered from the *Victor Pirolo* in the meadow.

"Only a single-fuse ground-circuit!" Arnott called. "Sort it out gently, please."

We heard the ping of a breaking lamp; a fuse blew out somewhere in the verandah roof, frightening a nest full of birds. The ground-circuit was open. We stopped and rubbed our tingling ankles.

"How rude—how very rude of you!" the maiden cried.

"Sorry, but we haven't time to look funny," said Arnott. "We've got to go to Chicago; and if I were you, young lady, I'd go into the cellars for the next two hours, and take mother with me."

Off he strode, with us at his heels, muttering indignantly, till the humor of the thing struck and doubled him up with laughter at the foot of the gangway ladder.

"The Board hasn't shown what you might call a fat spark on this occasion," said De Forest, wiping his eyes. "I hope I didn't look as big a fool as you did, Arnott! Hullo! What on earth is that? Dad coming home from Chicago?"

There was a rattle and a rush, and a five-plow cultivator, blades in air like so many teeth, trundled itself at us round the edge of the timber, fuming and sparking furiously.

"Jump!" said Arnott, as we bundled ourselves through the none-too-wide door. "Never mind about shutting it. Up!"

The *Victor Pirolo* lifted like a bubble, and the vicious machine shot just underneath us, clawing high as it passed.

"There's a nice little spit-kitten for you!" said Arnott, dusting his knees. "We ask her a civil question. First she circuits us and then she plays a cultivator at us!"

"And then we fly," said Dragomiroff. "If I were forty years more young, I would go back and kiss her. Ho! Ho!"

"I," said Pirolo, "would smack her! My pet ship has been chased by a dirty plow; a—how do you say?—agricultural implement."

"Oh, that is Illinois all over," said De Forest. "They don't content themselves with talking about privacy. They arrange to have it. And now, where's your alleged fleet, Arnott? We must assert ourselves against this wench."

Arnott pointed to the black heavens.

"Waiting on—up there," said he. "Shall I give them the whole installation, sir?"

"Oh, I don't think the young lady is quite worth that," said De Forest. "Get over Chicago, and perhaps we'll see something."

In a few minutes we were hanging at two thousand feet over an oblong block of incandescence in the center of the little town.

"That looks like the old City Hall. Yes, there's Salati's Statue in front of it," said Takahira. "But what on earth are they doing to the place? I thought they used it for a market nowadays! Drop a little, please."

We could hear the sputter and crackle of road-surfacing machines—the cheap Western type which fuse stone and rubbish into lava-like ribbed glass for their rough country roads. Three or four surfacers worked on each side of a square of ruins. The brick and stone wreckage crumbled, slid forward, and presently spread out into white-hot pools of sticky slag, which the leveling-rods smoothed more or less flat. Already a third of the big block had been so treated, and was cooling to dull red before our astonished eyes.

"It is the Old Market," said De Forest. "Well, there's nothing to prevent Illinois from making a road through a market. It doesn't interfere with traffic, that I can see."

"Hsh!" said Arnott, gripping me by the shoulder. "Listen! They're singing. Why on the earth are they singing?"

We dropped again till we could see the black fringe of people at the edge of that glowing square.

At first they only roared against the roar of the surfacers and levelers. Then the words came up clearly—the words of the Forbidden Song that all men knew, and none let pass their lips—poor Pat

MacDonough's Song, made in the days of the Crowds and the Plague—every silly word of it loaded to sparking-point with the Planet's inherited memories of horror, panic, fear and cruelty. And Chicago—innocent, contented little Chicago—was singing it aloud to the infernal tune that carried riot, pestilence and lunacy round our Planet a few generations ago!

> "Once there was The People—Terror gave it birth;
> Once there was The People, and it made a hell of earth!"

(Then the stamp and pause):

> "Earth arose and crushed it. Listen, oh, ye slain!
> Once there was The People—it shall never be again!"

The levelers thrust in savagely against the ruins as the song renewed itself again, again and again, louder than the crash of the melting walls.

De Forest frowned.

"I don't like that," he said. "They've broken back to the Old Days! They'll be killing somebody soon. I think we'd better divert 'em, Arnott."

"Ay, ay, sir." Arnott's hand went to his cap, and we heard the hull of the *Victor Pirolo* ring to the command: "Lamps! Both watches stand by! Lamps! Lamps! Lamps!"

"Keep still!" Takahira whispered to me. "Blinders, please, quartermaster."

"It's all right—all right!" said Pirolo from behind, and to my horror slipped over my head some sort of rubber helmet that locked with a snap. I could feel thick colloid bosses before my eyes, but I stood in absolute darkness.

"To save the sight," he explained, and pushed me on to the chart-room divan. "You will see in a minute."

As he spoke I became aware of a thin thread of almost intolerable light, let down from heaven at an immense distance—one vertical hairsbreadth of frozen lightning.

"Those are our flanking ships," said Arnott at my elbow. "That one is over Galena. Look south—that other one's over Keithburg. Vincennes is behind us, and north yonder is Winthrop Woods. The Fleet's in position, sir"—this to De Forest. "As soon as you give the word."

"Ah no! No!" cried Dragomiroff at my side. I could feel the old man tremble. "I do not know all that you can do, but be kind! I ask you to be a little kind to them below! This is horrible—horrible!"

"When a Woman kills a Chicken,
Dynasties and Empires sicken,"

Takahira quoted. "It is too late to be gentle now."

"Then take off my helmet! Take off my helmet!" Dragomiroff began hysterically.

Pirolo must have put his arm round him.

"Hush," he said, "I am here. It is all right, Ivan, my dear fellow."

"I'll just send our little girl in Bureau County a warning," said Arnott. "She don't deserve it, but we'll allow her a minute or two to take mamma to the cellar."

In the utter hush that followed the growling spark after Arnott had linked up his Service Communicator with the invisible Fleet, we heard MacDonough's Song from the city beneath us grow fainter as we rose to position. Then I clapped my hand before my mask lenses, for it was as though the floor of Heaven had been riddled and all the inconceivable blaze of suns in the making was poured through the manholes.

"You needn't count," said Arnott. I had had no thought of such a thing. "There are two hundred and fifty keels up there, five miles apart. Full power, please, for another twelve seconds."

The firmament, as far as eye could reach, stood on pillars of white fire. One fell on the glowing square at Chicago, and turned it black.

"Oh! Oh! Oh! Can men be allowed to do such things?" Dragomiroff cried, and fell across our knees.

"Glass of water, please," said Takahira to a helmeted shape that leaped forward. "He is a little faint."

The lights switched off, and the darkness stunned like an avalanche. We could hear Dragomiroff's teeth on the glass edge.

Pirolo was comforting him.

"All right, all ra-ight," he repeated. "Come and lie down. Come below and take off your mask. I give you my word, old friend, it is all right. They are my siege-lights. Little Victor Pirolo's leetle lights. You know *me!* I do not hurt people."

"Pardon!" Dragomiroff moaned. "I have never seen Death. I have never seen the Board take action. Shall we go down and burn them alive, or is that already done?"

"Oh, hush," said Pirolo, and I think he rocked him in his arms.

"Do we repeat, sir?" Arnott asked De Forest.

"Give 'em a minute's break," De Forest replied. "They may need it."

We waited a minute, and then MacDonough's Song, broken but defiant, rose from undefeated Chicago.

"They seem fond of that tune," said De Forest. "I should let 'em have it, Arnott."

"Very good, sir," said Arnott, and felt his way to the Communicator keys.

No lights broke forth, but the hollow of the skies made herself the mouth for one note that touched the raw fiber of the brain. Men hear such sounds in delirium, advancing like tides from horizons beyond the ruled foreshores of space.

"That's our pitch-pipe," said Arnott. "We may be a bit ragged. I've never conducted two hundred and fifty performers before." He pulled out the couplers, and struck a full chord on the Service Communicators.

The beams of light leaped down again, and danced, solemnly and awfully, a stilt-dance, sweeping thirty or forty miles left and right at each stiff-legged kick, while the darkness delivered itself—there is no scale to measure against that utterance—of the tune to which they kept time. Certain notes—one learned to expect them with terror—cut through one's marrow, but, after three minutes, thought and emotion passed in indescribable agony.

We saw, we heard, but I think we were in some sort swooning. The two hundred and fifty beams shifted, re-formed, straddled and split, narrowed, widened, rippled in ribbons, broke into a thousand white-hot parallel lines, melted and revolved in interwoven rings like old-fashioned engine-turning, flung up to the zenith, made as if to descend and renew the torment, halted at the last instant, twizzled insanely round the horizon, and vanished, to bring back for the hundredth time darkness more shattering than their instantly renewed light over all Illinois. Then the tune and lights ceased together, and we heard one single devastating wail that shook all the horizon as a rubbed wet finger shakes the rim of a bowl.

"Ah, that is my new siren," said Pirolo. "You can break an iceberg in half, if you find the proper pitch. They will whistle by squadrons now. It is the wind through pierced shutters in the bows."

I had collapsed beside Dragomiroff, broken and sniveling feebly, because I had been delivered before my time to all the terrors of

Judgment Day, and the Archangels of the Resurrection were hailing me naked across the Universe to the sound of the music of the spheres.

Then I saw De Forest smacking Arnott's helmet with his open hand. The wailing died down in a long shriek as a black shadow swooped past us, and returned to her place above the lower clouds.

"I hate to interrupt a specialist when he's enjoying himself," said De Forest. "But, as a matter of fact, all Illinois has been asking us to stop for these last fifteen seconds."

"What a pity." Arnott slipped off his mask. "I wanted you to hear us really hum. Our lower C can lift street-paving."

"It is Hell—Hell!" cried Dragomiroff, and sobbed aloud.

Arnott looked away as he answered:

"It's a few thousand volts ahead of the old shoot-'em-and-sink-'em game, but I should scarcely call it *that*. What shall I tell the Fleet, sir?"

"Tell 'em we're very pleased and impressed. I don't think they need wait on any longer. There isn't a spark left down there." De Forest pointed. "They'll be deaf and blind."

"Oh, I think not, sir. The demonstration lasted less than ten minutes."

"Marvellous!" Takahira sighed. "I should have said it was half a night. Now, shall we go down and pick up the pieces?"

"But first a small drink," said Pirolo. "The Board must not arrive weeping at its own works."

"I am an old fool—an old fool!" Dragomiroff began piteously. "I did not know what would happen. It is all new to me. We reason with them in Little Russia."

Chicago North landing-tower was unlighted, and Arnott worked his ship into the clips by her own lights. As soon as these broke out we heard groanings of horror and appeal from many people below.

"All right," shouted Arnott into the darkness. "We aren't beginning again!" We descended by the stairs, to find ourselves knee-deep in a groveling crowd, some crying that they were blind, others beseeching us not to make any more noises, but the greater part writhing face downward, their hands or their caps before their eyes.

It was Pirolo who came to our rescue. He climbed the side of a surfacing-machine, and there, gesticulating as though they could see, made oration to those afflicted people of Illinois.

"You stchewpids!" he began. "There is nothing to fuss for. Of course, your eyes will smart and be red tomorrow. You will look as if you and your wives had drunk too much, but in a little while you will see again as well as before. I tell you this, and I—*I* am Pirolo. Victor Pirolo!"

The crowd with one accord shuddered, for many legends attach to Victor Pirolo of Foggia, deep in the secrets of God.

"Pirolo?" An unsteady voice lifted itself. "Then tell us was there anything except light in those lights of yours just now?"

The question was repeated from every corner of the darkness. Pirolo laughed.

"No!" he thundered. (Why have small men such large voices?) "I give you my word and the Board's word that there was nothing except light—just light! You stchewpids! Your birthrate is too low already as it is. Someday I must invent something to send it up, but send it down—never!"

"Is that true?—We thought—somebody said—"

One could feel the tension relax all round.

"You *too* big fools," Pirolo cried. "You could have sent us a call and we would have told you."

"Send you a call!" a deep voice shouted. "I wish you had been at our end of the wire."

"I'm glad I wasn't," said De Forest. "It was bad enough from behind the lamps. Never mind! It's over now. Is there anyone here I can talk business with? I'm De Forest—for the Board."

"You might begin with me, for one—I'm Mayor," the bass voice replied.

A big man rose unsteadily from the street, and staggered towards us where we sat on the broad turf-edging, in front of the garden fences.

"I ought to be the first on my feet. Am I?" said he.

"Yes," said De Forest, and steadied him as he dropped down beside us.

"Hello, Andy. Is that you?" a voice called.

"Excuse me," said the Mayor; "that sounds like my Chief of Police, Bluthner!"

"Bluthner it is; and here's Mulligan and Keefe—on their feet."

"Bring 'em up please, Blut. We're supposed to be the Four in charge of this hamlet. What we says, goes. And, De Forest, what do you say?"

"Nothing—yet," De Forest answered, as we made room for the panting, reeling men. "*You*'ve cut out of system. Well?"

"Tell the steward to send down drinks, please," Arnott whispered to an orderly at his side.

"Good!" said the Mayor, smacking his dry lips. "Now I suppose

we can take it, De Forest, that henceforward the Board will administer us direct?"

"Not if the Board can avoid it," De Forest laughed. "The A.B.C.
is responsible for the planetary traffic only."

"*And all that that implies.*" The big Four who ran Chicago
chanted their Magna Carta like children at school.

"Well, get on," said De Forest wearily. "What is your silly trouble anyway?"

"Too much dam' Democracy," said the Mayor, laying his hand
on De Forest's knee.

"So? I thought Illinois had had her dose of that."

"She has. That's why. Blut, what did you do with our prisoners
last night?"

"Locked 'em in the water-tower to prevent the women killing
'em," the Chief of Police replied. "I'm too blind to move just yet,
but—"

"Arnott, send some of your people, please, and fetch 'em along,"
said De Forest.

"They're triple-circuited," the Mayor called. "You'll have to
blow out three fuses." He turned to De Forest, his large outline just
visible in the paling darkness. "I hate to throw anymore work on the
Board. I'm an administrator myself, but we've had a little fuss with
our Serviles. What? In a big city there's bound to be a few men and
women who can't live without listening to themselves, and who
prefer drinking out of pipes they don't own both ends of. They
inhabit flats and hotels all the year round. They say it saves 'em
trouble. Anyway, it gives 'em more time to make trouble for their
neighbors. We call 'em Serviles locally. And they are apt to be
tuberculous."

"Just so!" said the man called Mulligan. "Transportation is Civilization. Democracy is Disease. I've proved it by the blood-test,
every time."

"Mulligan's our Health Officer, and a one-idea man," said the
Mayor, laughing. "But it's true that most Serviles haven't much
control. They *will* talk; and when people take to talking as a business, anything may arrive—mayn't it, De Forest?"

"Anything—except the facts of the case," said De Forest, laughing.

"I'll give you those in a minute," said the Mayor. "Our Serviles
got to talking—first in their houses and then on the streets, telling
men and women how to manage their own affairs. (You can't teach
a Servile not to finger his neighbor's soul.) That's invasion of pri-

vacy, of course, but in Chicago we'll suffer anything sooner than make crowds. Nobody took much notice, and so I let 'em alone. My fault! I was warned there would be trouble, but there hasn't been a crowd or murder in Illinois for nineteen years."

"Twenty-two," said his Chief of Police.

"Likely. Anyway, we'd forgot such things. So, from talking in the houses and on the streets, our Serviles go to calling a meeting at the Old Market yonder." He nodded across the square where the wrecked buildings heaved up grey in the dawn-glimmer behind the square-cased statue of The Negro in Flames. "There's nothing to prevent anyone calling meetings except that it's against human nature to stand in a crowd, besides being bad for the health. I ought to have known by the way our men and women attended that first meeting that trouble was brewing. There were as many as a thousand in the market-place, touching each other. Touching! Then the Serviles turned in all tongue-switches and talked, and we—"

"What did they talk about?" said Takahira.

"First, how badly things were managed in the city. That pleased us Four—we were on the platform—because we hoped to catch one or two good men for City work. You know how rare executive capacity is. Even if we didn't it's—it's refreshing to find anyone interested enough in our job to damn our eyes. You don't know what it means to work, year in, year out, without a spark of difference with a living soul."

"Oh, don't we!" said De Forest. "There are times on the Board when we'd give our positions if anyone would kick us out and take hold of things themselves."

"But they won't," said the Mayor ruefully. "I assure you, sir, we Four have done things in Chicago, in the hope of rousing people, that would have discredited Nero. But what do they say? 'Very good, Andy. Have it your own way. Anything's better than a crowd. I'll go back to my land.' You *can't* do anything with folk who can go where they please, and don't want anything on God's earth except their own way. There isn't a kick or a kicker left on the Planet."

"Then I suppose that little shed yonder fell down by itself?" said De Forest. We could see the bare and still smoking ruins, and hear the slag-pools crackle as they hardened and set.

"Oh, that's only amusement. 'Tell you later. As I was saying, our Serviles held the meeting, and pretty soon we had to ground-circuit the platform to save 'em from being killed. And that didn't make our people any more pacific."

"How d'you mean?" I ventured to ask.

"If you've ever been ground-circuited," said the Mayor, "you'll know it don't improve any man's temper to be held up straining against nothing. No, sir! Eight or nine hundred folk kept pawing and buzzing like flies in treacle for two hours, while a pack of perfectly safe Serviles invades their mental and spiritual privacy, may be amusing to watch, but they are not pleasant to handle afterwards."

Pirolo chuckled.

"Our folk own themselves. They were of opinion things were going too far and too fiery. I warned the Serviles; but they're born house-dwellers. Unless a fact hits 'em on the head, they cannot see it. Would you believe me, they went on to talk of what they called 'popular government'? They did! They wanted us to go back to the old Voodoo-business of voting with papers and wooden boxes, and word-drunk people and printed formulas, and news-sheets! They said they practiced it among themselves about what they'd have to eat in their flats and hotels. Yes, sir! They stood up behind Bluthner's doubled ground-circuits, and they said that, in this present year of grace, *to* self-owning men and women, *on* that very spot! Then they finished"—he lowered his voice cautiously—"by talking about 'The People.' And then Bluthner he had to sit up all night in charge of the circuits because he couldn't trust his men to keep 'em shut."

"It was trying 'em too high," the Chief of Police broke in. "But we couldn't hold the crowd ground-circuited forever. I gathered in all the Serviles on charge of crowd-making, and put 'em in the water-tower, and then I let things cut loose. I had to! The District lit like a sparked gas-tank!"

"The news was out over seven degrees of country," the Mayor continued; "and when once it's a question of invasion of privacy, goodbye to right and reason in Illinois! They began turning out traffic-lights and locking up landing-towers on Thursday night. Friday, they stopped all traffic and asked for the Board to take over. Then they wanted to clean Chicago off the side of the Lake and rebuild elsewhere—just for a souvenir of 'The People' that the Serviles talked about. I suggested that they should slag the Old Market where the meeting was held, while I turned in a call to you all on the Board. That kept 'em quiet till you came along. And—and now *you* can take hold of the situation."

"Any chance of their quieting down?" De Forest asked.

"You can try," said the Mayor.

De Forest raised his voice in the face of the reviving crowd that had edged in towards us. Day was come.

"Don't you think this business can be arranged?" he began. But there was a roar of angry voices:

"We've finished with Crowds! We aren't going back to the Old Days! Take us over! Take the Serviles away! Administer direct or we'll kill 'em! Down with The People!"

An attempt was made to begin MacDonough's Song. It got no further than the first line, for the *Victor Pirolo* sent down a warning drone on one stopped horn. A wrecked side-wall of the Old Market tottered and fell inwards on the slag-pools. None spoke or moved till the last of the dust had settled down again, turning the steel case of Salati's Statue ashy grey.

"You see you'll just *have* to take us over," the Mayor whispered.

De Forest shrugged his shoulders.

"You talk as if executive capacity could be snatched out of the air like so much horsepower. Can't you manage yourselves on any terms?" he said.

"We can, if you say so. It will only cost those few lives to begin with."

The Mayor pointed across the square, where Arnott's men guided a stumbling group of ten or twelve men and women to the lake front and halted them under the Statue.

"Now I think," said Takahira under his breath, "there will be trouble."

The mass in front of us growled like beasts.

At that moment the sun rose clear, and revealed the blinking assembly to itself. As soon as it realized that it was a crowd we saw the shiver of horror and mutual repulsion shoot across it precisely as the steely flaws shot across the lake outside. Nothing was said, and, being half blind, of course it moved slowly. Yet in less than fifteen minutes most of that vast multitude—three thousand at the lowest count—melted away like frost on south eaves. The remnant stretched themselves on the grass, where a crowd feels and looks less like a crowd.

"These mean business," the Mayor whispered to Takahira. "There are a goodish few women there who've borne children. I don't like it."

The morning draft off the lake stirred the trees round us with promise of a hot day; the sun reflected itself dazzlingly on the canister-shaped covering of Salati's Statue; cocks crew in the gardens, and we could hear gate-latches clicking in the distance as people stumblingly resought their homes.

"I'm afraid there won't be any morning deliveries," said De Forest. "We rather upset things in the country last night."

"That makes no odds," the Mayor returned. "We're all provisioned for six months. *We* take no chances."

Nor, when you come to think of it, does anyone else. It must be three-quarters of a generation since any house or city faced a food shortage. Yet is there house or city on the Planet today that has not half a year's provisions laid in? We are like the shipwrecked seamen in the old books, who, having once nearly starved to death, ever afterwards hide away bits of food and biscuit. Truly we trust no Crowds, nor system based on Crowds!

De Forest waited till the last footstep had died away. Meantime the prisoners at the base of the Statue shuffled, posed and fidgeted, with the shamelessness of quite little children. None of them were more than six feet high, and many of them were as grey-haired as the ravaged, harassed heads of old pictures. They huddled together in actual touch, while the crowd, spaced at large intervals, looked at them with congested eyes.

Suddenly a man among them began to talk. The Mayor had not in the least exaggerated. It appeared that our Planet lay sunk in slavery beneath the heel of the Aerial Board of Control. The orator urged us to arise in our might, burst our prison doors and break our fetters (all his metaphors, by the way, were of the most medieval). Next he demanded that every matter of daily life, including most of the physical functions, should be submitted for decision at any time of the week, month, or year to, I gathered, anybody who happened to be passing by or residing within a certain radius, and that everybody should forthwith abandon his concerns to settle the matter, first by crowd-making, next by talking to the crowds made, and lastly by describing crosses on pieces of paper, which rubbish should later be counted with certain mystic ceremonies and oaths. Out of this amazing play, he assured us, would automatically arise a higher, nobler, and kinder world, based—he demonstrated this with the awful lucidity of the insane—based on the sanctity of the Crowd and the villainy of the single person. In conclusion, he called loudly upon God to testify to his personal merits and integrity. When the flow ceased, I turned bewildered to Takahira, who was nodding solemnly.

"Quite correct," said he. "It is all in the old books. He has left nothing out, not even the war-talk."

"But I don't see how this stuff can upset a child, much less a district," I replied.

"Ah, you are too young," said Dragomiroff. "For another thing, you are not a mamma. Please look at the mammas."

Ten or fifteen women who remained had separated themselves from the silent men, and were drawing in towards the prisoners. It reminded one of the stealthy encircling, before the rush in at the quarry, of wolves round musk-oxen in the North. The prisoners saw, and drew together more closely. The Mayor covered his face with his hands for an instant. De Forest, bareheaded, stepped forward between the prisoners and the slowly, stiffly moving line.

"That's all very interesting," he said to the dry-lipped orator. "But the point seems that you've been making crowds and invading privacy."

A woman stepped forward, and would have spoken, but there was a quick assenting murmur from the men, who realized that De Forest was trying to pull the situation down to ground-line.

"Yes! Yes!" they cried. "We cut out because they made crowds and invaded privacy! Stick to that! Keep on that switch! Lift the Serviles out of this! The Board's in charge! Hsh!"

"Yes, the Board's in charge," said De Forest. "I'll take formal evidence of crowd-making if you like, but the Members of the Board can testify to it. Will that do?"

The women had closed in another pace, with hands that clenched and unclenched at their sides.

"Good! Good enough!" the men cried. "We're content. Only take them away quickly."

"Come along up!" said De Forest to the captives. "Breakfast is quite ready."

It appeared, however, that they did not wish to go. They intended to remain in Chicago and make crowds. They pointed out that De Forest's proposal was gross invasion of privacy.

"My dear fellow," said Pirolo to the most voluble of the leaders, "you hurry, or your crowd that can't be wrong will kill you!"

"But that would be murder," answered the believer in crowds; and there was a roar of laughter from all sides that seemed to show the crisis had broken.

A woman stepped forward from the line of women, laughing, I protest, as merrily as any of the company. One hand, of course, shaded her eyes, the other was at her throat.

"Oh, they needn't be afraid of being killed!" she called.

"Not in the least," said De Forest. "But don't you think that, now the Board's in charge, you might go home while we get these people away?"

"I shall be home long before that. It—it has been rather a trying day."

She stood up to her full height, dwarfing even De Forest's six-foot-eight, and smiled, with eyes closed against the fierce light.

"Yes, rather," said De Forest. "I'm afraid you feel the glare a little. We'll have the ship down."

He motioned to the *Pirolo* to drop between us and the sun, and at the same time to loop-circuit the prisoners, who were a trifle unsteady. We saw them stiffen to the current where they stood. The woman's voice went on, sweet and deep and unshaken:

"I don't suppose you men realize how much this—this sort of thing means to a woman. I've borne three. We women don't want our children given to Crowds. It must be an inherited instinct. Crowds make trouble. They bring back the Old Days. Hate, fear, blackmail, publicity, 'The People'—*That! That! That!*" She pointed to the Statue, and the crowd growled once more.

"Yes, if they are allowed to go on," said De Forest. "But this little affair—"

"It means so much to us women that this—this little affair should never happen again. Of course, never's a big word, but one feels so strongly that it is important to stop crowds at the very beginning. Those creatures"—she pointed with her left hand at the prisoners swaying like seaweed in a tideway as the circuit pulled them— "those people have friends and wives and children in the city and elsewhere. One doesn't want anything done to *them*, you know. It's terrible to force a human being out of fifty or sixty years of good life. I'm only forty myself. *I* know. But, at the same time, one feels that an example should be made, because no price is too heavy to pay if—if these people and *all that they imply* can be put an end to. Do you quite understand, or would you be kind enough to tell your men to take the casing off the Statue? It's worth looking at."

"I understand perfectly. But I don't think anybody here wants to see the Statue on an empty stomach. Excuse me one moment." De Forest called up to the ship, "A flying loop ready on the port side, if you please." Then to the woman he said with some crispness, "You might leave us a little discretion in the matter."

"Oh, of course. Thank you for being so patient. I know my arguments are silly, but—" She half turned away and went on in a changed voice, "Perhaps this will help you to decide."

She threw out her right arm with a knife in it. Before the blade could be returned to her throat or her bosom it was twitched from her grip, sparked as it flew out of the shadow of the ship above, and fell flashing in the sunshine at the foot of the Statue fifty yards away. The outflung arm was arrested, rigid as a bar for an instant, till the releasing circuit permitted her to bring it slowly to her side. The other women shrank back silent among the men.

Pirolo rubbed his hands, and Takahira nodded.

"That was clever of you, De Forest," said he.

"What a glorious pose!" Dragomiroff murmured, for the frightened woman was on the edge of tears.

"Why did you stop me? I would have done it!" she cried.

"I have no doubt you would," said De Forest. "But we can't waste a life like yours on these people. I hope the arrest didn't sprain your wrist; it's so hard to regulate a flying loop. But I think you are quite right about those persons' women and children. We'll take them all away with us if you promise not to do anything stupid to yourself."

"I promise—I promise." She controlled herself with an effort. "But it is so important to us women. We know what it means; and I thought if you saw I was in earnest—"

"I saw you were, and you've gained your point. I shall take all your Serviles away with me at once. The Mayor will make lists of their friends and families in the city and the district, and he'll ship them after us this afternoon."

"Sure," said the Mayor, rising to his feet. "Keefe, if you can see, hadn't you better finish leveling off the Old Market? It don't look sightly the way it is now, and we shan't use it for crowds anymore."

"I think you had better wipe out that Statue as well, Mr. Mayor," said De Forest. "I don't question its merits as a work of art, but I believe it's a shade morbid."

"Certainly, sir. Oh, Keefe! Slag the Nigger before you go on to fuse the Market. I'll get to the Communicators and tell the District that the Board is in charge. Are you making any special appointments, sir?"

"None. We haven't men to waste on these backwoods. Carry on as before, but under the Board. Arnott, run your Serviles aboard, please. Ground ship and pass them through the bilge-doors. We'll wait till we've finished with this work of art."

The prisoners trailed past him, talking fluently, but unable to gesticulate in the drag of the current. Then the surfacers rolled up, two on each side of the Statue. With one accord the spectators looked elsewhere, but there was no need. Keefe turned on full power, and the thing simply melted within its case. All I saw was a surge of white-hot metal pouring over the plinth, a glimpse of Salati's inscription, "To the Eternal Memory of the Justice of the People," ere the stone base itself cracked and powdered into finest lime. The crowd cheered.

"Thank you," said De Forest; "but we want our breakfasts, and I expect you do too. Good-bye, Mr. Mayor! Delighted to see you at any time, but I hope I shan't have to, officially, for the next thirty years. Good-bye, madam. Yes. We're all given to nerves nowadays. I suffer from them myself. Good-bye, gentlemen all! You're under the tyrannous heel of the Board from this moment, but if ever you feel like breaking your fetters you've only to let us know. This is no treat to us. Good luck!"

We embarked amid shouts, and did not check our lift till they had dwindled into whispers. Then De Forest flung himself on the chart-room divan and mopped his forehead.

"I don't mind men," he panted, "but women are the devil!"

"Still the devil," said Pirolo cheerfully. "That one would have suicided."

"I know it. That was why I signaled for the flying loop to be clapped on her. I owe you an apology for that, Arnott. I hadn't time to catch your eye, and you were busy with our caitiffs. By the way, who actually answered my signal? It was a smart piece of work."

"Ilroy," said Arnott; "but he overloaded the wave. It may be pretty gallery-work to knock a knife out of a lady's hand, but didn't you notice how she rubbed 'em? He scorched her fingers. Slovenly, I call it."

"Far be it from me to interfere with Fleet discipline, but don't be too hard on the boy. If that woman had killed herself they would have killed every Servile and everything related to a Servile throughout the district by nightfall."

"That was what she was playing for," Takahira said. "And with our Fleet gone we could have done nothing to hold them."

"I may be ass enough to walk into a ground-circuit," said Arnott, "but I don't dismiss my Fleet till I'm reasonably sure that trouble is over. They're in position still, and I intend to keep 'em there till the Serviles are shipped out of the district. That last little crowd meant murder, my friends."

"Nerves! All nerves!" said Pirolo. "You cannot argue with agoraphobia."

"And it is not as if they had seen much dead—or *is* it?" said Takahira.

"In all my ninety years I have never seen death." Dragomiroff spoke as one who would excuse himself. "Perhaps that was why— last night—"

Then it came out as we sat over breakfast, that, with the exception of Arnott and Pirolo, none of us had ever seen a corpse, or knew in what manner the spirit passes.

"We're a nice lot to flap about governing the Planet," De Forest laughed. "I confess, *now* it's all over, that my main fear was I mightn't be able to pull it off without losing a life."

"I thought of that too," said Arnott; "but there's no death reported, and I've inquired everywhere. What are we supposed to do with our passengers? I've fed 'em."

"We're between two switches," De Forest drawled. "If we drop them in any place that isn't under the Board, the natives will make their presence an excuse for cutting out, same as Illinois did, and forcing the Board to take over. If we drop them in any place under the Board's control they'll be killed as soon as our backs are turned."

"If you say so," said Pirolo thoughtfully, "I can guarantee that they will become extinct in process of time, quite happily. What is their birthrate now?"

"Go down and ask 'em," said De Forest.

"I think they might become nervous and tear me to bits," the philosopher of Foggia replied.

"Not really? Well?"

"Open the bilge-doors," said Takahira with a downward jerk of the thumb.

"Scarcely—after all the trouble we've taken to save 'em," said De Forest.

"Try London," Arnott suggested. "You could turn Satan himself loose there, and they'd only ask him to dinner."

"Good man! You've given me an idea. Vincent! Oh, Vincent!" He threw the General Communicator open so that we could all hear, and in a few minutes the chartroom filled with the rich, fruity voice of Leopold Vincent, who has purveyed all London her choicest amusements for the last thirty years. We answered with expectant grins, as though we were actually in the stalls of, say, the Combination on a first night.

"We've picked up something in your line," De Forest began.

"That's good, dear man. If it's old enough. There's nothing to beat the old things for business purposes. Have you seen *London, Chatham, and Dover* at Earl's Court? No? I thought I missed you there. Im-mense! I've had the real steam locomotive engines built from the old designs and the iron rails cast specially by hand. Cloth cushions in the carriages, too! Im-mense! And paper railway tickets. And Polly Milton."

"Polly Milton back again!" said Arnott rapturously. "Book me two stalls for tomorrow night. What's she singing now, bless her?"

"The old songs. Nothing comes up to the old touch. Listen to this, dear men." Vincent carolled with flourishes:

> Oh, cruel lamps of London,
> If tears your light could drown,
> Your victims' eyes would weep them,
> Oh, lights of London Town!

"Then they weep."

"You see?" Pirolo waved his hands at us. "The old world always weeped when it saw crowds together. It did not know why, but it weeped. We know why, but we do not weep, except when we pay to be made to by fat, wicked old Vincent."

"Old, yourself!" Vincent laughed. "I'm a public benefactor, I keep the world soft and united."

"And I'm De Forest of the Board," said De Forest acidly, "trying to get a little business done. As I was saying, I've picked up a few people in Chicago."

"I cut out. Chicago is—"

"Do listen! They're perfectly unique."

"Do they build houses of baked mudblocks while you wait—eh? That's an old contact."

"They're an untouched primitive community, with all the old ideas."

"Sewing-machines and maypole-dances? Cooking on coal-gas stoves, lighting pipes with matches, and driving horses? Gerolstein tried that last year. An absolute blow-out!"

De Forest plugged him wrathfully, and poured out the story of our doings for the last twenty-four hours on the top-note.

"And they do it *all* in public," he concluded. "You can't stop 'em. The more public, the better they are pleased. They'll talk for hours—like you! Now you can come in again!"

"Do you really mean they know how to vote?" said Vincent. "Can they act it?"

"Act? It's their life to 'em! And you never saw such faces! Scarred like volcanoes. Envy, hatred, and malice in plain sight. Wonderfully flexible voices. They weep, too."

"Aloud? In public?"

"I guarantee. Not a spark of shame or reticence in the entire installation. It's the chance of your career."

"D'you say you've brought their voting props along—those papers and ballot-box things?"

"No, confound you! I'm not a luggage-lifter. Apply direct to the Mayor of Chicago. He'll forward you everything. Well?"

"Wait a minute. Did Chicago want to kill 'em? That 'ud look well on the Communicators."

"Yes! They were only rescued with difficulty from a howling mob—if you know what that is."

"But I don't," answered the Great Vincent simply.

"Well then, they'll tell you themselves. They can make speeches hours long."

"How many are there?"

"By the time we ship 'em all over they'll be perhaps a hundred, counting children. An old world in miniature. Can't you see it?"

"M-yes; but I've got to pay for it if it's a blow-out, dear man."

"They can sing the old war songs in the streets. They can get word-drunk, and make crowds, and invade privacy in the genuine old-fashioned way; and they'll do the voting trick as often as you ask 'em a question."

"Too good!" said Vincent.

"You unbelieving Jew! I've got a dozen head aboard here. I'll put you through direct. Sample 'em yourself."

He lifted the switch and we listened. Our passengers on the lower deck at once, but not less than five at a time, explained themselves to Vincent. They had been taken from the bosom of their families, stripped of their possessions, given food without finger-bowls, and cast into captivity in a noisome dungeon.

"But look here," said Arnott aghast; "they're saying what isn't true. My lower deck isn't noisome, and I saw to the finger-bowls myself."

"My people talk like that sometimes in Little Russia," said Dragomiroff. "We reason with them. We never kill. No!"

"But it's not true," Arnott insisted. "What can you do with people who don't tell facts? They're mad!"

"Hsh!" said Pirolo, his hand to his ear. "It is such a little time since all the Planet told lies."

We heard Vincent silkily sympathetic. Would they, he asked,

repeat their assertions in public—before a vast public? Only let Vincent give them a chance, and the Planet, they vowed, should ring with their wrongs. Their aim in life—two women and a man explained it together—was to reform the world. Oddly enough, this also had been Vincent's life-dream. He offered them an arena in which to explain, and by their living example to raise the Planet to loftier levels. He was eloquent on the moral uplift of a simple, old-world life presented in its entirety to a deboshed civilization.

Could they—would they—for three months certain, devote themselves under his auspices, as missionaries, to the elevation of mankind at a place called Earl's Court, which he said, with some truth, was one of the intellectual centers of the Planet? They thanked him, and demanded (we could hear his chuckle of delight) time to discuss and to vote on the matter. The vote, solemnly managed by counting heads—one head, one vote—was favorable. His offer, therefore, was accepted, and they moved a vote of thanks to him in two speeches—one by what they called the "proposer" and the other by the "seconder."

Vincent threw over to us, his voice shaking with gratitude:

"I've got 'em! Did you hear those speeches? That's Nature, dear men. Art can't teach *that*. And they voted as easily as lying. I've never had a troupe of natural liars before. Bless you, dear men! Remember, you're on my free lists forever, anywhere—all of you. Oh, Gerolstein will be sick—sick!"

"Then you think they'll do?" said De Forest.

"Do? The Little Village'll go crazy! I'll knock up a series of old-world plays for 'em. Their voices will make you laugh and cry. My God, dear men, where *do* you suppose they picked up all their misery from, on this sweet earth? I'll have a pageant of the world's beginnings, and Mosenthal shall do the music. I'll—"

"Go and knock up a village for 'em by tonight. We'll meet you at No. 15 West Landing Tower," said De Forest. "Remember the rest will be coming along tomorrow."

"Let 'em all come!" said Vincent. "You don't know how hard it is nowadays even for me, to find something that really gets under the public's damned iridium-plated hide. But I've got it at last. Goodbye!"

"Well," said De Forest when we had finished laughing, "if anyone understood corruption in London I might have played off Vincent against Gerolstein, and sold my captives at enormous prices. As it is, I shall have to be their legal adviser tonight when the contracts are signed. And they won't exactly press any commission on me, either."

"Meantime," said Takahira, "we cannot, of course, confine members of Leopold Vincent's last-engaged company. Chairs for the ladies, please, Arnott."

"Then I go to bed," said De Forest. "I can't face any more women!" And he vanished.

When our passengers were released and given another meal (finger-bowls came first this time) they told us what they thought of us and the Board; and, like Vincent, we all marveled how they had contrived to extract and secrete so much bitter poison and unrest out of the good life God gives us. They raged, they stormed, they palpitated, flushed and exhausted their poor, torn nerves, panted themselves into silence, and renewed the senseless, shameless attacks.

"But can't you understand," said Pirolo pathetically to a shrieking woman, "that if we'd left you in Chicago you'd have been killed?"

"No, we shouldn't. You were bound to save us from being murdered."

"Then we should have had to kill a lot of other people."

"That doesn't matter. We were preaching the Truth. You can't stop us. We shall go on preaching in London; and *then* you'll see!"

"You can see now," said Pirolo, and opened a lower shutter.

We were closing on the Little Village, with her three million people spread out at ease inside her ring of girdling Main-Traffic lights—those eight fixed beams at Chatham, Tonbridge, Redhill, Dorking, Woking, St. Albans, Chipping Ongar, and Southend.

Leopold Vincent's new company looked, with small pale faces, at the silence, the size, and the separated houses.

Then some began to weep aloud, shamelessly—always without shame.

MACDONOUGH'S SONG

Whether the State can loose and bind
  In Heaven as well as on Earth:
If it be wiser to kill mankind
  Before or after the birth—

These are matters of high concern
   Where State-kept schoolmen are;
But Holy State (we have lived to learn)
   Endeth in Holy War.

Whether The People be led by the Lord,
   Or lured by the loudest throat:
If it be quicker to die by the sword
   Or cheaper to die by vote—
These are the things we have dealt with once,
   (And they will not rise from their grave)
For Holy People, however it runs,
   Endeth in wholly Slave.

Whatsoever, for any cause,
   Seeketh to take or give,
Power above or beyond the Laws,
   Suffer it not to live!
Holy State or Holy King—
   Or Holy People's Will—
Have no truck with the senseless thing
   Order the guns and kill!
Saying—after—me:—

Once there was The People—Terror gave it birth;
Once there was The People and it made a Hell of
   Earth.
Earth arose and crushed it. Listen, O ye slain!
Once there was The People—it shall never be again!

In the Same Boat
FROM A DIVERSITY OF CREATURES
(1917)

This remarkable horror story was actually written in 1911, and reflects the interest RK displayed in abnormal psychology even before the shell-shock cases of World War I brought home—in the most literal sense—the awfulness of insanity on an unprecedented scale. In spite of which, it has a happy ending . . . though, Kipling being Kipling, it is not in the least the conventional kind.

It really needs no further introduction, save one mischievous comment: I can never help wondering whether this was where L. Ron Hubbard stole the idea for the prenatal traumas that in *Dianetics* he termed "engrams."

"A fox to every Spartan" refers to the legend of the Spartan boy who had stolen a fox and hidden it under his clothes. When he was caught and accused, although it began to bite him, he resisted the pain and denied the charge.

King's Counsel (currently Queen's Counsel) are lawyers entitled to plead before the higher courts of justice. The "Abernethy manner" I take to be a reference to the celebrated physician Dr. John Abernethy (1764–1831). *Post hoc ergo propter hoc* (after this, therefore on account of this) is the logical fallacy of assuming that because one event succeeds another there must be a connection between them. *Ipso facto* = by that self-same fact.

"Najdolene" actually existed; I recall seeing at least one advertisement for the stuff, though I'm unable to trace it. What it contained is anybody's guess. Patent medicine manufacturers were not then under any obligation to list their ingredients, and some of them were highly dangerous.

Nux vomica is the seed of an East Indian tree, *Strychnos nux-vomica*. It contains strychnine, $C_{21}H_{22}N_2O_2$, a strong poison sometimes utilized as a stimulant. Patent razors were safety razors; the implication is that cut-throat razors would have tempted him too easily to suicide.

Pounds, shillings, and pence were the British currency of the time. The "composite corridor-coach" was a passenger car with a vestibule (*cf.* "·007"). An ulster was a long loose overcoat, first made in Northern Ireland. Woking is a short distance west of London; the Necropolis is a large cemetery. "Bogie-girl" (in her dialect a bogy or bogie is a terrifying specter) implies that she is only the ghost of what she was. A wryneck is a kind of woodpecker, that can twist its neck around in alarming fashion. Farnborough is one of the stations used to mark their progress; now they are in Hampshire. The London and South Western was the railway company, now part of British Rail. Lancaster Gate and the Langham Hotel are in London. "Methody" = Methodist. A tub is a broad-beamed rowing-boat.

The reference to "Sir Pandarus of Troy" implies that Sir John Chartres is worried about the consequences of introducing Conroy to Miss Henschil because the condition they suffer from may be hereditary. (In legend, Pandaros the Lycian became incredibly debased, reduced from a valiant archer and a hero-god to a despicable procurer: hence the modern word "pander.")

The Cloister and the Hearth was a popular novel by Charles Reade. Pikelets are unsweetened cakes, small, round and rather thick, toasted and served with butter and/or a sweet or savory spread. For Naaman and Gehazi see the Second Book of Kings, Chapter 5.

"Bradshaw" was the standard railway timetable.

In the Same Boat

"A throbbing vein," said Dr. Gilbert soothingly, "is the mother of delusion."

"Then how do you account for my knowing when the thing is due?" Conroy's voice rose almost to a break.

"Of course, but you should have consulted a doctor before using—palliatives."

"It was driving me mad. And now I can't give them up."

"Not so bad as that! One doesn't form fatal habits at twenty-five. Think again. Were you ever frightened as a child?"

"I don't remember. It began when I was a boy."

"With or without the spasm? By the way, do you mind describing the spasm again?"

"Well," said Conroy, twisting in the chair, "I'm no musician, but suppose you were a violin-string—vibrating—and someone put his finger on you? As if a finger were put on the naked soul! Awful!"

"So's indigestion—so's nightmare—while it lasts."

"But the horror afterwards knocks me out for days. And the waiting for it . . . and then this drug habit! It can't go on!" He shook as he spoke, and the chair creaked.

"My dear fellow," said the doctor, "when you're older you'll know what burdens the best of us carry. A fox to every Spartan."

"That doesn't help *me*. I can't! I can't!" cried Conroy, and burst into tears.

"Don't apologize," said Gilbert, when the paroxysm ended. "I'm used to people coming a little—unstuck in this room."

"It's those tabloids!" Conroy stamped his foot feebly as he blew his nose. "They've knocked me out. I used to be fit once. Oh, I've tried exercise and everything. But—if one sits down for a minute when it's due—even at four in the morning—it runs up behind one."

"Ye-es. Many things come in the quiet of the morning. You always know when the visitation is due?"

"What would I give not to be sure!" he sobbed.

"We'll put that aside for the moment. I'm thinking of a case where what we'll call anemia of the brain was masked (I don't say cured) by vibration. He couldn't sleep, or thought he couldn't, but a steamer voyage and the thump of the screw—"

"A steamer? After what I've told you!" Conroy almost shrieked. "I'd sooner . . ."

"Of course *not* a steamer in your case, but a long railway journey the next time you think it will trouble you. It sounds absurd, but—"

"I'd try anything. I nearly have," Conroy sighed.

"Nonsense! I've given you a tonic that will clear *that* notion from your head. Give the train a chance, and don't begin the journey by bucking yourself up with tabloids. Take them along, but hold them in reserve—in reserve."

"D'you think I've self-control enough, after what you've heard?" said Conroy.

Dr. Gilbert smiled. "Yes. After what I've seen," he glanced round the room, "I have no hesitation in saying you have quite as much self-control as many other people. I'll write you later about your journey. Meantime, the tonic," and he gave some general directions before Conroy left.

An hour later Dr. Gilbert hurried to the links, where the others of his regular weekend game awaited him. It was a rigid round, played as usual at the trot, for the tension of the week lay as heavy on the two King's Counsels and Sir John Chartres as on Gilbert. The lawyers were old enemies of the Admiralty Court, and Sir John of the frosty eyebrows and Abernethy manner was bracketed with, but before, Rutherford Gilbert among nerve-specialists.

At the Club-house afterwards the lawyers renewed their squabble over a tangled collision case, and the doctors as naturally compared professional matters.

"Lies—all lies," said Sir John, when Gilbert had told him Conroy's trouble. "*Post hoc, propter hoc.* The man or woman who drugs is *ipso facto* a liar. You've no imagination."

"Pity you haven't a little—occasionally."

"I have believed a certain type of patient in my time. It's always the same. For reasons not given in the consulting-room they take to the drug. Certain symptoms follow. They will swear to you, and believe it, that they took the drug to mask the symptoms. What does your man use? Najdolene? I thought so. I had practically the duplicate of your case last Thursday. Same old Najdolene—same old lie."

"Tell me the symptoms, and I'll draw my own inferences, Johnnie."

"Symptoms! The girl was rank poisoned with Najdolene. Ramping, stamping possession. Gad, I thought she'd have the chandelier down."

"Mine came unstuck too, and he has the physique of a bull," said Gilbert. "What delusions had yours?"

"Faces—faces with mildew on them. In any other walk of life we'd call it the Horrors. She told me, of course, she took the drugs to mask the faces. *Post hoc, propter hoc* again. All liars!"

"What's that?" said the senior K.C. quickly. "Sounds professional."

"Go away! Not for you, Sandy." Sir John turned a shoulder against him and walked with Gilbert in the chill evening.

To Conroy in his chambers came, one week later, this letter:

DEAR MR. CONROY—If your plan of a night's trip on the 17th still holds good, and you have no particular destination in view, you could do me a kindness. A Miss Henschil, in whom I am interested, goes down to the West by the 10.8 from Waterloo (Number 3 platform) on that night. She is not exactly an invalid, but, like so many of us, a little shaken in her nerves. Her maid, of course, accompanies her, but if I knew you were in the same train it would be an additional source of strength. Will you please write and let me know whether the 10.8 from Waterloo, Number 3 platform, on the 17th, suits you, and I will meet you there? Don't forget my caution, and keep up the tonic.—Yours sincerely,

L. RUTHERFORD GILBERT.

"He knows I'm scarcely fit to look after myself," was Conroy's thought. "And he wants me to look after a woman!"

Yet, at the end of half an hour's irresolution, he accepted.

Now Conroy's trouble, which had lasted for years, was this:

On a certain night, while he lay between sleep and wake, he would be overtaken by a long shuddering sigh, which he learned to know was the sign that his brain had once more conceived its horror, and in time—in due time—would bring it forth.

Drugs could so well veil that horror that it shuffled along no worse than as a freezing dream in a procession of disorderly dreams; but over the return of the event drugs had no control. Once that sigh had passed his lips the thing was inevitable, and through the days granted before its rebirth he walked in torment. For the first two years he had striven to fend it off by distractions, but neither exercise nor drink availed. Then he had come to the tabloids of the excellent M. Najdol. These guarantee, on the label, "Refreshing and absolutely natural sleep to the soul-weary." They are carried in a case with a spring which presses one scented tabloid to the end of the tube, whence it can be lipped off in stroking the moustache or adjusting the veil.

Three years of M. Najdol's preparations do not fit a man for many careers. His friends, who knew he did not drink, assumed that Conroy had strained his heart through valiant outdoor exercises, and Conroy had with some care invented an imaginary doctor, symptoms, and regimen, which he discussed with them and with his mother in Hereford. She maintained that he would grow out of it, and recommended nux vomica.

When at last Conroy faced a real doctor, it was, he hoped, to be saved from suicide by a strait-waistcoat. Yet Dr. Gilbert had but given him more drugs—a tonic, for instance, that would couple railway carriages—and had advised a night in the train. Not alone the horrors of a railway journey (for which a man who dare keep no servant must e'en pack, label, and address his own bag), but the necessity for holding himself in hand before a stranger "a little shaken in her nerves."

He spent a long forenoon packing, because when he assembled and counted things his mind slid off to the hours that remained of the day before his night, and he found himself counting minutes aloud. At such times the injustice of his fate would drive him to revolts which no servant should witness, but on this evening Dr. Gilbert's tonic held him fairly calm while he put up his patent razors.

Waterloo Station shook him into real life. The change for his ticket needed concentration, if only to prevent shillings and pence turning into minutes at the booking-office; and he spoke quickly to a porter about the disposition of his bag. The old 10.8 from Waterloo to the West was an all-night caravan that halted, in the interests of the milk traffic, at almost every station.

Dr. Gilbert stood by the door of the one composite corridor-coach; an older and stouter man behind him. "So glad you're here!" he cried. "Let me get your ticket."

"Certainly not," Conroy answered. "I got it myself—long ago. My bag's in too," he added proudly.

"I beg your pardon. Miss Henschil's here. I'll introduce you."

"But—but," he stammered—"think of the state I'm in. If anything happens I shall collapse."

"Not you. You'd rise to the occasion like a bird. And as for the self-control you were talking of the other day"—Gilbert swung him round—"look!"

A young man in an ulster over a silk-faced frock-coat stood by the carriage window, weeping shamelessly.

"Oh, but that's only drink," Conroy said. "I haven't had one of my—my things since lunch."

"Excellent!" said Gilbert. "I knew I could depend on you. Come along. Wait for a minute, Chartres."

A tall woman, veiled, sat by the far window. She bowed her head as the doctor murmured Conroy knew not what. Then he disappeared and the inspector came for tickets.

"My maid—next compartment," she said slowly.

Conroy showed his ticket, but in returning it to the sleeve-pocket of his ulster the little silver Najdolene case slipped from his glove and fell to the floor. He snatched it up as the moving train flung him into his seat.

"How nice!" said the woman. She leisurely lifted her veil, unbuttoned the first button of her left glove, and pressed out from its palm a Najdolene case.

"Don't!" said Conroy, not realizing he had spoken.

"I beg your pardon." The deep voice was measured, even, and low. Conroy knew what made it so.

"I said 'don't'! He wouldn't like you to do it!"

"No, he would not." She held the tube with its ever-presented tabloid between finger and thumb. "But aren't you one of the—ah—'soul-weary' too?"

"That's why. Oh, please don't! Not at first. I—I haven't had one since morning. You—you'll set me off!"

"You? Are you so far gone as that?"

He nodded, pressing his palms together. The train jolted through Vauxhall points, and was welcomed with the clang of empty milk-cans for the West.

After long silence she lifted her great eyes, and, with an innocence that would have deceived any sound man, asked Conroy to call her maid to bring her a forgotten book.

Conroy shook his head. "No. Our sort can't read. Don't!"

"Were you sent to watch me?" The voice never changed.

"Me? I need a keeper myself much more—*this* night of all!"

"This night? Have you a night, then? They disbelieved *me* when I told them of mine." She leaned back and laughed, always slowly. "Aren't doctors stu-upid? They don't know."

She leaned her elbow on her knee, lifted her veil that had fallen, and, chin in hand, stared at him. He looked at her—till his eyes were blurred with tears.

"Have *I* been there, think you?" she said.

"Surely—surely," Conroy answered, for he had well seen the fear and the horror that lived behind the heavy-lidded eyes, the fine tracing on the broad forehead, and the guard set about the desirable mouth.

"Then—suppose we have one—just one apiece? I've gone without since this afternoon."

He put up his hand, and would have shouted, but his voice broke.

"Don't! Can't you see that it helps me to help you to keep it off? Don't let's both go down together."

"But I want one. It's a poor heart that never rejoices. Just one. It's my night."

"It's mine—too. My sixty-fourth, fifth, sixth, seventh." He shut his lips firmly against the tide of visualized numbers that threatened to carry him along.

"Ah, it's only my thirty-ninth." She paused as he had done. "I wonder if I shall last into the sixties. . . . Talk to me or I shall go crazy. You're a man. You're the stronger vessel. Tell me when you went to pieces."

"One, two, three, four, five, six, seven—eight—I beg your pardon."

"Not in the least. I always pretend I've dropped a stitch of my knitting. I count the days till the last day, then the hours, then the minutes. Do you?"

"I don't think I've done very much else for the last—" said Conroy, shivering, for the night was cold, with a chill he recognized.

"Oh, how comforting to find someone who can talk sense! It's not always the same date, is it?"

"What difference would that make?" He unbuttoned his ulster with a jerk. "You're a sane woman. Can't you see the wicked—wicked—wicked" (dust flew from the padded armrest as he struck it) "unfairness of it? What have *I* done?"

She laid her large hand on his shoulder very firmly.

"If you begin to think over that," she said, "you'll go to pieces and be ashamed. Tell me yours, and I'll tell you mine. Only be quiet—be quiet, lad, or you'll set me off!" She made shift to soothe him, though her chin trembled.

"Well," said he at last, picking at the armrest between them, "mine's nothing much, of course."

"Don't be a fool! That's for doctors—and mothers."

"It's Hell," Conroy muttered. "It begins on a steamer—on a stifling hot night. I come out of my cabin. I pass through the saloon where the stewards have rolled up the carpets, and the boards are bare and hot and soapy."

"I've traveled too," she said.

"Ah! I come on deck. I walk down a covered alleyway. Butcher's meat, bananas, oil, that sort of smell."

Again she nodded.

"It's a lead-colored steamer, and the sea's lead-colored. Perfectly smooth sea—perfectly still ship, except for the engines running, and her waves going off in lines and lines and lines—dull grey. All this time I know something's going to happen."

"*I* know. Something going to happen," she whispered.

"Then I hear a thud in the engine-room. Then the noise of machinery falling down—like fire-irons—and then two most awful yells. They're more like hoots, and I know—I know while I listen—that it means that two men have died as they hooted. It was their last breath hooting out of them—in most awful pain. Do you understand?"

"I ought to. Go on."

"That's the first part. Then I hear bare feet running along the alleyway. One of the scalded men comes up behind me and says quite distinctly, 'My friend! All is lost!' Then he taps me on the shoulder and I hear him drop down dead." He panted and wiped his forehead.

"So that is your night?" she said.

"That is my night. It comes every few weeks—so many days after I get what I call sentence. Then I begin to count."

"Get sentence? D'you mean *this?*" She half closed her eyes, drew a deep breath, and shuddered. " 'Notice' I call it. Sir John thought it was all lies."

She had unpinned her hat and thrown it on the seat opposite, showing the immense mass of her black hair, rolled low in the nape of the columnar neck and looped over the left ear. But Conroy had no eyes except for her grave eyes.

"Listen now!" said she. "I walk down a road, a white sandy road near the sea. There are broken fences on either side, and Men come and look at me over them."

"Just men? Do they speak?"

"They try to. Their faces are all mildewy—eaten away," and she hid her face for an instant with her left hand. "It's the Faces—the Faces!"

"Yes. Like my two hoots. *I* know."

"Ah! But the place itself—the bareness—and the glitter and the salt smells, and the wind blowing the sand! The Men run after me and I run. . . . I know what's coming too. One of them touches me."

"Yes! What comes then? We've both shirked that."

"One awful shock—not palpitation, but shock, shock, shock!"

"As though your soul were being stopped—as you'd stop a finger-bowl humming?" he said.

"Just that," she answered. "One's very soul—the soul that one lives by—stopped. So!"

She drove her thumb deep into the armrest. "And now," she whined to him, "now that we've stirred each other up this way, mightn't we have just one?"

"No," said Conroy, shaking. "Let's hold on. We're past"—he peered out of the black windows—"Woking. There's the Necropolis. How long till dawn?"

"Oh, cruel long yet. If one dozes for a minute, it catches one."

"And how d'you find that this"—he tapped the palm of his glove—"helps you?"

"It covers up the thing from being too real—if one takes enough—you know. Only—only—one loses everything else. I've been no more than a bogie-girl for two years. What would you give to be real again? This lying's such a nuisance."

"One must protect oneself—and there's one's mother to think of," he answered.

"True. I hope allowances are made for us somewhere. Our burden—can you hear?—our burden is heavy enough."

She rose, towering into the roof of the carriage. Conroy's ungentle grip pulled her back.

"Now *you* are foolish. Sit down," said he.

"But the cruelty of it! Can't you see it? Don't you feel it? Let's take one now—before I—"

"Sit down!" cried Conroy, and the sweat stood again on his forehead. He had fought through a few nights, and had been defeated on more, and he knew the rebellion that flares beyond control to exhaustion.

She smoothed her hair and dropped back, but for a while her head and throat moved with the sickening motion of a captured wryneck.

"Once," she said, spreading out her hands, "I ripped my counterpane from end to end. That takes strength. I had it then. I've little now. 'All dorn,' as my little niece says. And you, lad?"

" 'All dorn'! Let me keep your case for you till the morning."

"But the cold feeling is beginning."

"Lend it me, then."

"And the drag down my right side. I shan't be able to move in a minute."

"I can scarcely lift my arm myself," said Conroy. "We're in for it."

"Then why are you so foolish? You know it'll be easier if we have only one—only one apiece."

She was lifting the case to her mouth. With tremendous effort Conroy caught it. The two moved like jointed dolls, and, when their hands met it was as wood on wood.

"You must—not!" said Conroy. His jaws stiffened, and the cold climbed from his feet up.

"Why—must—I—not?" She repeated the words idiotically.

Conroy could only shake his head, while he bore down on the hand and the case in it.

Her speech went from her altogether. The wonderful lips rested half over the even teeth, the breath was in the nostrils only, the eyes dulled, the face set grey, and through the glove the hand struck like ice.

Presently her soul came back and stood behind her eyes—only thing that had life in all that place—stood and looked for Conroy's soul. He too was fettered in every limb, but somewhere at an immense distance he heard his heart going about its work as the engine-room carries on through and beneath the all but overwhelming wave. His one hope, he knew, was not to lose the eyes that clung to his, because there was an Evil abroad which would possess him if he looked aside by a hairbreadth.

The rest was darkness through which some distant planet spun while cymbals clashed. (Beyond Farnborough the 10.8 rolls out many empty milk-cans at every halt.) Then a body came to life with intolerable pricklings. Limb by limb, after agonies of terror, that body returned to him, steeped in most perfect physical weariness such as follows a long day's rowing. He saw the heavy lids droop over her eyes—the watcher behind them departed—and, his soul sinking into assured peace, Conroy slept.

Light on his eyes and a salt breath roused him without shock. Her hand still held his. She slept, forehead down upon it, but the movement of his waking waked her too, and she sneezed like a child.

"I—I think it's morning," said Conroy.

"And nothing has happened! Did you see your Men? I didn't see my Faces. Does it mean we've escaped? Did—did you take any after I went to sleep? I'll swear *I* didn't," she stammered.

"No, there wasn't any need. We've slept through it."

"No need! Thank God! There was no need! Oh, look!"

The train was running under red cliffs along a sea-wall washed by waves that were colorless in the early light. Southward the sun rose mistily upon the Channel.

She leaned out of the window and breathed to the bottom of her lungs, while the wind wrenched down her disheveled hair and blew it below her waist.

"Well!" she said with splendid eyes. "Aren't you still waiting for something to happen?"

"No. Not till next time. We've been let off," Conroy answered, breathing as deeply as she.

"Then we ought to say our prayers."

"What nonsense! Someone will see us."

"We needn't kneel. Stand up and say 'Our Father.' We *must!*"

It was the first time since childhood that Conroy had prayed. They laughed hysterically when a curve threw them against an armrest.

"Now for breakfast!" she cried. "My maid—Nurse Blaber—has the basket and things. It'll be ready in twenty minutes. Oh! Look at my hair!" and she went out laughing.

Conroy's first discovery, made without fumbling or counting letters on taps, was that the London and South Western's allowance of washing-water is inadequate. He used every drop, rioting in the cold tingle on neck and arms. To shave in a moving train balked him, but the next halt gave him a chance, which, to his own surprise, he took. As he stared at himself in the mirror he smiled and nodded. There were points about this person with the clear, if sunken, eye and the almost uncompressed mouth. But when he bore his bag back to his compartment, the weight of it on a limp arm humbled that new pride.

"My friend," he said, half aloud, "you go into training. You're putty."

She met him in the spare compartment, where her maid had laid breakfast.

"By Jove!" he said, halting at the doorway, "I hadn't realized how beautiful you were!"

"The same to you, lad. Sit down. I could eat a horse."

"I shouldn't," said the maid quietly. "The less you eat the better." She was a small, freckled woman, with light fluffy hair and pale-blue eyes that looked through all veils.

"This is Miss Blaber," said Miss Henschil. "He's one of the soul-weary too, Nursey."

"I know it. But when one has just given it up a full meal doesn't agree. That's why I've only brought you bread and butter."

She went out quietly, and Conroy reddened.

"We're still children, you see," said Miss Henschil. "But I'm well enough to feel some shame of it. D'you take sugar?"

They starved together heroically, and Nurse Blaber was good enough to signify approval when she came to clear away.

"Nursey?" Miss Henschil insinuated, and flushed.

"Do you smoke?" said the nurse coolly to Conroy.

"I haven't in years. Now you mention it, I think I'd like a cigarette—or something."

"I used to. D'you think it would keep me quiet?" Miss Henschil said.

"Perhaps. Try these." The nurse handed them her cigarette case.

"Don't take anything else," she commanded, and went away with the tea-basket.

"Good!" grunted Conroy, between mouthfuls of tobacco.

"Better than nothing," said Miss Henschil; but for a while they felt ashamed, yet with the comfort of children punished together.

"Now," she whispered, "who were you when you were a man?"

Conroy told her, and in return she gave him her history. It delighted them both to deal once more in worldly concerns—families, names, places, and dates—with a person of understanding.

She came, she said, of Lancashire folk—wealthy cotton-spinners, who still kept the broadened *a* and slurred aspirate of the old stock. She lived with an old masterful mother in an opulent world north of Lancaster Gate, where people in Society gave parties at a Mecca called the Langham Hotel.

She herself had been launched into Society there, and the flowers at the ball had cost eighty-seven pounds; but, being reckoned peculiar, she had made few friends among her own sex. She had attracted many men, for she was a beauty—*the* beauty, in fact, of Society, she said.

She spoke utterly without shame or reticence, as a life-prisoner tells his past to a fellow-prisoner; and Conroy nodded across the smoke-rings.

"Do you remember when you got into the carriage?" she asked. "(Oh, I wish I had some knitting!) Did you notice aught, lad?"

Conroy thought back. It was ages since. "Wasn't there someone outside the door—crying?" he asked.

"He's—he's the little man I was engaged to," she said. "But I made him break it off. I told him 'twas no good. But he won't, yo' see."

"*That* fellow? Why, he doesn't come up to your shoulder."

"That's naught to do with it. I think all the world of him. I'm a foolish wench"—her speech wandered as she settled herself cosily, one elbow on the armrest. "We'd been engaged—I couldn't help that—and he worships the ground I tread on. But it's no use. I'm not responsible, you see. His two sisters are against it, though I've the money. They're right, but they think it's the dri-ink," she drawled. "They're Methody—the Skinners. You see, their grandfather that started the Patton Mills, he died o' the dri-ink."

"I see," said Conroy. The grave face before him under the lifted veil was troubled.

"George Skinner." She breathed it softly. "I'd make him a good wife, by God's gra-ace—if I could. But it's no use. I'm not responsible. But he'll not take 'No' for an answer. I used to call him 'Toots.' He's of no consequence, yo' see."

"That's in Dickens," said Conroy, quite quickly. "I haven't thought of Toots for years. He was at Doctor Blimber's."

"And so—that's my trouble," she concluded, ever so slightly wringing her hands. "But I—don't you think—there's hope now?"

"Eh?" said Conroy. "Oh yes! This is the first time I've turned my corner without help. With your help, I should say."

"It'll come back, though."

"Then shall we meet it in the same way? Here's my card. Write me your train, and we'll go together."

"Yes. We must do that. But between times—when we want—" She looked at her palm, the four fingers working on it. "It's hard to give 'em up."

"But think what we have gained already, and let me have the case to keep."

She shook her head, and threw her cigarette out of the window. "Not yet."

"Then let's lend our cases to Nurse, and we'll get through today on cigarettes. I'll call her while we feel strong."

She hesitated, but yielded at last, and Nurse accepted the offerings with a smile.

"*You'll* be all right," she said to Miss Henschil. "But if I were you"—to Conroy—"I'd take strong exercise."

When they reached their destination Conroy set himself to obey Nurse Blaber. He had no remembrance of that day, except one streak of blue sea to his left, gorse-bushes to his right, and, before him, a coast-guard's track marked with white-washed stones that he counted up to the far thousands. As he returned to the little town he saw Miss Henschil on the beach below the cliffs. She kneeled at Nurse Blaber's feet, weeping and pleading.

Twenty-five days later a telegram came to Conroy's rooms: *"Notice given. Waterloo again. Twenty-fourth."* That same evening he was wakened by the shudder and the sigh that told him his sentence had gone forth. Yet he reflected on his pillow that he had, in spite of lapses, snatched something like three weeks of life, which included several rides on a horse before breakfast—the hour one most craves Najdolene; five consecutive evenings on the river at Hammersmith in a tub where he had well stretched the white arms that passing crews mocked at; a game of rackets at his club; three dinners, one small dance, and one human flirtation with a human woman. More notable still, he had settled his month's accounts, only once confusing petty cash with the days of grace allowed him. Next morning he rode his hired beast in the park victoriously. He saw Miss Henschil on horseback near Lancaster Gate, talking to a young man at the railings.

She wheeled and cantered toward him.

"By Jove! How well you look!" he cried, without salutation. "I didn't know you rode."

"I used to once," she replied. "I'm all soft now."

They swept off together down the ride.

"Your beast pulls," he said.

"Wa-ant him to. Gi-gives me something to think of. How've you been?" she panted. "I wish chemists' shops hadn't red lights."

"Have you slipped out and bought some, then?"

"You don't know Nursey. Eh, but it's good to be on a horse again! This chap cost me two hundred."

"Then you've been swindled," said Conroy.

"I know it, but it's no odds. I must go back to Toots and send him away. He's neglecting his work for me."

She swung her heavy-topped animal on his none too sound hocks. "Sentence come, lad?"

"Yes. But I'm not minding it so much this time."

"Waterloo, then—and God help us!" She thundered back to the little frock-coated figure that waited faithfully near the gate.

Conroy felt the spring sun on his shoulders and trotted home. That evening he went out with a man in a pair oar, and was rowed

to a standstill. But the other man owned he could not have kept the
pace five minutes longer.

He carried his bag all down Number 3 platform at Waterloo, and
hove it with one hand into the rack.

"Well done!" said Nurse Blaber, in the corridor. "We've improved too."

Dr. Gilbert and an older man came out of the next compartment.

"Hallo!" said Gilbert. "Why haven't you been to see me, Mr.
Conroy? Come under the lamp. Take off your hat. No—no. Sit, you
young giant. Ve-ry good. Look here a minute, Johnnie."

A little, round-bellied, hawk-faced person glared at him.

"Gilbert was right about the beauty of the beast," he muttered.
"D'you keep it in your glove now?" he went on, and punched
Conroy in the short ribs.

"No," said Conroy meekly, but without coughing. "Nowhere—
on my honor! I've chucked it for good."

"Wait till you are a sound man before you say *that*, Mr. Conroy."
Sir John Chartres stumped out, saying to Gilbert in the corridor,
"It's all very fine, but the question is shall I or we 'Sir Pandarus of
Troy become,' eh? We're bound to think of the children."

"Have you been vetted?" said Miss Henschil, a few minutes after
the train started. "May I sit with you? I—I don't trust myself yet.
I can't give up as easily as you can, seemingly."

"Can't you? I never saw any one so improved in a month."

"Look here!" She reached across to the rack, single-handed lifted
Conroy's bag, and held it at arm's length. "I counted ten slowly.
And I didn't think of hours or minutes," she boasted.

"Don't remind me," he cried.

"Ah! Now I've reminded myself. I wish I hadn't. Do you think it'll
be easier for us tonight?"

"Oh, don't." The smell of the carriage had brought back all his
last trip to him, and Conroy moved uneasily.

"I'm sorry. I've brought some games," she went on. "Draughts
and cards—but they all mean counting. I wish I'd brought chess, but
I can't play chess. What can we do? Talk about something."

"Well, how's Toots, to begin with?" said Conroy.

"Why? Did you see him on the platform?"

"No. Was he there? I didn't notice."

"Oh yes. He doesn't understand. He's desperately jealous. I told
him it doesn't matter. Will you please let me hold your hand? I
believe I'm beginning to get the chill."

"Toots ought to envy me," said Conroy.

"He does. He paid you a high compliment the other night. He's taken to calling again—in spite of all they say."

Conroy inclined his head. He felt cold, and knew surely he would be colder.

"He said," she yawned. "(Beg your pardon.) He said he couldn't see how I could help falling in love with a man like you; and he called himself a damned little rat, and he beat his head on the piano last night."

"The piano? You play, then?"

"Only to him. He thinks the world of my accomplishments. Then I told him I wouldn't have you if you were the last man on earth instead of only the best-looking—not with a million in each stocking."

"No, not with a million in each stocking," said Conroy vehemently. "Isn't that odd?"

"I suppose so—to anyone who doesn't know. Well, where was I? Oh, George as good as told me I was deceiving him, and he wanted to go away without saying good-night. He hates standing a-tiptoe, but he must if I won't sit down."

Conroy would have smiled, but the chill that foreran the coming of the Lier-in-Wait was upon him, and his hand closed warningly on hers.

"And—and so—" she was trying to say, when her hour also overtook her, leaving alive only the fear-dilated eyes that turned to Conroy. Hand froze on hand and the body with it as they waited for the horror in the blackness that heralded it. Yet through the worst Conroy saw, at an uncountable distance, one minute glint of light in his night. Thither would he go and escape his fear; and behold, that light was the light in the watch-tower of her eyes, where her locked soul signaled to his soul: "Look at me!"

In time, from him and from her, the Thing sheered aside, that each soul might step down and resume its own concerns. He thought confusedly of people on the skirts of a thunderstorm, withdrawing from windows where the torn night is, to their known and furnished beds. Then he dozed, till in some drowsy turn his hand fell from her warmed hand.

"That's all. The Faces haven't come," he heard her say. "All—thank God! I don't feel even I need what Nursey promised me. Do you?"

"No." He rubbed his eyes. "But don't make too sure."

"Certainly not. We shall have to try again next month. I'm afraid it will be an awful nuisance for you."

"Not to me, I assure you," said Conroy, and they leaned back and laughed at the flatness of the words, after the hells through which they had just risen.

"And now," she said, strict eyes on Conroy, *"why* wouldn't you take me—not with a million in each stocking?"

"I don't know. That's what I've been puzzling over."

"So have I. We're as handsome a couple as I've ever seen. Are you well off, lad?"

"They call me so," said Conroy, smiling.

"That's North country." She laughed again. "Setting aside my good looks and yours, I've four thousand a year of my own, and the rents should make it six. That's a match some old cats would lap tea all night to fettle up."

"It is. Lucky Toots!" said Conroy.

"Ay," she answered, "he'll be the luckiest lad in London if I win through. Who's yours?"

"No—no one, dear. I've been in Hell for years. I only want to get out and be alive and—so on. Isn't that reason enough?"

"Maybe, for a man. But I never minded things much till George came. I was all stu-upid like."

"So was I, but now I think I can live. It ought to be less next month, oughtn't it?" he said.

"I hope so. Ye-es. There's nothing much for a maid except to be married, and *I* ask no more. Whoever yours is, when you've found her, she shall have a wedding present from Mrs. George Skinner that—"

"But she wouldn't understand it any more than Toots."

"He doesn't matter—except to me. I can't keep my eyes open, thank God! Good-night, lad."

Conroy followed her with his eyes. Beauty there was, grace there was, strength, and enough of the rest to drive better men than George Skinner to beat their heads on piano-tops—but for the new-found life of him Conroy could not feel one flutter of instinct or emotion that turned to herward. He put up his feet and fell asleep, dreaming of a joyous, normal world recovered—with interest on arrears. There were many things in it, but no one face of any one woman.

Thrice afterward they took the same train, and each time their trouble shrank and weakened. Miss Henschil talked of Toots, his multiplied calls, the things he had said to his sisters, the much worse things his sisters had replied; of the late (he seemed very dead to them) M. Najdol's gifts for the soul-weary; of shopping, of house rents, and the cost of really artistic furniture and linen.

Conroy explained the exercises in which he delighted—mighty labors of play undertaken against other mighty men, till he sweated and, having bathed, slept. He had visited his mother, too, in Hereford, and he talked something of her and of the home-life, which his body, cut out of all clean life for five years, innocently and deeply enjoyed. Nurse Blaber was a little interested in Conroy's mother, but, as a rule, she smoked her cigarette and read her paper-backed novels in her own compartment.

On their last trip she volunteered to sit with them, and buried herself in *The Cloister and the Hearth* while they whispered together. On that occasion (it was near Salisbury) at two in the morning, when the Lier-in-Wait brushed them with his wing, it meant no more than that they should cease talk for the instant, and for the instant hold hands, as even utter strangers on the deep may do when their ship rolls underfoot.

"But still," said Nurse Blaber, not looking up, "I think your Mr. Skinner might feel jealous of all this."

"It would be difficult to explain," said Conroy.

"Then you'd better not be at my wedding," Miss Henschil laughed.

"After all we've gone through, too. But I suppose you ought to leave me out. Is the day fixed?" he cried.

"Twenty-second of September—in spite of both his sisters. I can risk it now." Her face was glorious as she flushed.

"My dear chap!" He shook hands unreservedly, and she gave back his grip without flinching. "I can't tell you how pleased I am!"

"Gracious Heavens!" said Nurse Blaber, in a new voice. "Oh, I beg your pardon. I forgot I wasn't paid to be surprised."

"What at? Oh, I see!" Miss Henschil explained to Conroy. "She expected you were going to kiss me, or I was going to kiss you, or something."

"After all you've gone through, as Mr. Conroy said."

"But I couldn't, could you?" said Miss Henschil, with a disgust as frank as that on Conroy's face. "It would be horrible—horrible. And yet, of course, you're wonderfully handsome. How d'you account for it, Nursey?"

Nurse Blaber shook her head. "I was hired to cure you of a habit, dear. When you're cured I shall go on to the next case—that senile-decay one at Bournemouth I told you about."

"And I shall be left alone with George! But suppose it isn't cured," said Miss Henschil of a sudden. "Suppose it comes back again. What can I do? I can't send for *him* in this way when I'm a married woman!" She pointed like an infant.

"I'd come, of course," Conroy answered. "But, seriously, that is a consideration."

They looked at each other, alarmed and anxious, and then toward Nurse Blaber, who closed her book, marked the place, and turned to face them.

"Have you ever talked to your mother as you have to me?" she said.

"No. I might have spoken to dad—but mother's different. What d'you mean?"

"And you've never talked to your mother either, Mr. Conroy?"

"Not till I took Najdolene. Then I told her it was my heart. There's no need to say anything, now that I'm practically over it, is there?"

"Not if it doesn't come back, but—" She beckoned with a stumpy, triumphant finger that drew their heads close together. "You know I always go in and read a chapter to mother at tea, child."

"I know you do. You're an angel." Miss Henschil patted the blue shoulder next her. "Mother's Church of England now," she explained. "But she'll have her Bible with her pikelets at tea every night like the Skinners."

"It was Naaman and Gehazi last Tuesday that gave me a clue. I said I'd never seen a case of leprosy, and your mother said she'd seen too many."

"Where? She never told me," Miss Henschil began.

"A few months before you were born—on her trip to Australia—at Mola or Molo something or other. It took me three evenings to get it all out."

"Ay—mother's suspicious of questions," said Miss Henschil to Conroy. "She'll lock the door of every room she's in, if it's but for five minutes. She was a Tackberry from Jarrow way, yo' see."

"She described your men to the life—men with faces all eaten away, staring at her over the fence of a lepers' hospital in this Molo Island. They begged from her, and she ran, she told me, all down the street, back to the pier. One touched her and she nearly fainted. She's ashamed of that still."

"My men? The sand and the fences?" Miss Henschil muttered.

"Yes. You know how tidy she is and how she hates wind. She remembered that the fences were broken—she remembered the wind blowing. Sand—sun—salt wind—fences—faces—I got it all out of her, bit by bit. You don't know what I know! And it all happened three or four months before you were born. There!" Nurse Blaber slapped her knee with her little hand triumphantly.

"Would that account for it?" Miss Henschil shook from head to foot.

"Absolutely. I don't care who you ask! You never imagined the thing. It was *laid* on you. It happened on earth to *you!* Quick, Mr. Conroy, she's too heavy for me! I'll get the flask."

Miss Henschil leaned forward and collapsed, as Conroy told her afterwards, like a factory chimney. She came out of her swoon with teeth that chattered on the cup.

"No—no," she said, gulping. "It's not hysterics. Yo' see I've no call to hev 'em anymore. No call—no reason whatever. God be praised! Can't you *feel* I'm a right woman now?"

"Stop hugging me!" said Nurse Blaber. "You don't know your strength. Finish the brandy and water. It's perfectly reasonable, and I'll lay long odds Mr. Conroy's case is something of the same. I've been thinking—"

"I wonder—" said Conroy, and pushed the girl back as she swayed again.

Nurse Blaber smoothed her pale hair. "Yes. Your trouble, or something like it, happened somewhere on earth or sea to the mother who bore you. Ask her, child. Ask her and be done with it once for all."

"I will," said Conroy. . . . "There ought to be—" He opened his bag and hunted breathlessly.

"Bless you! Oh, God bless you, Nursey!" Miss Henschil was sobbing. "You don't know what this means to me. It takes it all off—from the beginning."

"But doesn't it make any difference to you now?" the nurse asked curiously. "Now that you're rightfully a woman?"

Conroy, busy with his bag, had not heard. Miss Henschil stared across, and her beauty, freed from the shadow of any fear, blazed up within her. "I see what you mean," she said. "But it hasn't changed anything. I want Toots. *He* has never been out of his mind in his life—except over silly me."

"It's all right," said Conroy, stooping under the lamp, Bradshaw in hand. "If I change at Templecombe—for Bristol (Bristol—Hereford—yes)—I can be with mother for breakfast in her room and find out."

"Quick, then," said Nurse Blaber. "We've passed Gillingham quite a while. You'd better take some of our sandwiches." She went out to get them. Conroy and Miss Henschil would have danced, but there is no room for giants in a South-Western compartment.

"Good-bye, good luck, lad. Eh, but you've changed already—like me. Send a wire to our hotel as soon as you're sure," said Miss Henschil. "What should I have done without you?"

"Or I?" said Conroy. "But it's Nurse that's saving us really."

"Then thank her," said Miss Henschil, looking straight at him. "Yes, I would. She'd like it."

When Nurse Blaber came back after the parting at Templecombe her nose and her eyelids were red, but, for all that, her face reflected a great light even while she sniffed over *The Cloister and the Hearth*.

Miss Henschil, deep in a house furnisher's catalogue, did not speak for twenty minutes. Then she said, between adding totals of best, guest, and servants' sheets, "But why should our times have been the same, Nursey?"

"Because a child is born somewhere every second of the clock," Nurse Blaber answered. "And besides that, you probably set each other off by talking and thinking about it. You shouldn't, you know."

"Ay, but you've never been in Hell," said Miss Henschil.

The telegram handed in at Hereford at 12.46 and delivered to Miss Henschil on the beach of a certain village at 2.7 ran thus:

" '*Absolutely confirmed. She says she remembers hearing noise of accident in engine-room returning from India eighty-five.*' "

"He means the year, not the thermometer," said Nurse Blaber, throwing pebbles at the cold sea.

" '*And two men scalded thus explaining my hoots.*' (The idea of telling me that!) '*Subsequently silly clergyman passenger ran up behind her calling for joke, "Friend, all is lost," thus accounting very words.*' "

Nurse Blaber purred audibly.

" '*She says only remembers being upset minute or two. Unspeakable relief. Best love Nursey, who is jewel. Get out of her what she would like best.*' Oh, I oughtn't to have read that," said Miss Henschil.

"It doesn't matter. I don't want anything," said Nurse Blaber, "and if I did I shouldn't get it."

The Eye of Allah
FROM *DEBITS AND CREDITS* (1926)

By this stage I trust the reader will have noticed that one of RK's greatest gifts was his ability to take a stock theme and, without resorting to twist endings (he wrote virtually no stories of that kind), treat it in a wholly individual way. Examples in this book include "A Matter of Fact" and " 'Wireless' "; in the companion volume of Fantasy I would cite particularly " 'They' ", which I have termed a ghost story in reverse.

This time it's the turn of that hardy science fiction standby, the alternative history story, built around the question "What if events had worked out otherwise?" But RK stood it on its head. This is the tale of how a history different from ours *was stopped from happening.* . . .

We are in the mid–thirteenth century. The monastery of St. Illod's is imaginary, but the monks appear to belong to the Benedictine order. This would accord with the various offices the characters hold. The Cantor (Latin, = singer) and his deputy not only instructed the novices in music but often taught them to read, as well: hence their responsibility for the library and the scriptorium—which was where, before the invention of printing, Bibles, Books of Hours and other works were copied out by hand, either plainly, like the Gospels for the abbot at Evesham, or in illuminated (color-illustrated) form.

Fitz is the Norman version of French *fils*, son. It was often used to indicate that a man's father was not married to his mother but had acknowledged paternity. Otho is

the equivalent of modern German Otto. Burgos is in
Northern Spain; it is famous for its splendid cathedral, to
which John refers a few lines lower down. A Papal Legate
was and is the counterpart of an ambassador in the service
of the Pope. (This one, Falcodi, went on to become Pope
himself, as Clement IV.)

The Magnificat is a text from Luke I, used as a canticle
at evensong in the Church of England and Episcopalian
rite: "My soul doth magnify the Lord . . ." Arabesque is
a form of ornament developed by Moorish painters, who
being forbidden to represent animals or humans by the
Prophet's injunction against iconolatry (image-worship)
evolved complex designs derived from plants and Arabic
writing. Diaper-work = the repetition of a pattern over a
large area.

Absolution is general forgiveness of sins. The tonsure, a
shaven area on the crown of the head, marked John as a
monk, entitling him to "benefit of clergy"—the right to
be tried for an offense by an ecclesiastical, rather than a
secular, court. Ultramarine is a blue pigment made from
ground lapis-lazuli; its name means "more than sea-blue."
Vermilion red is prepared from an ore containing mercu-
ric sulphide. "Indulgences" (what Chaucer's Pardoner had
for sale) were a means of raising money for the Church;
their purchase was supposed to release the buyer from
part of his or her time in Purgatory. It was one of the
abuses railed against by Luther.

Abana and Pharphar are rivers. This is a reference to
the same chapter of Second Kings that was mentioned in
"In the Same Boat." Traditionally, St. Luke's profession
was that of medicine.

The next section of the conversation masterfully con-
veys what it must have been like in the late Middle Ages
to live with a sort of imaginary Thought Police inside
your head—a predicament many people still suffer from
today. And the reference to the Conquered Countries
(those from which the Christians had driven back the
Moors) reflects RK's liking for situations where people of
different backgrounds and cultures could establish mutual
tolerance and respect.

Fairings = trinkets bought at a fair; the term is used
ironically. The dried beetles would be kermes insects,

Coccus ilicis, so called after the kermes oak, *Quercus coccifera,* on which they breed; the name is *qirmiz* in both Persian and Arabic. Cornelian is a semiprecious stone, a form of chalcedony. At seventy, Brother Martin would have been exceptionally old—John Paston (1378–1444), he of *The Paston Letters,* was exempted from most of his legal duties in 1437 "on account of his great age" . . . and he was only fifty-five!

Vellum, prior to the advent of good-quality paper, was the medium of choice for illuminated books; it was a fine parchment made from the skin of calves, kids, or lambs too young to bear marring scars. *De Virtutibus Herbarum* = Of the Virtues of Plants. Scullions = kitchen-hands. Durham is in the north of England, site of an old cathedral and a respected university. Torre I take to be Torremolinos on the south coast of Spain, though it might be Torre del Greco, south of Naples. "In the world" means outside the seclusion of his Order.

Roger is probably Roger of Salerno, in southern Italy, where there was a famous school of medicine and anatomy. The other Roger is certainly Roger Bacon, to whom have been attributed many discoveries including gunpowder and ether. *Physicus* = physician; *sacerdos* = priest. The Viaticum is the communion wafer given to those at point of death.

Vespers is the evening service; prime, the first service of the new day, held at sunrise and sometimes earlier.

"By way of the leads" = across a portion of the roof, sheathed in lead to make it rainproof. A triforium is a gallery or arcade surmounting an aisle alongside a church or chapel. Bernard is Bernard of Clairvaux (1091–1153) who wrote the hymn they listen to. *De Contemptu Mundi* = Of Despising the World. *Hora novissima—tempora pessima sunt* = The latest hour, the times are at their worst. *Ecce minaciter, imminet Arbiter* = Behold, threatening, the Judge arrives. *Ille supremus* = He, the supreme. *Imminet, ut mala terminet* = He comes to put an end to evil things.

Utque (I suspect this should be *utique*) *malum late solet immedicabile cancer* = Anyhow, a bad untreatable cancer usually becomes widespread (we would say metastatises). There is a neat but rather nasty play on words concealed in this phrase, for *solere* meant not only "to do as a mat-

ter of custom" but also "to have sex." *Hocus-pocus* is
mock-Latin of the kind used by fairground charlatans, as
"abracadabra" is mock-Arabic or Hebrew.

The Abbot removes his ring to show that he is, so to
say, temporarily off duty. Compline and Matins are late
and early services in the daily ritual. A silver-point was
used before the invention of the "lead" pencil: one scored
lines with it, then emphasized them by blowing on or rubbing in opaque dust, rather like looking for fingerprints.

Varro was a Roman poet who wrote a treatise on farming, *De Re Rustica* (Of Country Matters). It contains a re-
markably early reference (27 B.C.!) to the germ-theory of
disease. Trust RK to have spotted it!

The Demon of Socrates was a concept RK (who called
his a *daemon*, as do I) was very well acquainted with: less
kind and less forgiving than the traditional Muse. For
"Shall mortal man. . . ?" see the Book of Job. Peter Pere-
grinus taught at the University of Paris, where Roger
Bacon was a student. Paul of Aegina influenced the other
Roger in the same way. Apuleius is not the Lucius
Apuleius who wrote one of the earliest of all novels, and
one of the funniest, *The Golden Ass*, but "Pseudo-
Apuleius," author of a book on herbal medicine.

The association of the woman from whom Jesus "cast
out seven devils" with Mary of Magdala is questionable
(M. R. James, in *The Apocryphal Gospels*, speaks of "reckless identification of all the Maries"), but it would have
been accepted at the time RK is writing of. Grisaille is a
technique of painting with grayish tints in imitation of
bas-reliefs. "Broke" is correct, not a mistake for "broken," but = compelled to endure, as is a horse. *Non nobis*
(supply *gloria*) = not to us the glory, a stock quotation
from Psalm 115. The Snakes of Aesculapius are symbols
of immortality (because a snake casts its old skin), and
one still sees them, and his staff, on doctors' car-window
stickers.

(It occurs to me, as I write, that underlying all these
brilliant descriptions of "devils" may have been RK's acquaintance with that most dreadful of then-incurable diseases: syphilis. Its terminal stage, from which among
others Frederick Delius and Sir Winston Churchill's father suffered, was known as G.P.I.—general paralysis of

the insane. Moreover, by 1920 it had been established what organisms caused such terrible conditions as gas-gangrene, which literally rots the limbs from off your living body. Certainly the rods, chains, and ladders correspond exactly to infective microbes: e.g., *bacillus* = little rod.)

"Count everything unknown . . ." is a deliberate misapplication of a phrase from Tacitus: *omne ignotum pro magnifico*—anything unknown passes for marvelous.

Now, suddenly, we are truly in a science fiction world. *The Shell Book of Firsts* dates the first microscope (it would have had a single intensely magnifying lens, like John's, plus a mirror to reflect light from beneath the specimen) to 1590—over *three hundred years* later than the setting of this story. RK has created a universe where it has already been invented, in the East. One can almost hear the foundations of time grinding on their bedrock . . . Ah, but watch!

Watch his onslaught against the bigotry that, like the lynch law which condemned Salati's "nigger" to the flames, would do the same to these sane albeit inquisitive people, were they so foolish as to risk a declaration of the truth—reduce them all to "fifty pounds of ashes at the stake!"

Thus through the fear of being burnt alive there dies another, maybe better, Earth.

The Eye of Allah

The Cantor of St. Illod's being far too enthusiastic a musician to concern himself with its Library, the Sub-Cantor, who idolized every detail of the work, was tidying up, after two hours' writing and dictation in the Scriptorium. The copying-monks handed him in their sheets—it was a plain Four Gospels ordered by an Abbot at Evesham—and filed out to vespers. John Fitz Otho, better known as John of Burgos, took no heed. He was burnishing a tiny boss of gold in his miniature of the Annunciation for his Gospel of St. Luke, which it was hoped that Cardinal Falcodi, the Papal Legate, might later be pleased to accept.

"Break off, John," said the Sub-Cantor in an undertone.

"Eh? Gone, have they? I never heard. Hold a minute, Clement."

The Sub-Cantor waited patiently. He had known John more than a dozen years, coming and going at St. Illod's, to which monastery John, when abroad, always said he belonged. The claim was gladly allowed for, more even than other Fitz Othos, he seemed to carry all the Arts under his hand, and most of their practical receipts under his hood.

The Sub-Cantor looked over his shoulder at the pinned-down sheet where the first words of the magnificat were built up in gold washed with red-lac for a background to the Virgin's hardly yet fired halo. She was shown, hands joined in wonder, at a lattice of infinitely intricate arabesque, round the edges of which sprays of orange-bloom seemed to load the blue hot air that carried back over the minute parched landscape in the middle distance.

"You've made her all Jewess," said the Sub-Cantor, studying the olive-flushed cheek and the eyes charged with foreknowledge.

"What else was Our Lady?" John slipped out the pins. "Listen, Clement. If I do not come back, this goes into my Great Luke, whoever finishes it." He slid the drawing between its guard-papers.

"Then you're for Burgos again—as I heard?"

"In two days. The new Cathedral yonder—but they're slower than the Wrath of God, those masons—is good for the soul."

"*Thy* soul?" The Sub-Cantor seemed doubtful.

"Even mine, by your permission. And down south—on the edge of the Conquered Countries—Granada way—there's some Moorish diaper-work that's wholesome. It allays vain thought and draws it toward the picture—as you felt, just now, in my Annunciation."

"She—it was very beautiful. No wonder you go. But you'll not forget your absolution, John?"

"Surely." This was a precaution John no more omitted on the eve of his travels than he did the recutting of the tonsure which he had provided himself with in his youth, somewhere near Ghent. The mark gave him privilege of clergy at a pinch, and a certain consideration on the road always.

"You'll not forget, either, what we need in the Scriptorium. There's no more true ultramarine in this world now. They mix it with that German blue. And as for vermilion—"

"I'll do my best always."

"And Brother Thomas" (this was the Infirmarian in charge of the monastery hospital) "he needs—"

"He'll do his own asking. I'll go over his side now, and get me re-tonsured."

John went down the stairs to the lane that divides the hospital and cook-house from the back-cloisters. While he was being barbered, Brother Thomas (St. Illod's meek but deadly persistent Infirmarian) gave him a list of drugs that he was to bring back from Spain by hook, crook, or lawful purchase. Here they were surprised by the lame, dark Abbot Stephen, in his fur-lined night-boots. Not that Stephen de Sautré was any spy; but as a young man he had shared an unlucky Crusade, which had ended, after a battle at Mansura, in two years' captivity among the Saracens at Cairo where men learn to walk softly. A fair huntsman and hawker, a reasonable disciplinarian, but a man of science above all, and a Doctor of Medicine under one Ranulphus, Canon of St. Paul's, his heart was more in the monastery's hospital work than its religious. He checked their list interestedly, adding items of his own. After the Infirmarian had withdrawn, he gave John generous absolution, to cover lapses by the way; for he did not hold with chance-bought Indulgences.

"And what seek you *this* journey?" he demanded, sitting on the bench beside the mortar and scales in the little warm cell for stored drugs.

"Devils, mostly," said John, grinning.

"In Spain? Are not Abana and Pharphar—?"

John, to whom men were but matter for drawings, and well-born to boot (since he was a de Sanford on his mother's side), looked the Abbot full in the face and—"Did *you* find it so?" said he.

"No. They were in Cairo too. But what's your special need of 'em?"

"For my Great Luke. He's the master-hand of all Four when it comes to devils."

"No wonder. He was a physician. You're not."

"Heaven forbid! But I'm weary of our Church-pattern devils. They're only apes and goats and poultry conjoined. Good enough for plain red-and-black Hells and Judgment Days—but not for me."

"What makes you so choice in them?"

"Because it stands to reason and Art that there are all musters of devils in Hell's dealings. Those Seven, for example, that were haled out of the Magdalene. They'd be she-devils—no kin at all to the beaked and horned and bearded devils-general."

The Abbot laughed.

"And see again! The devil that came out of the dumb man. What use is snout or bill to *him*? He'd be faceless as a leper. Above all—God send I live to do it!—the devils that entered the Gadarene swine. They'd be—they'd be—I know not yet what they'd be, but they'd be surpassing devils. I'd have 'em diverse as the Saints themselves. But now, they're all one pattern, for wall, window, or picture-work."

"Go on, John. You're deeper in this mystery than I."

"Heaven forbid! But I say there's respect due to devils, damned tho' they be."

"Dangerous doctrine."

"My meaning is that if the shape of anything be worth man's thought to picture to man, it's worth his best thought."

"That's safer. But I'm glad I've given you Absolution."

"There's less risk for a craftsman who deals with the outside shapes of things—for Mother Church's glory."

"Maybe so, but John"—the Abbot's hand almost touched John's sleeve—"tell me, now, is—is she Moorish or—or Hebrew?"

"She's mine," John returned.

"Is that enough?"

"I have found it so."

"Well—ah well! It's out of my jurisdiction, but—how do they look at it down yonder?"

"Oh, they drive nothing to a head in Spain—neither Church nor King, bless them! There's too many Moors and Jews to kill them all, and if they chased 'em away there'd be no trade nor farming. Trust me, in the Conquered Countries, from Seville to Granada, we live lovingly enough together—Spaniard, Moor, and Jew. Ye see, we ask no questions."

"Yes—yes," Stephen sighed. "And always there's the hope, she may be converted."

"Oh yes, there's always hope."

The Abbot went on into the hospital. It was an easy age before Rome tightened the screw as to clerical connections. If the lady were not too forward, or the son too much his father's beneficiary in ecclesiastical preferments and levies, a good deal was overlooked. But, as the Abbot had reason to recall, unions between Christian and Infidel led to sorrow. Nonetheless, when John with mule, mails, and man, clattered off down the lane for Southampton and the sea, Stephen envied him.

He was back, twenty months later, in good hard case, and loaded down with fairings. A lump of richest lazuli, a bar of orange-hearted vermilion, and a small packet of dried beetles which make most glorious scarlet, for the Sub-Cantor. Besides that, a few cubes of milky marble, with yet a pink flush in them, which could be slaked and ground down to incomparable background-stuff. There were quite half the drugs that the Abbot and Thomas had demanded, and there was a long deep-red cornelian necklace for the Abbot's Lady—Anne of Norton. She received it graciously, and asked where John had come by it.

"Near Granada," he said.

"You left all well there?" Anne asked. (Maybe the Abbot had told her something of John's confession.)

"I left all in the hands of God."

"Ah me! How long since?"

"Four months less eleven days."

"Were you—with her?"

"In my arms. Childbed."

"And?"

"The boy too. There is nothing now."

Anne of Norton caught her breath.

"I think you'll be glad of that," she said after a while.

"Give me time, and maybe I'll compass it. But not now."

"You have your handwork and your art and—John—remember there's no jealousy in the grave."

"Ye-es! I have my Art, and Heaven knows I'm jealous of none."

"Thank God for that at least," said Anne of Norton, the always ailing woman who followed the Abbot with her sunk eyes. "And be sure I shall treasure this"—she touched the beads—"as long as I shall live."

"I brought—trusted—it to you for that," he replied, and took leave. When she told the Abbot how she had come by it, he said nothing, but as he and Thomas were storing the drugs that John handed over in the cell which backs on to the hospital kitchen-chimney, he observed, of a cake of dried poppy-juice: "This has power to cut off all pain from a man's body."

"I have seen it," said John.

"But for pain of the soul there is, outside God's Grace, but one drug; and that is a man's craft, learning, or other helpful motion of his own mind."

"That is coming to me, too," was the answer.

John spent the next fair May day out in the woods with the monastery swineherd and all the porkers; and returned loaded with flowers and sprays of spring, to his own carefully kept place in the north bay of the Scriptorium. There, with his traveling sketchbooks under his left elbow, he sunk himself past all recollections in his Great Luke.

Brother Martin, Senior Copyist (who spoke about once a fortnight), ventured to ask, later, how the work was going.

"All here!" John tapped his forehead with his pencil. "It has been only waiting these months to—ah God!—be born. Are ye free of your plain-copying, Martin?"

Brother Martin nodded. It was his pride that John of Burgos turned to him, in spite of his seventy years, for really good pagework.

"Then see!" John laid out a new vellum—thin but flawless. "There's no better than this sheet from here to Paris. Yes! Smell it if you choose. Wherefore—give me the compasses and I'll set it out for you—if ye make one letter lighter or darker than its next, I'll stick ye like a pig."

"Never, John!" the old man beamed happily.

"But I will! Now, follow! Here and here, as I prick, and in script of just this height to the hair's breadth, ye'll scribe the thirty-first and thirty-second verses of Eighth Luke."

"Yes, the Gadarene Swine! *'And they besought him that he would not command them to go out into the abyss. And there was a herd of many swine'* "—Brother Martin naturally knew all the Gospels by heart.

"Just so! Down to *'and he suffered them.'* Take your time to it. My Magdalene has to come off my heart first."

Brother Martin achieved the work so perfectly that John stole some soft sweetmeats from the Abbot's kitchen for his reward. The old man ate them; then repented; then confessed and insisted on penance. At which, the Abbot, knowing there was but one way to reach the real sinner, set him a book called *De Virtutibus Herbarum* to fair-copy. St. Illod's had borrowed it from the gloomy Cistercians, who do not hold with pretty things, and the crabbed text kept Martin busy just when John wanted him for some rather specially spaced letterings.

"See now," said the Sub-Cantor improvingly. "You should not do such things, John. Here's Brother Martin on penance for your sake—"

"No—for my Great Luke. But I've paid the Abbot's cook. I've drawn him till his own scullions cannot keep straight-faced. *He'll* not tell again."

"Unkindly done! And you're out of favor with the Abbot too.

He's made no sign to you since you came back—never asked you to high table."

"I've been busy. Having eyes in his head, Stephen knew it. Clement, there's no Librarian from Durham to Torre fit to clean up after you."

The Sub-Cantor stood on guard; he knew where John's compliments generally ended.

"But outside the Scriptorium—"

"Where I never go." The Sub-Cantor had been excused even digging in the garden, lest it should mar his wonderful book-binding hands.

"In all things outside the Scriptorium you are the master-fool of Christendie. Take it from me, Clement. I've met many."

"I take everything from you," Clement smiled benignly. "You use me worse than a singing-boy."

They could hear one of that suffering breed in the cloister below, squalling as the Cantor pulled his hair.

"God love you! So I do! But have you ever thought how I lie and steal daily on my travels—yes, and for aught you know, murder—to fetch you colors and earths?"

"True," said just and conscience-stricken Clement. "I have often thought that were I in the world—which God forbid!—I might be a strong thief in some matters."

Even Brother Martin, bent above his loathed *De Virtutibus*, laughed.

But about mid-summer, Thomas the Infirmarian conveyed to John the Abbot's invitation to supper in his house that night, with the request that he would bring with him anything that he had done for his Great Luke.

"What's toward?" said John, who had been wholly shut up in his work.

"Only one of his 'wisdom' dinners. You've sat at a few since you were a man."

"True: and mostly good. How would Stephen have us—?"

"Gown and hood over all. There will be a doctor from Salerno—one Roger, an Italian. Wise and famous with the knife on the body. He's been in the Infirmary some ten days, helping me—even me!"

"Never heard the name. But our Stephen's *physicus* before *sacerdos*, always."

"And his Lady has a sickness of some time. Roger came hither in chief because of her."

"Did he? Now I think of it, I have not seen the Lady Anne for a while."

"Ye've seen nothing for a long while. She has been housed near a month—they have to carry her abroad now."

"So bad as that, then?"

"Roger of Salerno will not yet say what he thinks. But—"

"God pity Stephen! . . . Who else at table, beside thee?"

"An Oxford friar. Roger is his name also. A learned and famous philosopher. And he holds his liquor too, valiantly."

"Three doctors—counting Stephen. I've always found that means two atheists."

Thomas looked uneasily down his nose. "That's a wicked proverb," he stammered. "You should not use it."

"Hoh! Never come you the monk over me, Thomas! You've been Infirmarian at St. Illod's eleven years—and a lay-brother still. Why have you never taken orders, all this while?"

"I—I am not worthy."

"Ten times worthier than that new fat swine—Henry Who's-his-name—that takes the Infirmary Masses. He bullocks in with the Viaticum, under your nose, when a sick man's only faint from being bled. So the man dies—of pure fear. Ye know it! I've watched your face at such times. Take Orders, Didymus. You'll have a little more medicine and a little less Mass with your sick then; and they'll live longer."

"I am unworthy—unworthy," Thomas repeated pitifully.

"Not you—but—to your own master you stand or fall. And now that my work releases me for a while, I'll drink with any philosopher out of any school. And Thomas," he coaxed, "a hot bath for me in the Infirmary before vespers."

When the Abbot's perfectly cooked and served meal had ended, and the deep-fringed naperies were removed, and the Prior had sent in the keys with word that all was fast in the Monastery, and the keys had been duly returned with the word, "Make it so till Prime," the Abbot and his guests went out to cool themselves in an upper cloister that took them, by way of the leads, to the South Choir side of the Triforium. The summer sun was still strong, for it was barely six o'clock, but the Abbey Church, of course, lay in her wonted darkness. Lights were being lit for choir-practice thirty feet below.

"Our Cantor gives them no rest," the Abbot whispered. "Stand by this pillar and we'll hear what he's driving them at now."

"Remember all!" the Cantor's hard voice came up. "This is the soul of Bernard himself, attacking our evil world. Take it quicker than yesterday, and throw all your words clean-bitten from you. In the loft there! Begin!"

The organ broke out for an instant, alone and raging. Then the voices crashed together into that first fierce line of the *"De Contemptu Mundi."*

"Hora novissima—tempora pessima"—a dead pause till the assenting *sunt* broke, like a sob, out of the darkness, and one boy's voice, clearer than silver trumpets, returned the long-drawn *vigilemus.*

"Ecce minaciter, imminet Arbiter" (organ and voices were leashed together in terror and warning, breaking away liquidly to the *"ille supremus"*). Then the tone-colors shifted for the prelude to—*"Imminet, imminet, ut mala terminet—"*

"Stop! Again!" cried the Cantor; and gave his reasons a little more roundly than was natural at choir-practice.

"Ah! Pity o' man's vanity! He's guessed we are here. Come away!" said the Abbot. Anne of Norton, in her carried chair, had been listening too, further along the dark Triforium, with Roger of Salerno. John heard her sob. On the way back, he asked Thomas how her health stood. Before Thomas could reply the sharp-featured Italian doctor pushed between them. "Following on our talk together, I judged it best to tell her," said he to Thomas.

"What?" John asked simply enough.

"What she knew already." Roger of Salerno launched into a Greek quotation to the effect that every woman knows all about everything.

"I have no Greek," said John stiffly. Roger of Salerno had been giving them a good deal of it, at dinner.

"Then I'll come to you in Latin. Ovid hath it nearly. *'Utque malum late solet immedicabile cancer'*—but doubtless you know the rest, worthy Sir."

"Alas! My school-Latin's but what I've gathered by the way from fools professing to heal sick women. *'Hocus-pocus—'* but doubtless you know the rest, worthy Sir."

Roger of Salerno was quite quiet till they regained the dining-room, where the fire had been comforted and the dates, raisins, ginger, figs, and cinnamon-scented sweetmeats set out, with the choicer wines, on the after-table. The Abbot seated himself, drew off his ring, dropped it, that all might hear the tinkle, into an empty silver cup, stretched his feet towards the hearth, and looked at the great gilt and carved rose in the barrel-roof. The silence that keeps from Compline to Matins had closed on their world. The bull-necked Friar watched a ray of sunlight split itself into colors on the rim of a crystal salt-cellar; Roger of Salerno had re-opened some discussion with Brother Thomas on a type of spotted fever that was baffling them both in England and abroad; John took note of the keen profile, and—it might serve as a note for the Great Luke—his hand moved to his bosom. The Abbot saw, and nodded permission. John whipped out silver-point and sketchbook.

"Nay—modesty is good enough—but deliver your own opinion," the Italian was urging the Infirmarian. Out of courtesy to the foreigner nearly all the talk was in table-Latin; more formal and more copious than monk's patter. Thomas began with his meek stammer.

"I confess myself at a loss for the cause of the fever unless—as Varro saith in his *De Re Rustica*—certain small animals which the eye cannot follow enter the body by nose and mouth, and set up grave diseases. On the other hand, this is not in Scripture."

Roger of Salerno hunched head and shoulders like an angry cat. "Always *that!*" he said, and John snatched down the twist of the thin lips.

"Never at rest, John," the Abbot smiled at the artist. "You should break off every two hours for prayers, as we do. St. Benedict was no fool. Two hours is all that a man can carry the edge of his eye or hand."

"For copyists—yes. Brother Martin is not sure after one hour. But when a man's work takes him, he must go on till it lets him go."

"Yes, that is the Demon of Socrates," the Friar from Oxford rumbled above his cup.

"The doctrine leans toward presumption," said the Abbot. "Remember, 'Shall mortal man be more just than his Maker?' "

"There is no danger of justice"; the Friar spoke bitterly. "But at least Man might be suffered to go forward in his Art or his thought. Yet if Mother Church sees or hears him move anyward, what says she? 'No!' Always 'No.' "

"But if the little animals of Varro be invisible"—this was Roger of Salerno to Thomas—"how are we any nearer to a cure?"

"By experiment"—the Friar wheeled round on them suddenly. "By reason and experiment. The one is useless without the other. But Mother Church—"

"Ay!" Roger de Salerno dashed at the fresh bait like a pike. "Listen, Sirs. Her bishops—our Princes—strew our roads in Italy with carcasses that they make for their pleasure or wrath. Beautiful corpses! Yet if I—if we doctors—so much as raise the skin of one of them to look at God's fabric beneath, what says Mother Church? 'Sacrilege! Stick to your pigs and dogs, or you burn!' "

"And not Mother Church only!" the Friar chimed in. *"Every* way we are barred—barred by the words of some man, dead a thousand years, which are held final. Who is any son of Adam that his one say-so should close a door towards truth? I would not except even Peter Peregrinus, my own great teacher."

"Nor I Paul of Aegina," Roger of Salerno cried. "Listen, Sirs! Here is a case to the very point. Apuleius affirmeth, if a man eat fasting of the juice of the cut-leaved buttercup—*sceleratus* we call it, which means 'rascally' "—this with a condescending nod towards John—"his soul will leave his body laughing. Now this is the lie more dangerous than truth, since truth of a sort is in it."

"He's away!" whispered the Abbot despairingly.

"For the juice of that herb, I know by experiment, burns, blisters, and wries the mouth. I know also the *rictus,* or pseudo-laughter on the face of such as have perished by the strong poisons of herbs allied to this ranunculus. Certainly that spasm resembles laughter. It seems then, in my judgment, that Apuleius, having seen the body of one thus poisoned, went off at score and wrote that the man died laughing."

"Neither staying to observe, nor to confirm observation by experiment," added the Friar, frowning.

Stephen the Abbot cocked an eyebrow toward John.

"How think *you?*" said he.

"I'm no doctor," John returned, "but I'd say Apuleius in all these years might have been betrayed by his copyists. They take short cuts to save 'emselves trouble. Put case that Apuleius wrote the soul *seems* to leave the body laughing, after this poison. There's not three copyists in five (*my* judgment) would not leave out the 'seems to.' For who'd question Apuleius? If it seemed so to him, so it must be. Otherwise any child knows cut-leaved buttercup."

"Have you knowledge of herbs?" Roger of Salerno asked curtly.

"Only, that when I was a boy in convent, I've made tetters round my mouth and on my neck with buttercup-juice, to save going to prayer o' cold nights."

"Ah!" said Roger. "I profess no knowledge of tricks." He turned aside, stiffly.

"No matter! Now for your own tricks, John," the tactful Abbot broke in. "You shall show the doctors your Magdalene and your Gadarene Swine and the devils."

"Devils? Devils? *I* have produced devils by means of drugs; and have abolished them by the same means. Whether devils be external to mankind or immanent, I have not yet pronounced." Roger of Salerno was still angry.

"Ye dare not," snapped the Friar from Oxford. "Mother Church makes Her own devils."

"Not wholly! Our John has come back from Spain with brand-new ones." Abbot Stephen took the vellum handed to him, and laid it tenderly on the table. They gathered to look. The Magdalene was drawn in palest, almost transparent, grisaille, against a raging, swaying background of woman-faced devils, each broke to and by her special sin, and each, one could see, frenziedly straining against the Power that compelled her.

"I've never seen the like of this grey shadow work," said the Abbot. "How came you by it?"

"*Non nobis!* It came to me," said John, not knowing he was a generation or so ahead of his time in the use of that medium.

"Why is she so pale?" the Friar demanded.

"Evil has all come out of her—she'd take any color now."

"Ay, like light through glass. *I* see."

Roger of Salerno was looking in silence—his nose nearer and nearer the page. "It is so," he pronounced finally. "Thus it is in epilepsy—mouth, eyes, and forehead—even to the droop of her wrist there. Every sign of it! She will need restoratives, that woman, and, afterwards, sleep natural. No poppy-juice, or she will vomit on her waking. And thereafter—but I am not in my Schools." He drew himself up. "Sir," said he, "you should be of Our calling. For, by the Snakes of Aesculapius, you *see!*"

The two struck hands as equals.

"And how think you of the Seven Devils?" the Abbot went on.

These melted into convoluted flower- or flame-like bodies, ranging in color from phosphorescent green to the black purple of outworn iniquity, whose hearts could be traced beating through their substance. But, for sign of hope and the sane workings of life, to be regained, the deep border was of conventionalized spring flowers and birds, all crowned by a kingfisher in haste, atilt through a clump of yellow iris.

Roger of Salerno identified the herbs and spoke largely of their virtues.

"And now, the Gadarene Swine," said Stephen. John laid the picture on the table.

Here were devils dishoused, in dread of being abolished to the

Void, huddling and hurtling together to force lodgment by every opening into the brute bodies offered. Some of the swine fought the invasion, foaming and jerking; some were surrendering to it, sleepily, as to a luxurious back-scratching; others, wholly possessed, whirled off in bucking droves for the lake beneath. In one corner the freed man stretched out his limbs all restored to his control, and Our Lord, seated, looked at him as questioning what he would make of his deliverance.

"Devils indeed!" was the Friar's comment. "But wholly a new sort."

Some devils were mere lumps, with lobes and protuberances—a hint of a fiend's face peering through jelly-like walls. And there was a family of impatient, globular devilings who had burst open the belly of their smirking parent, and were revolving desperately toward their prey. Others patterned themselves into rods, chains, and ladders, single or conjoined, round the throat and jaws of a shrieking sow, from whose ear emerged the lashing, glassy tail of a devil that had made good his refuge. And there were granulated and conglomerate devils, mixed up with the foam and slaver where the attack was fiercest. Thence the eye carried on to the insanely active backs of the downward-racing swine, the swineherd's aghast face, and his dog's terror.

Said Roger of Salerno, "I pronounce that these were begotten of drugs. They stand outside the rational mind."

"Not these," said Thomas the Infirmarian, who as a servant of the Monastery should have asked his Abbot's leave to speak. "Not *these*—look!—in the bordure."

The border to the picture was a diaper of irregular but balanced compartments or cellules, where sat, swam, or weltered, devils in blank, so to say—things as yet uninspired by Evil—indifferent, but lawlessly outside imagination. Their shapes resembled, again, ladders, chains, scourges, diamonds, aborted buds, or gravid phosphorescent globes—some well-nigh star-like.

Roger of Salerno compared them to the obsessions of a Churchman's mind.

"Malignant?" the Friar from Oxford questioned.

" 'Count everything unknown for horrible,' " Roger quoted with scorn.

"Not I. But they are marvelous—marvelous. I think—"

The Friar drew back. Thomas edged in to see better, and half opened his mouth.

"Speak," said Stephen, who had been watching him. "We are all in a sort doctors here."

"I would say then"—Thomas rushed at it as one putting out his life's belief at the stake—"that these lower shapes in the bordure may not be so much hellish and malignant as models and patterns upon which John has tricked out and embellished his proper devils among the swine above there!"

"And that would signify?" said Roger of Salerno sharply.

"In my poor judgment, that he may have seen such shapes—without help of drugs."

"Now who—*who*," said John of Burgos, after a round and unregarded oath, "has made thee so wise of a sudden, my Doubter?"

"I wise? God forbid! Only John, remember—one winter six years ago—the snowflakes melting on your sleeve at the cookhouse-door. You showed me them through a little crystal, that made small things larger."

"Yes. The Moors call such a glass the Eye of Allah," John confirmed.

"You showed me them melting—six-sided. You called them, then, your patterns."

"True. Snowflakes melt six-sided. I have used them for diaper-work often."

"Melting snowflakes as seen through a glass? By art optical?" the Friar asked.

"Art optical? *I* have never heard!" Roger of Salerno cried.

"John," said the Abbot of St. Illod's commandingly, "was it—is it so?"

"In some sort," John replied, "Thomas has the right of it. Those shapes in the bordure were my workshop-patterns for the devils above. In *my* craft, Salerno, we dare not drug. It kills hand and eye. My shapes are to be seen honestly, in nature."

The Abbot drew a bowl of rose-water towards him. "When I was prisoner with—with the Saracens after Mansura," he began, turning up the fold of his long sleeve, "there were certain magicians—physicians—who could show—" he dipped his third finger delicately in the water—"all the firmament of Hell, as it were, in—" he shook off one drop from his polished nail on to the polished table—"even such a supernaculum as this."

"But it must be foul water—not clean," said John.

"Show us then—all—all," said Stephen. "I would make sure—once more." The Abbot's voice was official.

John drew from his bosom a stamped leather box, some six or

eight inches long, wherein, bedded on faded velvet, lay what looked like silver-bound compasses of old box-wood, with a screw at the head which opened or closed the legs to minute fractions. The legs terminated, not in points, but spoon-shapedly, one spatula pierced with a metal-lined hole less than a quarter of an inch across, the other with a half-inch hole. Into this latter John, after carefully wiping with a silk rag, slipped a metal cylinder that carried glass or crystal, it seemed, at each end.

"Ah! Art optic!" said the Friar. "But what is that beneath it?"

It was a small swiveling sheet of polished silver no bigger than a florin, which caught the light and concentrated it on the lesser hole. John adjusted it without the Friar's proffered help.

"And now to find a drop of water," said he, picking up a small brush.

"Come to my upper cloister. The sun is on the leads still," said the Abbot, rising.

They followed him there. Halfway along, a drip from a gutter had made a greenish puddle in a worn stone. Very carefully, John dropped a drop of it into the smaller hole of the compass-leg, and, steadying the apparatus on a coping, worked the screw in the compass-joint, screwed the cylinder, and swung the swivel of the mirror till he was satisfied.

"Good!" He peered through the thing. "My Shapes are all here. Now look, Father! If they do not meet your eye at first, turn this nicked edge here, left- or right-handed."

"I have not forgotten," said the Abbot, taking his place. "Yes! They are here—as they were in my time—my time past. There is no end to them, I was told . . . There *is* no end!"

"The light will go. Oh, let me look! Suffer me to see, also!" the Friar pleaded, almost shouldering Stephen from the eye-piece. The Abbot gave way. His eyes were on time past. But the Friar, instead of looking, turned the apparatus in his capable hands.

"Nay, nay," John interrupted, for the man was already fiddling at the screws. "Let the Doctor see."

Roger of Salerno looked, minute after minute. John saw his blue-veined cheekbones turn white. He stepped back at last, as though stricken.

"It is a new world—a new world and—Oh, God Unjust!—I am old!"

"And now Thomas," Stephen ordered.

John manipulated the tube for the Infirmarian, whose hands shook, and he too looked long. "It is Life," he said presently in a

breaking voice. "No Hell! Life created and rejoicing—the work of
the Creator. They live, even as I have dreamed. Then it was no sin
for me to dream. No sin—O God—no sin!"

He flung himself on his knees and began hysterically the *Benedicite omnia Opera.*

"And now I will see how it is actuated," said the Friar from
Oxford, thrusting forward again.

"Bring it within. The place is all eyes and ears," said Stephen.

They walked quietly back along the leads, three English counties
laid out in evening sunshine around them; church upon church,
monastery upon monastery, cell after cell, and the bulk of a vast
cathedral moored on the edge of the banked shoals of sunset.

When they were at the after-table once more they sat down, all
except the Friar who went to the window and huddled bat-like over
the thing. "I see! I see!" he was repeating to himself.

"He'll not hurt it," said John. But the Abbot, staring in front of
him, like Roger of Salerno, did not hear. The Infirmarian's head was
on the table between his shaking arms.

John reached for a cup of wine.

"It was shown to me," the Abbot was speaking to himself, "in
Cairo, that man stands ever between two Infinities—of greatness
and littleness. Therefore, there is no end—either to life—or—"

"And *I* stand on the edge of the grave," snarled Roger of Salerno.
"Who pities *me?*"

"Hush!" said Thomas the Infirmarian. "The little creatures shall
be sanctified—sanctified to the service of His sick."

"What need?" John of Burgos wiped his lips. "It shows no more
than the shapes of things. It gives good pictures. I had it at Granada.
It was brought from the East, they told me."

Roger of Salerno laughed with an old man's malice. "What of
Mother Church? Most Holy Mother Church? If it comes to Her ears
that we have spied into Her Hell without Her leave, where do we
stand?"

"At the stake," said the Abbot of St. Illod's, and, raising his voice
a trifle, "You hear that? Roger Bacon, heard you that?"

The Friar turned from the window, clutching the compasses
tighter.

"No, no!" he appealed. "Not with Falcodi—not with our English-hearted Foulkes made Pope. He's wise—he's learned. He reads
what I have put forth. Foulkes would never suffer it."

" 'Holy Pope is one thing, Holy Church another,' " Roger
quoted.

"But, I—*I* can bear witness it is no Art Magic," the Friar went on. "Nothing is it, except Art optical—wisdom after trial and experiment, mark you. I can prove it, and—my name weighs with men who dare think."

"Find them!" croaked Roger of Salerno. "Five or six in all the world. That makes less than fifty pounds by weight of ashes at the stake. I have watched such men—reduced."

"I will not give this up!" The Friar's voice cracked in passion and despair. "It would be to sin against the Light."

"No, no! Let us—let us sanctify the little animals of Varro," said Thomas.

Stephen leaned forward, fished his ring out of the cup, and slipped it on his finger. "My sons," he said, "we have seen what we have seen."

"That it is no magic but simple Art," the Friar persisted.

"Avails nothing. In the eyes of Mother Church we have seen more than is permitted to man."

"But it was Life—created and rejoicing," said Thomas.

"To look into Hell as we shall be judged—as we shall be proved—to have looked, is for priests only."

"Or green-sick virgins on the road to sainthood who, for cause any midwife could give you—"

The Abbot's half-lifted hand checked Roger of Salerno's outpouring.

"Nor may even priests see more in Hell than Church knows to be there. John, there is respect due to Church as well as to Devils."

"My trade's the outside of things," said John quietly. "I have my patterns."

"But you may need to look again for more," the Friar said.

"In my craft, a thing done is done with. We go on to new shapes after that."

"And if we trespass beyond bounds, even in thought, we lie open to the judgment of the Church," the Abbot continued.

"But thou knowest—*knowest!*" Roger of Salerno had returned to the attack. "Here's all the world in darkness concerning the causes of things—from the fever across the lane to thy Lady's—thine own Lady's—eating malady. Think!"

"I have thought upon it, Salerno! I have thought indeed."

Thomas the Infirmarian lifted his head again; and this time he did not stammer at all. "As in the water, so in the blood must they rage and war with each other! I have dreamed these ten years—I thought it was a sin—but my dreams and Varro's are true! Think on it again! Here's the Light under our very hand!"

"Quench it! You'd no more stand to roasting than—any other. I'll give you the case as Church—as I myself—would frame it. Our John here returns from the Moors, and shows us a hell of devils contending in the compass of one drop of water. Magic past clearance! You can hear the faggots crackle."

"But thou knowest! Thou hast seen it all before! For man's poor sake! For old friendship's sake—Stephen!" The Friar was trying to stuff the compasses into his bosom as he appealed.

"What Stephen de Sautré knows, you his friends know also. I would have you, now, obey the Abbot of St. Illod's. Give to me!" He held out his ringed hand.

"May I—may John here—not even make a drawing of one—one screw?" said the broken Friar, in spite of himself.

"Nowise!" Stephen took it over. "Your dagger, John. Sheathed will serve."

He unscrewed the metal cylinder, laid it on the table, and with the dagger's hilt smashed some crystal to sparkling dust which he swept into a scooped hand and cast behind the hearth.

"It would seem," said he, "the choice lies between two sins. To deny the world a Light which is under our hand, or to enlighten the world before her time. What you have seen, I saw long since among the physicians at Cairo. And I know what doctrine they drew from it. Hast *thou* dreamed, Thomas? I also—with fuller knowledge. But this birth, my sons, is untimely. It will be but the mother of more death, more torture, more division, and greater darkness in this dark age. Therefore I, who know both my world and the Church, take this Choice on my conscience. Go! It is finished."

He thrust the wooden part of the compasses deep among the beech logs till all was burned.

Unprofessional
FROM *LIMITS AND RENEWALS* (1932)

Of this story the celebrated surgeon Sir John Bland-Sutton
said, "Kipling has here foretold the course of medical research, as far ahead as his 'Easy as A.B.C.' foretold the
progress of aviation."

Sir John was even more right than he could have
known. On January 5, 1987, the BBC broadcast a program
in the *Horizon* series (known as *Nova* in the States), entitled "The 25-Hour Clock"—a significant title! Note that,
in mice, RK's "tides . . . slipped a little round the clock
according to the season of each litter's birth."

The said program reported, *inter alia,* how doctors at
the Masonic Hospital in Minneapolis had found that the
effectiveness of drugs can be enhanced by taking into account the time at which they are administered—or, more
precisely, the patient's circadian rhythms, the "biological
clock."

And, just as RK predicted, this phenomenon is especially marked in cancer cases . . .

The setting is London; references are to London streets.
No Man's Land = the territory between the front lines in
World War I, shot over from both sides. Schermoltz's
was a medical supply firm. *Padrone* (Italian) = proprietor.
Zillebeeke was the scene of a battle in Flanders. A pill-box
in this context is a small concrete blockhouse.

Vaughan is referred to as "Doctor," in quotes, because
in Britain surgeons are invariably Mr., and they take some
pride in this traditional form of address. Jutland saw the

only major sea-battle of World War I. The ship's compasses Frost refers to were of course magnetic ones. The
new shirts would have been "marked" with laundry-proof
ink or sewn-on name-tapes. Barker's was and still is a department store in Kensington.

The Lock Hospital, in Southwark, was for patients
dying of venereal disease, particularly syphilis. It became
internationally famous because of a song, "The Unfortu-
nate Rake," which in America evolved into both "The
Streets of Laredo" (a.k.a. "The Dying Cowboy") and "St.
James Infirmary Blues."

Unprofessional

Since Astronomy is even less remunerative than Architecture, it
was well for Harries that an uncle of his had once bought a
desert in a far country, which turned out to overlie oil. The result
for Harries, his only nephew, was over a million pounds invested,
plus annual royalties.

When the executors had arranged this, Harries, who might have
been called an almost-unpaid attaché at Washe Observatory, gave
a dinner to three men, whom he had tried and proved beneath
glaring and hostile moons in No Man's Land.

Vaughan, Assistant Surgeon at St. Peggoty's, was building himself
a practice near Sloane Street. Loftie, pathologist, with the beginnings of a reputation, was—for he had married the unstable daughter of one of his earlier London landladies—bacteriological advisor
to a Public Department, on five hundred and seventy pounds per
annum, and a prospect of being graded for pension. Ackerman, also
a St. Peggoty's man, had been left a few hundreds a year just after
he had qualified, and so had given up all serious work except
gastronomy and the allied arts.

Vaughan and Loftie knew of Harries' luck, which Harries explained in detail at the dinner, and stated what, at the lowest count,
his income would be.

"Now," said he, " 'Tacks' can tell you."

Ackerman made himself small in his chair, as though it had been
the shell-hole whence he had once engineered their retreat.

"We know each other fairly well," he began. "We've seen each other stripped to the Ultimate Atom pretty often? We needn't camouflage? Agreed? You're always saying what you'd do if you were independent. Have you changed your minds?"

"Not me," said Vaughan, whose oft-told dream was a nursing-home of his own near Sloane Street. He had marked the very house for it.

"Do you think I'd keep on with this sewage job if it wasn't for the pension?" Loftie asked. He had followed research the more keenly since, at twenty-two, he had wrecked his own happiness.

"Be free, then," said Ackerman. "Take three thousand—"

"Hold on," Harries broke in plaintively. "I said 'up to five.' "

"Sorry, old man! I was trying for the commission. Take up to five thousand a year from Harries for as long as you choose—for life, if you like. Then research on your own lines, Loftie, and—and—let the Bull know if you stumble on anything. That's the idea, isn't it?"

"Not all." Harries surged a little in his seat. "A man's entitled to use a telescope as well as a microscope, isn't he? Well—I've got notions I want to test. They mean keeping one's eyes open and—logging the exact times that things happen."

"That's what you said when you lectured our company about Astrology—that night under Arras. D'you mean 'planetary influences?' " Loftie spoke with a scientist's scorn.

"This isn't my lecture." Harries flushed. "This is my gamble. We can't tell on what system this dam' dynamo of our universe is wound, but we know we're in the middle of every sort of wave, as we call 'em. They used to be 'influences.' "

"Like Venus, Cancer, and that lot?" Vaughan inquired.

"Yes—if you choose. Now I want Vaughan to start his clinic, and give me a chance to test my notions occasionally. No! Not faith-healing! Loftie can worry his cells and tissues with radium as much as he likes. But—"

"We're only on the threshold of radium," Loftie snapped.

"Then get off it!" was the blasphemous retort. "Radium's a *post hoc*, not a *propter*. I want you merely to watch some of your cell-growths all round the clock. Don't think! *Watch*—and put down the times of any changes you see."

"Or imagine?" Loftie supplemented.

"You've got it. Imagination *is* what we want. This rigid 'thinking' game is hanging up research. You told me yourself, the other night, it was becoming all technique and no advance," Harries ended.

"That's going too far. We're on the edge of big developments."

"All the better! Take the money and go ahead. Think of your lab, Lofter! Stoves, filters, sterilizers, frigidaria—everything you choose to indent for!"

"I've brought along Schermoltz's last catalog. You might care to look at it, later." Ackerman passed the pamphlet into Loftie's stretched hand.

"Five thousand a year," Loftie muttered and turned the enthralling pages. "God! What one could afford! . . . But I'm not worth the money, Bull. Besides, it's robbery. . . . You'll never arrive at anything by this astrology nonsense."

"But *you* may, on your lines. What do you suppose is the good of Research?"

"God knows," Loftie replied, devouring the illustrations. "Only—only it looks—sometimes—as if He were going to tell."

"That's all we want," Harries coaxed. "Keep your eye on Him, and if He seems inclined to split about anything, put it down."

"I've had my eye on that house for the last half-year. You could build out a lift-shaft at the back." Vaughan looked and spoke into the future.

Here the *padrone* came in to say that if more drinks were needed, they should be ordered.

Ackerman ordered; Harries stared at the fire; Loftie sank deeper into the catalog; and Vaughan into his vision of the desirable house for his clinic. The *padrone* came back with a loaded tray.

"It's too much money to take—even from you, Bull." Vaughan's voice was strained. "If you'd lend me a few hundred for my clinic, I could . . ."

Loftie came out of the catalog and babbled to the same effect, while he reckoned up for just how many pounds a week the horror that defiled his life and lodgings could be honorably removed from both till it drank itself dead.

Harries reared up over them like a walrus affronted.

"Do you remember the pill-box at Zillebeeke, and the skeleton in the door? Who pinched the bombs for us *then?*" he champed.

"Me and The Lofter," said Vaughan, sullen as a schoolboy.

"What for?"

"Because we dam' well needed 'em."

"We need 'em worse now! We're up against the beggar in the pill-box. He's called Death—if you've ever heard of him. This stuff of mine isn't money, you imbeciles! It's a service-issue—same as socks. We—we haven't kept on saving each other's silly lives for *this!* Oh, don't let me down! Can't you *see?*" The big voice quavered.

"Kamerad, Bull! I'll come in," said Loftie. Vaughan's hands had gone up first, and he was the first to recover himself, saying: "What about 'Tacks?' He isn't let off, is he?"

"No. I'm going to make commission out of the lot of you," said Ackerman. "Meantime! Come on, me multimillionaires! The Bald-headed Beggar in the pill-box is old, but the night is yet young."

The effects of five thousand a year are stimulating.

A mere Cabinet Minister, dependent on elections for his place, looking in on a Committee where Loftie was giving technical evidence, asked in too loud a whisper, if that all-but-graded Civil Servant were "one of my smell-and-tell temporaries." Loftie's resignation was in that evening. Vaughan, assisted by an aunt, started a little nursing-home near Sloane Street, where his new household napery lift and drying-cupboards almost led to his capture by "just the kind of girl, my dear, to make an ideal wife for a professional man."

Harries continued to observe the heavens, and commissioned Ackerman to find a common meeting-place. This—Simson House was its name—had been a small boys' school in a suburb without too many trams. Ackerman put in floods of water, light and power, an almost inspired kitchen-range, a house-man and his cook-wife, and an ex-Navy petty rating as valet-plumber, steward-engineer, and butler-electrician; set four cots in four little bedrooms, and turned the classroom in the back garden into a cement-floored hall of great possibilities, which Harries was the first to recognize. He cut off a cubicle at one end of it, where he stored books, clocks, and apparatus. Next, Loftie clamored for a laboratory and got it, dust-and air-tight, with lots of the Schermoltz toys laid out among taps and sinks and glass shelves. Hither he brought various numbered odds-and-ends which Vaughan and other specialists had sent him in the past, and on which, after examination, he had pronounced verdicts of importance to unknown men and women. Some of the samples—mere webs of cancerous tissue—he had, by arts of his own, kept alive in broths and salts after sentence had been executed on their sources of origin.

There were two specimens—Numbers 127 and 128—from a rarish sort of affliction in exactly the same stage of development and precisely the same position, in two women of the same age and physique, who had come up to Vaughan on the same afternoon, just after Vaughan had been appointed Assistant Surgeon at St. Peg-goty's. And when the absurdly identical operations were over, a man, whose praise was worth having, but whose presence had made Vaughan sweat into his palms, had complimented him. So far as St. Peggoty's knew, both cases were doing well several months after. Harries found these samples specially interesting, and would pore over them long times on end, for he had always used the microscope very neatly.

"Suppose you watch what these do for a while," he suggested to Loftie one day.

"*I* know what they'll do well enough," the other returned. He was hunting a line of his own in respect to brain-cells.

"Then couldn't you put Frost on to watch 'em with a low-power lens?" Harries went on. "He's a trained observer in his own line. What? Of *course* he's at your disposition, old man. *You* could make anything of him. Oh, by the way, do you happen to remember what time of day you operated on One-twenty-Seven and Eight?"

"Afternoon, of course—at St. Peggoty's—between three and five. It's down somewhere."

"It don't matter. I only wanted to get an idea. Then you'll turn on Frost to watch 'em? Thanks awfully."

Frost, the valet-plumber, etc., was ex-captain of a turret, with the hard blue eye of the born gun-layer—a middle-aged, uncomely man, no mean mechanic, and used to instruments of precision. He liked sitting in a warm room, looking through a microscope at what he called "muckings," with instructions to "watch 'em all round the clock and log all changes." But no sooner did he begin than Loftie, jealous as two women, and knowing what beginner's luck may do, stood watch and watch with him. Loftie was in hard work on his brain-cells, and the monotony of this sentry-go made him fear that his mind might build theories on self-created evidence. So he told Frost, after a while, that the whole thing was absurd, as well as bad for the eyes. "Isn't it?" he added.

"I don't know how it is with *you,* sir," Frost replied. "It some-times makes *me* feel as if I were seeing a sort of ripple strike up along the edges of 'em. Like broken water, with the sun tipping it. Like Portland Race in open-and-shut weather."

"That's eye-strain. But when does it come on—with you?"

"Sometimes through the middle watch—from twelve to four A.M. Then, again, it will come on through the first and second dog-watches—four to eight P.M., sir."

"No matter which—what sample—you are looking at?" Loftie asked keenly.

"I'd say it depended on the sample. Now, One-twenty-Eight—'seems to me—plays up in the middle watch—from midnight on—and One-twenty-Seven in the afternoon. I've logged it all."

Three months later, at Simson House, Loftie told the others that, while not in the least departing from his own theories, there was a phenomenon, which for the sake of brevity he would call "tide," in Samples 127 and 128. It occurred at certain hours, which had all been noted and passed on to Harries—"for what *that* may be worth."

Harries smiled, and hired an expensive expert to photo the two samples and film them; which took several weeks and cost some hundreds of pounds. They all checked the magnified "tides" by some curious tables which Harries had worked out—"for what *that's* worth," as Loftie said.

Harries said it was worth the expense, and took to spending a good deal of his leisure at Simson House. Vaughan, too, reeking of ether, would put in for shelter there, as the hunt after him (which his aunt whipped) quickened with his successes. Loftie had been almost a fixture in his lab from the first; and poor "Tacks," who could no more have made a dishonest penny than he could have saved an honest one, catered for them so lavishly that even the cook shied at the weekly bills, which Harries flatly refused to audit.

Three months after their first film's "release," Loftie read them a typed paper before dinner, asserting there was "tide" in the normal cells of all tissues which he and his helper, Frost, had observed; but he could see no sign of "tide" in the malignant areas. He detailed tests and observations till they yawned. Then Frost ran the latest film for them—in slow and quick time—and they sat round the fire.

"I'm not committing myself to anything," said Loftie, speaking like a badly shaken human being, "but every dam' tissue up till now seems to have its own time for its own tides. Samples from the same source have the same tides in strength and time. But, as I showed you just now, there are minute constant variations—reactions to something or other—in each tide, as individual as finger-prints. I wouldn't stake my reputation on it except to you. But I *know* it's so."

"What do you suppose it means?" Vaughan half-whispered.

"As I read it," Harries spoke quietly, "the minor differences in those 'tides' in the tissues are due to interferences with the main or external influence—whichever it may be—which sets up, or which *is,* the main tide in all matter. They both come from with*out*. Not with*in*."

"How far out?" Vaughan asked.

"Can't tell—yet—to a few light-years. I've been trying to disentangle the minor interferences or influences—which may be due to the nearer—er—influences—from the main tide. In *my* opinion—"

"Stop!" Loftie cried shrilly. "You swore us all not to theorize before a year."

"Hear me out! I've verified some of my calculations at *my* end of the game, and they justify me in saying that . . . we are all justified in getting tight tonight."

So, then, they did: being drunk with the ferment of their own speculations before they went to table. Loftie, whom Ackerman confined to strong beer as best for tired brain-cells, rose up above the savory, and said that he was "the Servant of the Infil-tresimally Minute, but not of that fat tape-worm, Tacks." Harries described to them the vasts of the Ultimate Heavens fizzing in spirals "with— or rather like—champagne," but all one generating station of one Power drawn from the Absolute, and of one essence and substance with all things. Then he slept soundly. Vaughan—the professional man—merely wanted to telephone for a taxi that he might drive to discredit a hated West End rival by calling him to his bedroom window and there discussing "dichotomy"—a hard word at 3 A.M.

Then they packed Loftie off for a month's holiday, with a cubic meter of seven-and-sixpenny detective novels, *plus* Vaughan's aunt to see that he ate and dressed properly. On his return, he began certain experiments with mice, which Frost took charge of in the boiler-room, because he remembered when their ancestors served in the earliest submarines. It seemed that "tides" worked in their tissues also; but slipped a little round the clock according to the season of each litter's birth.

And there were born to them mice among mice with prodigious "tides." Some of these, inoculated at the flood, threw off the trouble, and were promoted by Frost to the rating of pets. Treated on their lowest ebbs, they perished less quickly than the average. Harries kept careful count of their times in all things and ways, and had Frost sling some of their cages on various compass-bearings or set them out in moonlight or thunderstorms.

This last was too much for Loftie, who returned once more to the legitimate drama of cultures and radium emanations, and the mysteries of malignant cells which never acknowledge any "tide." At the end of three weeks, he, and Frost, broke off the campaign.

He said to Harries one evening after watching their usual film: "What do you suppose germs think of?"

"If you've got as far as that," was the answer, "you'll develop an imagination one day."

Then Vaughan came in full of trouble. His matron had been immobilized by sciatica, and his household staff had taken base advantages. He needed at once, some table-napkins, some bath towels, two jacketed water-jugs and a metal—not china—bedroom breakfast-set. Ackerman said he would speak to Frost and see what could be spared from the ship.

While they were laughing at Vaughan, St. Peggoty's rang him up. He replied: "Well, well! If it was coming, it was to be expected now. . . . One of my beds empty? . . . You can have it. . . . Send her over to me. . . . You *must!* . . . I'll warn my people to expect her? . . . Oh? *That's* all right. . . . I'll send the car. . . . Yes, and all other expenses. . . . Because I operated on her originally, of course. We'll expect her at nine, then. . . . Righto! . . . Not in the least. Thank you, old man."

He then telephoned his home to prepare for a patient, and returned to the still circle by the fire.

"It's one of those twin cases of mine," he explained. "One of 'em's back again. Recurrence—in the scar—after eighteen months."

"That means?" said Harries.

"With that particular kind of trouble—three—five months' reprieve—perhaps. Then final recurrence. The other one's all right, so far, they say."

"She would be. This one is One-twenty-Eight," said Loftie.

"How do you make that out?"

Frost had entered and was going through Vaughan's indent with Ackerman.

"Frost, what is One-twenty-Eight's timing?" Loftie interposed.

"One-two-Eight, sir? Flood from midnight till four A.M.—ebb from four to eight P.M. . . . Yes, sir, I can make the table-linen all right, *and* the jugs. But we're short on bath-towels just now."

"Would it prove anything if she lasted out nine months?" Harries picked up the thread of talk with Vaughan.

"No. There are rallies and reserves."

"A full year?"

"*I* should accept that. But I know who wouldn't." Vaughan gave a great name.

"Thanks for reminding me," said Ackerman over his shoulder. "Frost, the bathroom hot-water pipe has got arterial sclerosis, too. Operate on it."

"When shall *you* operate, Taffy?" Harries held on.

"Tomorrow at a quarter to ten. I always feel fittest then."

"Think of the patient for a change. Suppose you stand-to at a few minutes to midnight tomorrow? I'll telephone you zero from here."

Vaughan seemed a shade taken aback. "Midnight? Oh, certainly," he said. "But I'll have to warn my anaesthetist."

"And Ferrers'll swear you've taken to drink or drugs," said Ackerman. "Besides, think of your poor matron and the nurse who's got to have her evening off? *Much* better let the woman conk out in Trades Union hours, Taffy."

"Dry up, *padrone*," said Loftie. "No need to bring in Ferrers. I'll take his place—if you think I'm safe."

Since this was as if Raeburn had volunteered to prime a canvas for Sir Benjamin West, Vaughan accepted, and they sat down to eat.

When he and Loftie had refreshed their memories of One-two-Eight's construction and arrangements, they asked Harries why he had chosen that time for the operation. Harries said that by his reckonings it should fall nearer the woman's birthday. His guess at its actual date he wrote down and was passing it to Vaughan, when Vaughan's Nursing Home reported the arrival of the patient, not unduly fatigued and most anxious to thank "Doctor" Vaughan for the amazing kindness which had rescued her from the open ward.

The table listened to Vaughan's reply, soothing and sustaining, and, by tone, assuming the happiest issue out of this annoying little set-back. When he hung up, he said: "She—wants it the day after tomorrow, because that's her birthday. She thinks it'll be lucky."

"Make it midnight, then, of the day after tomorrow, and look at the date I wrote down. . . . No! The Devil has nothing to do with it. By the way—if it won't cramp your style—could you set the table on—" Harries gave a compass bearing.

"Don't be shy," said Ackerman. "He'd stand her on her head to operate now, if the Bull told him. Are you off, Taffy? Frost'll put all your towels and pots in a taxi. Sorry if I've hurt your feelings."

Loftie's account of the operation did not interest Frost so much as the samples he brought back. It took both of them three or four days to plant them out properly. In return, Frost told Loftie that "our end of the show," with Major Harries at the sidereal clock, waiting "till the sights came on," and Captain Ackerman at the telephone, waiting to pass the range to Captain Vaughan in Sloane Street, was "just like Jutland."

"Now, this lady of ours," he said after a busy silence. "How would she lie in her bed?"

Loftie gave a bearing which he had heard Harries give Vaughan.

"I expect Major Harries knows, if anyone," was Frost's placid comment. "It's the same as ships' compasses varying according as their heads lay when they were building."

"It's crazy mad. That's all!"

"Which was what the Admiralty said at first about steam in the Navy," Frost grinned.

He put away a set of sealed cover-glasses and reverently returned some lenses to their velvet shrines.

"Not to talk of that lady of ours—" he straightened up as he spoke—"some of my mice aren't behaving as I could wish."

"Which?" said Loftie. There were several types of experiments under way.

"One or two of some that recovered after inoculation—since discharged and promoted to pets. But it looks as if they'd had a relapse. They're highly restless—always trying to escape out—as if they were wild, not white. I don't like it."

"Clean up, then," Loftie answered, "and we'll go down to the boiler-room."

In one of the cages there, a doe with a plum-colored saddle was squeaking, as she strove desperately to work through the wires with semitransparent hand-like forefeet. Frost set the cage on a table under an electric and handed her dossier to Loftie. This gave her birth, age, date and nature of inoculation, date also when her system seemed to have cleared itself of the dose; and, of course, the times and strengths of her "tides." It showed dead-ebb for her at that hour.

"What does she think she's doing?" Loftie whispered. "It isn't her natural squeak, either."

They watched. She labored increasingly at the barrier; sat up as though most intently listening; leaped forward and tore into her task beneath the glare of the basement-bulb.

"Turn it out," said Loftie. "It's distressing her."

Frost obeyed. In a few seconds the little noises changed to a flutter and ceased.

"I thought so! Now we'll look again," said Loftie. "Oh! Oh! God!"

"Too late," Frost cried. "She's broke her neck! Fair broken her pretty little neck between the wires! How did she do it?"

"In convulsion," Loftie stammered. "Convulsion at the last. She pushed and pushed with her head in the wires and that acted as a wedge . . . and . . . what do *you* think?"

"I expect I'm thinking pretty much the same as you are, sir." Frost replaced the cage under the leads and fuses which he had painted man-o'-war fashion. "It looks like two tides meeting," he added. "That always sets up a race, and a race is worst at ebb. She must have been caught on her ebb—an' knocked over! Pity! There ought to be some way of pulling 'em through it."

"Let's see if there isn't," said Loftie, and lifted out the tiny warm body with a needed droplet of blood on the end of the nose.

One-two-Eight (Mrs. Berners) made a good recovery, and since she seemed alone in the world, Vaughan said that, as payment, she must stay on in his home and complete it to his satisfaction. She was touchingly grateful. After a few months (her strength returning) she asked to do something for her benefactors. No one seemed to look after the linen at Mr. Vaughan's. Might she repair, count, store, and, even, give it out—for she had had experience in that line as a house-keeper. Her prayer was granted, and the work of getting at the things Vaughan had started the Home with; had bought, but had never entered; had raided from Ackerman, and thought—or worse, was quite sure—that he had sent back; or had lost by laundries and through servants, did her good. It also brought her over to Simson House to return things to Frost, where Harries and Ackerman complimented her on her appearance, and Loftie asked her to administer his chance-bought body-line. She was delighted. She told them that, when she had nothing to do, she mostly felt in people's way, and as if she ought to go on elsewhere. Loftie asked her why. She answered that, when her troubles were on her, they kept her busy, if it was only at trying not to cry. But now that they had been removed—and by *such* kind gentlemen—the busiest day was none too full for her. She had a trick of tossing her head sideways and upwards, sometimes in the midst of her overseeings, and would say: "Well, well! I can't keep at this all the time. I must be off elsewhere where I'm wanted"—Loftie's Home or Simson House as the case might be.

They discussed her at long and at large, one evening, throughout a film which—Vaughan and Loftie collaborating—was based on her more recent productions.

Vaughan was well satisfied. "You see! Nothing has struck back. I know that her strength—notice how the tides have steadied—and our new blankets weigh a bit, too—is above normal. She has covered seven months and twenty-three days, and—I tell *you*—her scar is simply beautiful."

"We'll take your word," said Harries. "Now bring on your mouse-film, Loftie."

And Loftie, while Frost slowed, speeded, or went back at command, spoke of mice that had recovered apparently from certain infections, but had fallen later into a characteristic unease, followed by nervous crises—as shown—culminating in what seemed to be attempts at suicide.

In every case where an attempt had succeeded, the vacuoles—the empty centers—which do not take stain—of the brain-cells over a minute area seemed to have blown out, apparently as—("This'll interest you, I know. I hired it from the Dominion Weather Bureau last week.") as—a house explodes through its own windows under the vacuum set up by a tornado. They then beheld a three-story, clapboarded hotel vomiting itself outwards, while the black hook of a tornado's tip writhed and fished above it.

Sometimes, Loftie went on, an affected mouse would recover, after nervous upheavals very like those of tetanus—as they had seen—followed by collapse and amazingly sub-normal temperatures, and then a swift resumption of normal life. They could draw their own conclusions.

Ackerman broke their stillness. "Frost, go back, please, to that bit showing the movement of their heads when the attacks are coming on." Frost began again.

"Who's *that* like?" Ackerman called out suddenly. "Am I wrong?"

"No, sir," Frost groaned out of the dark. Then they all saw.

" 'Well, *I* can't stay here! I've got to move on elsewhere where I'm wanted,' " Ackerman quoted half-aloud. "And her hands working! The forefeet—I mean her hands! Look! It's *her!*"

"That's exactly her listening attitude, too," said Harries. "I never noticed it before."

"Why would you—with nothing to check it by?" said Loftie. "What does it mean?"

"It means she's as likely as not to chuck herself under a lorry some day, between here and Sloane Street," Frost interrupted, as though he had full knowledge and right.

"How do you know?" Vaughan began. "She's absolutely normal."

The flexes of the camera had not been disconnected, so they were still darkling.

"She's *not!* She's all astray. God knows where she's straying; but she's not here, more'n the dead." Frost repacked the camera and went out. They gathered round Harries.

"As I read it," he laid down, after some preliminaries, "she has been carried—yes, tided—over the time that her trouble ought to have finished her. That is two or three months now, isn't it, Taffy? *But,* she wasn't saved by the knife. She was saved by the knife at the proper time of tide."

"She has lasted seven months and twenty-three days. Most unusual, I grant, with that type of growth; but not conclusive," was Vaughan's retort.

"Hear me out. *Qua* Death, as created or evolved, on this planet (He needn't exist elsewhere, you know), and especially *qua* the instrument of decay that was to kill her, she's some odd weeks owing to the grave. *But, qua* the influence—tide, if you like— external to this swab of culture which we call our world, she has been started on a new tide of life. The gamble is that, after crises, something like those we've seen in the mice, that tide may carry her beyond the—er—the demand of the grave. It's beginning to be pull-devil, pull-baker between 'em now, I should imagine."

"I see your line, Bull," said Loftie. "When ought her crises to be due? Because—it's all as insane as the rest—but there may be an off-chance of—"

"The suicidal tendency comes first," said Ackerman. "Why not have her watched when she goes out? Taffy's nurses can keep an eye on her indoors."

"You've been reading my sleuth-tales," Loftie smiled.

"Make it so, then. Any decent inquiry-agency would undertake it, I suppose," said Harries.

"I'll leave the choice to Frost. I'll only take the commission. We're in for a wildish time. She's a woman—not a white mouse!" Ackerman said, and added thoughtfully: "*But* the champion ass, as distinguished from mere professional fool, of us all, is Taffy!"

Vaughan had ordered her never to go afoot between Simson House and the Nursing Home, and, also, to take taxis to and from her little "exercise walks" in the parks, where she so often picked up the nice elderly lady's-maid with the pom, the sales-lady from the Stores, and other well-spoken lady strangers near her own class (at ever so many shillings an hour). Of Mr. Frost she saw but little that summer, owing to the pressure of his duties and some return, they told her, of rheumatism contracted in the defense of his country. The worst that came to her was a slight attack of stiff neck, caught from sitting in a draft. As to her health, she admitted that sometimes she felt a bit flustered in the head, but otherwise could not be better.

She was recounting her mercies, a little fulsomely as usual, to Loftie one afternoon in the common-room of Simson House, where she had brought him some new shirts marked. Frost had taken them upstairs, and Loftie had hinted that he must get back to his work. She flicked her head sideways and said that she was busy, too. In the same breath, but in a whisper, she ran on: "I don't want to die, Mr. Loftie. But I've *got* to. I've really *got* to get out of this. I'm wanted elsewhere, but"—she shivered—"I don't like going."

Then she raced, with lowered head, straight towards the wall. Loftie snatched at her dress, turned her, so that she struck the wall with her shoulder and fell—and Frost came down to find him grappling with her, not inexpertly.

She broke away and skimmed across the room. Frost ran and tripped her, and brought her down. She would have beaten her head on the floor, but he jerked it up, his palm beneath her chin, and dragged her to her feet. Then he closed.

She was silent, absorbed in this one business of driving to the nearest wall through whatever stood between. Small and fragile though she was, she flung the twelve-stone Frost clear of her again and again; and a side-pushing stroke of her open palm spun Loftie half across the hall. The struggle lasted without a break, but her breath had not quickened, when like a string she relaxed, repeating that she did not want to die. As she cried to Loftie to hold her, she slipped away between them, and they had to chase her round the furniture.

They backed her down on the couch at last, Loftie clinging to her knees, while Frost's full strength and weight forced the thin arms over her head. Again the body gave, and the low, casual whisper began: "After what you said outside Barker's in the wet, you don't think I *really* want to die. Mr. Frost? I don't—not a mite. But I've *got* to. I've got to go where I'm wanted."

Frost had to kneel on her right arm then, holding her left down with both hands. Loftie, braced against the sofa, mastered her feet, till the outbreak passed in shudders that shook all three. Her eyes were shut. Frost raised an eyelid with his thumb and peered closely.

"Lor'!" said she, and flushed to the temples. The two shocked men leapt clear at once. She lifted a hand to her disordered hair. "Who's done this?" she said. "Why've I come all over like this? I ought to be busy dying." Loftie was ready to throw himself on her again, but Frost held up a hand.

"You can suit yourself about that, Mrs. Berners," he said. "What I've been at you all this time to find out is, what you've done with our plated toast-rack, towels, et cetera."

He shook her by the shoulders, and the rest of her pale hair descended.

"One plated toast-rack and two egg-cups, which went over to Mr. Vaughan's on indent last April twenty-eighth, together with four table-napkins and six sheets. I ask because I'm responsible for 'em at this end."

"But I've got to die."

"So we've all, Mrs. Berners. But before you do, I want to know what you did with. . . ." He repeated the list and the date. "You know the routine between the houses as well as I do. I sent 'em by Mr. Ackerman's orders, on Mr. Vaughan's indent. When do you check your linen? Monthly or quarterly?"

"Quarterly. But I'm wanted elsewhere."

"If you aren't a little more to the point, Mrs. Berners, I'll tell you where you *will* be wanted before long, and what for. I'm not going to lose my character on account of your carelessness—if no worse. An' here's Mr. Loftie. . . ."

"Don't drag me in," Loftie whispered, with male horror.

"Leave us alone! I know me class, sir. . . . Mr. Loftie who has done everything for you."

"It was Mr. Vaughan. *He* wouldn't let me die." She tried to stand, fell back, and sat up on the couch.

"You won't get out of it that way. Cast back in your memory and see if you can clear yourself!" Frost began anew, scientifically as a female inquisitor; mingling details, inferences, dates, and innuendoes with reminders of housekeeping ritual: never overwhelming her, save when she tried to ride off on her one piteous side-issue, but never accepting an answer. Painfully, she drew out of her obsession, protesting, explaining, striving to pull her riven wits into service; but always hunted from one rambling defense to the next, till, with eyes like those of a stricken doe, she moaned: "Oh, Fred! Fred! The only thing I've ever took—*you* said so outside Barker's—was your own 'ard 'eart."

Frost's face worked, but his voice was the petty-officer's with the defaulter.

"No such names between us, Mrs. Berners, till this is settled."

He crumpled his wet eyes, as though judging an immense range. Then observed deliberately:

"Ask *me*—I'd say you're a common thief."

She stared at him for as long as a shell might take to travel to an horizon. Then came the explosion of natural human wrath—she would not stoop to denial, she said—till, choking on words of abuse, she hit him weakly over the mouth, and dropped between his feet.

"She's come back!" said Frost, his face transfigured. "What next?"

"My room. Tell Cook to put her to bed. Fill every hot-water bottle we've got, and warm the blankets. I'll telephone the Home. Then we'll risk the injections."

Frost slung her, limp as a towel, over his shoulder, and, turning, asked: "This—all these symptoms don't need to be logged, sir—do they? We—we know something like 'em?"

Loftie nodded assent.

She came up shuddering out of the seven days' chill of the cheated grave, and Vaughan's nurses told her what a dreadful thing was this "suppressed influenza" which had knocked her out, but that she might report for duty in a few weeks. Ackerman, who loved Vaughan more than the others put together, testified on their next film-night that Taffy was almost worthy to be called a medical man for his handling of the case.

"Tacks," said Vaughan kindly, "you are as big a dam' fool about my job as I was about Frost. I injected what the Lofter gave me, at the times that Harries told me. The rest was old wives' practice."

"She always looked like a wet hen," said Harries. "Now she goes about like a smiling sheep. I wish I'd seen her crises. Did you or Frost time 'em, Lofter?"

"It wasn't worth it," was the light answer. "Just hysteria. But she's covered her full year now. D'you suppose we've held her?"

"I should say yes. I don't know how you feel, but"—Vaughan beamed—"the more I see of her scar, the more pleased I am. Ah! That was a lovely bit of work, even if I *am* only a carpenter, Tacks!"

"But, speaking with some relation to ordinary life, what does all this lunacy of ours prove?" Ackerman demanded.

"Not a dam' thing, except that it may give us some data and inferences which may serve as some sort of basis for some detail of someone else's work in the future," Harries pronounced. "The main point, as I read it, is that it makes one—not so much think—Research is gummed up with thinking—as imagine a bit."

"That'll be possible, too—by the time Frost and I have finished with this film," said Loftie.

It included a sequence of cultures, from mice who had overcome their suicidal fits, attenuated through a human being who, very obligingly, in the intervals of running the camera, described the effects of certain injections on his own rugged system. The earlier ones, he admitted, had "fair slung him round the deck."

"It was chuck it and chance it," Loftie apologized. "You see, we couldn't tell, all this summer, when Mrs. Berners might play up for the grave. So I rather rushed the injections through Frost. I haven't worked out my notes yet. You'll get 'em later."

He stayed to help Frost put back some of the more delicate gear, while the others went to change.

"Not to talk about that lady of ours," Frost said presently. "My first—though, of course, her mother never warned me—drank a bit. She disgraced me all round Fratton pretty much the whole of one commission. And she died in Lock 'Ospital. So, I've had *my* knock."

"Some of us seem to catch it. I've had mine, too," Loftie answered.

"*I* never heard that. But"—the voice changed—"I knew it—surer than if I'd been told."

"Yes. God help us!" said Loftie, and shook his hand. Frost, not letting go of it, continued: "One thing more, sir. I didn't properly take it in at the time—not being then concerned—but—that first operation on that lady of mine, was it of a nature that'll preclude—so to say—expectations of—of offspring?"

"Absolutely, old man." Loftie's free hand dropped on Frost's shoulder.

"Pity! There ought to be some way of pulling 'em through it—somehow—oughtn't there?"

The Fairies' Siege
ENLARGED FROM *KIM* (1901)

When Tom Doherty, publisher of Tor Books—to whom I
am greatly indebted because thanks to him this labor of
love, which I have nurtured among my ambitions for lo!
these many years, has finally attained publication—
accepted the companion collection of Kipling's Fantasy,
he requested that it conclude with that splendid poem
"When Earth's Last Picture Is Painted." I was happy to
oblige. (How often these days do publishers specially request inclusion of a poem?)

But it struck me that for symmetry's sake the SF collection should also terminate with a poetical envoi. So I
chose this.

What do fairies have to do with science fiction? Well,
RK wasn't thinking of fluffy creatures in ballet skirts—
rather, of beings with more than mortal powers. And who
knows? Perhaps one day his, and our, dreams may indeed
come true, and if they do, then we shall be as they.

Sic fiat.

The Fairies' Siege

I have been given my charge to keep—
Well have I kept the same!
Playing with strife for the most of my life,

But this is a different game.
I'll not fight against swords unseen,
Or spears that I cannot view—
Hand him the keys of the place on your knees—
'Tis the Dreamer whose dreams come true!

Ask him his terms and accept them at once.
Quick, ere we anger him, go!
Never before have I flinched from the guns,
But this is a different show.
I'll not fight with the Herald of God
(I know what his Master can do!)
Open the gate, he must enter in state,
'Tis the Dreamer whose dreams come true!

I'd not give way for an Emperor,
I'd hold my road for a King—
To the Triple Crown I would not bow down—
But this is a different thing.
I'll not fight with the Powers of Air,
Sentry, pass him through!
Drawbridge let fall, 'tis the Lord of us all,
The Dreamer whose dreams come true!